The Landfill Lofts
Wade Fleming

Copyright © 2021 Wade Fleming
All rights reserved.
ISBN 9798485761349

For my boys.

March 7, 2082

"You spend all your days thinking your life is this one thing, this one way. And then one day it's something completely different and you're no longer at all the person you were before, or maybe you never were that person. And that's not something that happens to everyone. But that's what happened to me."

Lucian Gavril was listless and numb as he spoke into his phone, a thin and nearly weightless touchscreen, about the size of his hand. Dissatisfied but unable to muster the energy to say anything more, he put his phone on the desk in front of him, and made no further effort to move.

Natalie Ross, a tall and sinewy police officer, was patrolling along a strip of weatherworn apartment buildings when the sun emerged from the clouds. She squinted as she flipped down the car's visor and strained as she reached for a bottle of water rolling along the floor on the passenger side. Each movement was born of contempt. Keeping her eyes on the road, she took a mouthful, and her mannerisms turned in an instant: water was the elixir.

She set the bottle down with some care, but her rigidity returned thereafter. She adjusted a tiny, one-button, wireless clip that was attached to the collar of her shirt, ensuring it was in place before she began speaking:

Constable Natalie Ross, badge number 38523, operating out of the Terrace Bay detachment of the Great Lakes Regional Police Service. I don't know why I was selected to do this, but I was, so I'm doing it. I'll have this clip on for a few shifts and…

I should have started the way they told me to—Natalie Ross, forty-two years old, my pronouns are she and her, and I am a police officer. I will be contributing to this project by explaining the intricacies of some of the work I do on shift, and giving a view into what it's like serving the public in law enforcement here in Canada and the United States in 2082. I'm currently in my cruiser, on patrol along Lake Superior in Canada. My thoughts might be a little disjointed, as I'll need to stop when calls come in or whenever I need to exit my cruiser.

I shouldn't say that I don't know why they selected me. I know that it makes sense to choose me because I adhere to the service's standards, and I take that very seriously. I have decent rapport in the community and a strong record in terms of my enforcement actions, limited complaints against me, not many use-of-force incidents. And most of the other officers don't have much to say. I don't like to talk either, but the service knows I can talk when they need me to.

There wasn't really much of a directive given as to what I should discuss. It feels a little strange. But I guess... let's see... I can say that policing here and now is challenging. A century ago, it used to be that many officers didn't even need to carry a firearm. That's certainly not the case anymore, even though there aren't many guns on the street now. Sometimes it feels like our guiding principles are limited, or change too often, and there are no objective measures with which to gauge our long-term success or lack thereof. I don't mean for that to sound like a knock against the service, the government, the Oversight Committee, or any of my colleagues. It's just an honest feeling. I can explain it in a scenario, like if—

Cst. Ross noticed a young but haggard man—fists clenched, screaming his demands—standing over a fallen boy; the boy was tall for his age but boney and baby-faced, clearly not a teenager yet. She stopped her vehicle, radioed for assistance, and exited with haste.

"I just want your water. Gimme that blue gold, kid. Run it!"

"Police—stop!" Natalie announced.

The man turned to her with contempt and advanced on her as though she was a minor inconvenience to be brushed aside. A smirk came upon his face as his pace quickened.

She took a step backward, and with a quick movement, drew her soft-control pistol and fired a rubber bullet to the centre of his left quadriceps. It hit him like a strike from a ballpeen hammer. The man jolted and stumbled hard; the pain surged through his body in a rush of nauseating heat.

"Oh you stupid cunt," he spit through his teeth as he continued limping toward her.

Ross took a bladed stance, holstered her weapon with another sharp movement, and began backing away slowly with her hands outstretched and a pleading, fearful look on her face. But when the man drew within an arm's reach, she used her left hand to push his face to her right side, while simultaneously yanking his left wrist downward and using her right leg to sweep his weak leg out from under him. It appeared easy, like an adult wrestling a child.

Ross maintained control of the man's wrist as his back hit the pavement, and she drove her left knee into his chest, taking the wind out of him. She braced his left arm against the inside of her right knee, pushed it hard to hyperextend the elbow, and as he pulled the arm toward his own body to cradle it, she drove his palm toward his own wrist, straining the tendons as he screamed in agony.

With the man fully focused on nursing his injuries, Natalie cracked him with a quick palm-strike to the nose, causing him to turn over and turtle, pain still searing in his leg. From back-mount, she grabbed a fistful of hair and shoved his face into the pavement as she retrieved her cuffs with her free hand. She cuffed him quickly and moved to side-control, keeping two hands on the subject's back as she scanned the area for any other threats. The sequence took all of ten seconds.

The boy had scampered off. With the man in cuffs and now compliant, Ross was methodical: she breathed slowly and deeply and gave her subject calm and clear instructions. She retrieved a needle and a knife from his pockets. She then got him into the cruiser without further issue. Backup arrived in time to slow down and drive past with little more than a glance in Ross' direction. She entered the driver's seat, sat silently for a beat, held her hand to her heart, and took another series of deep, deliberate breaths.

"Now when I'm up here, I'm going to be talking, but I'm not talking to you, so I'd appreciate if you stay quiet unless you need medical assistance."

Now I'll explain what just happened, because it's the type of incident I see every day on shift. People will take advantage of any opportunity where they see a weakness or vulnerability. Each item you own has value here, which sounds obvious, but what I mean is that whatever you have on you, wherever you go, someone wants to snatch it. There is no such thing as a worthless trinket. People will steal your family photos if you leave your doors unlocked—I've actually seen that happen. If your shoes have soles, someone wants to take them from you. And if you carry water outside your home, well, calling that an error in judgment would be a monumental understatement.

Natalie parked her vehicle at the Terrace Bay detachment, and then exited to escort the man she'd just apprehended into the staff sergeant's office and then into cells. After completing the transfer, she returned to her cruiser.

So just now, I apprehended a subject who was attacking a young boy and then turned his attack on me when I intervened. I used my softy, which is a firearm that projects non-lethal ammunition. The softy pistol can be holstered on your hip, thigh, arm, or ankle, or on your vest. It depends what you want, for comfort and practicality. There are benefits and drawbacks to each spot. When the temperature gets too hot, I wear mine on my hip, but mostly, I keep it on my arm. It's light and small, so it doesn't get in the way much. It's on a sliding rail along my dominant wrist, and is drawn via a short, crisp movement, like flicking open a jackknife; we call it a Bickle release. It's our only tool that we take home at the end of our shifts, not including our implanted tools. We're expected to practice using it daily. I use a sandbag in my apartment.

Getting off track here... I used to avoid using my tools at all costs, even the softy. But since they transferred me back to uniform, I don't hesitate. It's not because I'm bitter. It's actually because I'm more careful now. The softy is great if you use it the right way.

When this subject came toward me, I fired a round into his left quad muscle. It's a shot I intentionally directed in a place on his body that will have limited or no long-term damage, but the acute effect left him limping toward me, so he was immediately fighting me with about a seventy percent handicap. Others on my platoon think I'm crazy because I'm the only officer who will use and then holster my tool before I've detained an assailant. But that's why my subjects don't end up dead. They say I could just keep my softy drawn, but that can get messy, and at close range, it's usually more beneficial for me to just have both hands free rather than to have a softy ready to fire.

After I fired and hit the target, he kept coming at me, limping and grunting, and I holstered and prepared myself. I put a frightened look on my face and let him catch up to me, so that he would assume I was going to passively take his beating. Men are strange that way. Begging and pleading makes them slow down. They're enjoying themselves too much, which gives me more time to think. It's as though he'd already forgotten that I shot him and could easily do it again. Then as he got close, I hit a foot sweep, went knee on belly, briefly cranked a straight armbar and a wristlock, broke his nose, turned him over, and cuffed him.

That all sounds like a lot. Like a brag, maybe. But it's just leverage and timing—that's how I got him. It's easy if no one believes you can do it.

With the morning's shift briefing completed, S/Sgt. Pete Canizales spent two extra minutes alone in the briefing room. He closed the door, dimmed the lights, sat down, and shut his eyes for fifteen seconds. Next, he pulled out his phone and watched a compilation video of elaborate dominoes setups being knocked over. He paused the video after exactly ninety seconds, and left the room to join his officers.

Pete approached Cormac Dawson, a densely muscled detective constable with a tight crew cut and clean shaved face.

"Take your pin to your cruiser. Make sure you're mic'd up all day today."

"This is that project they first started in Albany, right?" Cormac was curious.

"Yeah, I think it came from Brooklyn."

"Oh I heard Albany."

"Anything south of Syracuse is Brooklyn to me."

Cormac let out a short laugh. "And what's the directive, again?"

"Isn't one. I'll see if I can get some specs by tomorrow. Communication's been slow and sparse on the project. I've got you and Ross doing recordings. I don't care if you're mindful what you say or how you say it. It can all be edited and it's not my project or my concern. Just talk. Say what you're doing and how you do it. We can be done with it after a few shifts."

"Understood."

"The whole thing is weird. I don't even know if Albany actually started it, or if it comes from one of the chiefs, the government, or oversight. I don't really care at this point."

"Typical bureaucratic garbage."

Pete responded with a short grunt, but his attention had been drawn to another officer, Oshun Briggs, who was using a window as a mirror, turning and flexing, adjusting his duty belt.

"Briggs."

"Yes, Staff."

"You'd be surprised how often no one is looking at you."

While Briggs pondered how to respond, Pete looked back to Dawson: "What's your workout plan for this shift?"

"Running."

"Treadmill?"

"Never. Treadmills are speed inhibitors. I don't need all those numbers in my face. Turns your mind into a little bitch, thinking you can't go any longer or faster. I pound the pavement, Staff."

"We need to get you off the Outreach Program and in as the strength and conditioning trainer. Put that request in writing for me, when you want it."

"Yes, sir."

Pete scanned the room, now mostly cleared out. Briggs met Pete's eyes for a brief moment, but he quickly looked away and increased his pace toward the exit. Expressionless, Pete turned back to Cormac: "Time to put in work."

"Work!"

Detective Constable Cormac Dawson, twenty-eight years old, he him, GLR Police. Currently on duty out of our Terrace Bay detachment, en route to the outpost in Jackfish, then to our Red Rock detachment. So lots of driving today. This is something I do bi-weekly.

I work CID—criminal investigations—but I'm also a mental health outreach officer and I'm one of our leads for the ongoing community policing initiative. That's why I need to make my rounds to check in with officers, ride with them for some public outreach, take note of any changes in morale, see if there's any civil unrest. Usually there's a boiling point around the time of the lotto announcements, so I like to make my rounds at that time, trying to get in on the action in the street, as a way to balance out the monotony of this mental health gig. And actually, the lotto messes with officers too, so it's good to be checking in with them at the same time.

Aside from that, this part of the job is honestly just a good chance for me to de-stress. I like the drive. And I use it as a chance to connect with some of my contacts that supply me with information, related to my real job in CID, I mean.

For sure I like touching base with my brothers around the region, though I'm not really trained to supply the type of support they need. I'm the one who gets the extra stipend for taking on the role, but even I get jaded about it sometimes. Like, these guys don't need me to bring them donuts and give them fist bumps. They need extra weeks of vacation, and days off where they don't have to supply specific reasons or get doctors' notes. But the union was gutted well before I got here, so I'm just working with what I've been given.

I'm an action junkie though. People give me shit because they say this is just an extra day off, but like I said, I want to see the action while I'm on the road. I liked being in uniform before, on patrol. So this is a little chance to reconnect with that. If you think about those people who are so low, their crimes so petty, some might say they're not worth the time of day—those are the people I want to spend my time on. My eyes don't drip for them, and I don't care about what circumstances brought them to me.

Lucian Gavril, towering but slender, bordering on emaciated, emerged from his basement and managed a half smile to greet his wife, Ava, who had just returned home from work. Ava had straight black hair, shoulder length, and a long-distance runner's build, but with the solid, toned forearms of a woman accustomed to labour—built to carry buckets. She maintained a gentle touch as she placed a hand on Lucian's shoulder and looked up at him, smiling.

"How's David?"

"He's fine," Lucian said, looking into her eyes. The sight of

Ava seemed to be helping him emerge from a trance. "Been home for an hour. He told me he had a good day, then went straight to his room."

"Did they have anything for him to eat today?"

"You know how he is." Lucian's smile was genuine by then, nothing forced. "He wouldn't tell me anything. How was your day? 'Good'. What did you learn? 'I dunno'. Did you play tag or soccer or what? 'I can't remember'. Seems like he's in a good mood though, so I imagine they had something filling, at least."

"Okay good. Something more than dry cereal and a multivitamin this time then. And did you get any call-backs today?"

Lucian sighed and turned his head. Ava pressed her hand a little tighter to his shoulder, then ran it down his arm and tried a bigger smile: "It's okay. I'm sorry to ask right away. I know there'll be more work soon."

"Yeah well."

"Maybe a call will come tomorrow."

"Maybe."

Lucian started to return to the basement, but Ava stopped him. "Stay up with me this time. You don't have to be by yourself. We'll find something to cook together."

Lucian halted at the top of the stairs, but only for a moment. He took in a breath through his teeth. "I've got work to do."

'Consider yourself lucky.' That's what they always tell us.

Natalie sat in the Terrace Bay detachment rec room during her one-hour self-care allotment.

I decided to use my break to do this recording project, as it was too much of a distraction on patrol. Though it's going to be hard this way too because I have to eat.

She stopped the recording in order to shovel mashed potatoes into her mouth. As if on cue, Cst. Colton Oakshot entered the room.

"Just starting your break?" Oakshot asked.

She nodded, raised her eyebrows, grunted.

"Must been nice."

"Mmhmm," she managed, swallowing too much and then smothering a choked cough.

Oakshot left the room as quickly as he'd entered. There was no one else in the room to share her annoyed look with, so she rolled her eyes and moved on. She began spreading thick layers of peanut butter across four saltine crackers. She sliced a piece of banana onto each cracker, and delicately pressed them together into two sandwiches. She licked the knife clean, drank a tiny sip of water, and shoved one of the cracker-sandwiches into her mouth. Then Oakshot re-entered the room.

"Forgot what I came in here for. What are you working on after self-care?"

She waved her hand in a circular motion around her mouth—can't you see I'm eating—with her eyes wide. He waited, confused. She looked down in disbelief, trying to lick the thick peanut butter clean from the inside of her mouth while holding her hand up to block Oakshot from the sight of it, as Oakshot continued to watch and wait.

With extra effort, she swallowed too quickly, jagged bits of cracker stinging her throat, and then took a bigger drink of water than she would have hoped, clearing her throat as best she could.

"Not sure," was all she said.

"Cool." And he left again, this time with a snack in hand.

Natalie paused, took a deep breath, ate her other cracker-sandwich slowly—making a mess of it by trying to bite it into little pieces—and then returned to her voice recording:

So I was just interrupted by Oakshot, who actually often goes by Scattershot, because of the broad strokes of anger he directs at whichever civilian might be near him. But whatever, his blood runs hot.

Anyway, the man enters a room like a piano falling from a balcony. I think he plans to come to the break room whenever someone's alone in here. The place is supposed to be a sanctuary. He said something for no reason other than to fill the air, then he left, so I started eating again. Then the asshole immediately came back in to ask me something.

He's got this saccharine sweet voice that just annoys the hell out of me. It's like he's talking down to everyone because he likes them so much. Then he'll just explode with rage at some random target—scattered. And he's always making these trumpet sounds with his mouth—

This is not relevant to the project, I know. But I just had to say it out loud. Please excuse my language and my… tone. Eating is important to me. That feels strange to say, because obviously eating is vital. But I mean I value my eating time more than almost anything. When I'm on shift, I eat once a day, and I cherish that time. I had some leftovers and then I was having peanut butter on crackers, and I'm serious when I say that I could live off peanut butter on crackers. But I absolutely despise being interrupted while eating. When I'm eating, that's all I'm doing…

I seriously just contemplated throwing this pin into the garbage, but then I know I'd have to explain that to someone who gets paid to scorn front-liners, so I opted not to.

Okay what I was saying was, they tell us we should think of ourselves as being lucky. The truth is not that we're lucky, but that we're better off: we're better off than the overwhelming majority of the people on the planet. Most people scavenge for food every day, and ration their water with a spinal surgeon's precision. Locally, some of the worst calls are when we have to defend dumpsters at the restaurants and grocery stores—keeping people from trying to get to the food-waste that can't be composted or recycled somehow. But it's not the people dumpster-diving that I would call degenerates or animals. It's the people who are so intent on turning profits that they can't handle the idea of someone eating the expired chocolate bar for free. The citizens who live in our low-income neighbourhoods have no savings, no land, and no chance of getting a steady job and a liveable wage, so they do what they have to do. I'd do the same, but I'm better off, for now.

As cops, we get paid okay, and our housing is provided. I'm careful with my pay cheques and my credit, but I'm in a better position than most because I don't have any dependents. My fresh water is relatively limited, but like I said, I'm careful. And I finish my food—nothing gets wasted.

Though they pay us pretty well, we have to make sacrifices. It's all very clear during the interview process—the metal grafts under the skin, the probes they put in our brains to dull our pain receptors, and the wakefulness pills. We become 'fuel injected'. That's what they say to make us feel like it's not wrong… like it's cool instead. The meatheads amongst us just run with the idea. I call those guys the false-alphas: they're just loud assholes who try to impose their will on a world that's too complex for them. A world that has *moved beyond a man's inflated sense of self-importance. These false-alphas have a motto for us, and they've posted it all over the station: 'Our eyes don't drip and our hearts don't bleed'.*

Everybody knows, but people want the job anyway. Working with the Great Lakes Regional Police Service is one of the most desirable jobs available, mostly because we have a twenty-and-out policy. Put in your twenty years, retire with the best severance package a regular job can offer. No real pensions anymore, but we get something at least, which is important, because you can't stay on past the twenty year mark unless you're working in upper management by then. So while you're working, you have to be careful with your money, or else you'll be desperate for a new career as soon as you get let go.

Otherwise, while we're working, they take care of us pretty well, but it's really just because they have to. They have to do more for us because of the bad things they—because of the toll the job takes on us. You'd think there's a better way to balance that out, but it's not my job to fight for that, and I don't have the energy. So I gladly accept my three weeks of consecutive vacation each year.

We're the only service that works legally across two different countries, all around the Great Lakes. And the service has good funding. But it's a touchy area to police, as the landfill cops operate within our jurisdiction and there are some knuckle-draggers working for the independent security companies, doing patrols of the wealthiest estates.

So we have to deescalate a lot of confrontations, and we have to be vigilant, because people occasionally try to steal the garbage or equipment from the landfill. It's easy to stop them, but it's hard to stop people from killing each other. Beyond the landfill, the threat of theft is constant in the city streets, and increasingly, people have a penchant for killing thieves who have no choice but to steal—I guess I shouldn't say 'no choice'. We all have a choice. You can see my job's not fun, but this is the choice I made. We work long hours; it's designed that way as a cost-saving measure. Long hours and short turnarounds mean they can hire fewer people, as long as we can sustain the workload. Obviously they've found a way to make that happen.

And that is why this one hour, the hour where I eat and I am not on duty, is so important to me. I work for twenty-three hours per day and I don't go home for seven days. This is my hour. And I don't get paid for this hour. It's mine.

Now let's say it's the first day I'm on shift, so I'm coming from home. I tool up and go to shift briefing at 0600. For the next twenty-three-and-a-half hours after briefing, this is what I do, in general: I hit the road in my cruiser, and usually there's a response-call within ten minutes, so I don't hit the road with any plan. Throughout the shift, I'll find my way back to the station to do reports—which to my understanding are just as cumbersome as they were fifty years ago, or even more so—then I usually get my ninety minutes of workout time in right after that. And that is paid time, we have to log the exercise, and it's all recorded and reviewed by management. I hit the road some more, I work front desk, I complete two hours of mandatory hand-to-hand combat or high-risk scenario training with a small group. Road, reports, desk. And I eat a huge meal when I get my hour.

We work twenty-three hour shifts, seven days on, two days off, with a third day off after every fourth rotation. We shower at the station during our days on.

This is the rock that I push.

Cormac Dawson left the Terrace Bay detachment, but remained indoors as he walked through the halls of the Northern Great Lakes Community Village Complex, which all the locals knew as The Blade. The nickname referred to the blade of a snowplow, not slicing or stabbing, but scraping clean. The building was chevron shaped, with its centre point driving into the prevailing northwest winds. It towered over old-town Terrace Bay, standing ten stories tall and extending five hundred metres in either direction from its apex. In its shadow were the new housing and community developments, sheltered from the storms and treacherous winter winds. At its leading edge grew a peculiar area that was a mix of the old town and new construction, with relatively wealthy citizens moving into town in the new builds, while their neighbours nearby struggled to keep the lights on in their old homes.

Much of the ground level of The Blade housed shops and restaurants, set deep into the building. To maintain efficiency in the most extreme winter weather conditions, the upper stories had bands of triple-glazed windows, laid into the solid concrete construction.

With durability and ease of construction the key concerns, almost all new buildings were constructed with concrete. Local granite was used as the aggregate, giving the new developments the same colour pallet as the surrounding hills and The Blade. The new districts, as well as the infill of empty lots in the old town, continued this aesthetic and acted as an extension of The Blade, both physically as well as in the collective consciousness of the people who lived in and around the area. Whether you were in The Blade or miles away from it, its shadow loomed large and its purpose and value were always near the front of your mind.

Besides the police station, The Blade also housed many of the city's important amenities: a fire and emergency services station, a grocery store, a health and fitness centre, a boutique hotel, a museum, provincial and city government offices, a courthouse, a movie theatre, a hospital and scientific research facility, and a private school. Further, The Blade was home to a handful of the area's socioeconomic elite, who lived there in ninth and tenth floor studio apartments, sacrificing space for access.

Every visit to The Blade came with pocket searches, illness screenings, a multimodal biometrics exam, and a biometrics-of-intent test, all completed by members of the Canadian Armed Forces. Facial and voice recognition, an iris scan, and both an electrocardiogram and an electroencephalogram were common at The Blade's entrance. The entire facility was supremely secure, with dozens of military members, police officers, and private security workers in the building at any given time.

On foot, Cormac's movements were assured, his steps firm. He made a point of not locking eyes with any civilians, but of noting their movements and expressions in his periphery. He kept his eyes forward as he passed an armed security guard while entering Milly's Café; he often stopped there early in his walk, as it was the one expensive pleasure he allowed himself on a daily basis. His orders were often done at random, as he enjoyed any hot drink: a flat white on this day.

"Morning, Detective." The security guard stood up from his high stool and put both hands down to adjust his duty belt as he spoke.

"Yeah," Cormac replied, and kept moving. He took ten paces before stopping to take full satisfaction in his first drink. He drank in tiny, savoured sips, even after the cup was half-empty and the coffee well below its peak temperature.

Passing the grocery store, Cormac spotted another security guard barking orders at a customer and trying to open the man's reusable grocery bag. Despite the comprehensive security measures in place at The Blade, there remained an ever-present distrust of and distaste for authority among many citizens. These people accepted the lengthy process to enter The Blade, but once inside, they were more than willing to cause a scene in the name of their perceived rights, and most would not roll over based on the hunches of security officers. Cormac flashed his badge before he spoke: "Problem here?"

"Got a feeling about this one. I'm trying to check receipts but he's giving me trouble over it."

"I've only got four items in here. He just watched me check out, and he's been staring at me like he wants to fuck me."

"Shut your mouth, you—"

"Enough!" Cormac looked for somewhere to set his coffee, flustered at having to separate with it. "If there's nothing to hide and you're in a hurry, just give me the bag and let's be done with it... four items. Receipt matches. Clothing doesn't have any bulging pockets, nowhere to hide anything." He turned to the security guard, venom in his voice as he continued, "So unless you want to get his pants off."

He handed the bag back to the civilian, continuing to look at the security officer as he did so. He turned left and right, having forgotten where he set his coffee.

"Christ," he muttered, picking up the cup and moving on.

The grocery store was the end of the line—the final section of The Blade. A few more paces and he was at the main entrance, where numerous soldiers divided civilians, scanning, searching, and questioning as needed. These were professionals with one simple but vital task, and the shoppers seeking entrance understood the routine and the necessity.

Just outside the entrance, uniformed officers Colton Oakshot and Naseer Aleem stood side-by-side in silence, waiting for Cormac.

"Let's walk and talk, boys. I got shit to do today."

"Yessir," Oakshot replied, and the three men walked along the imaginary line between the neighbourhoods on either side of The Blade.

They hadn't walked another block before there was a clear drop in the number of people in sight. Dozens with medical masks, piling around the entrance to The Blade, had turned to a sparse spatter of walkers and runners, all in an apparent hurry, collars turned up, chins tucked, eyes on the pavement. It was a town designed for pedestrian traffic, with wide sidewalks and ample bike lanes, as well as a well-funded and affordable public transit system. But people often took to the sidewalks with great haste, worried about the weather or the potential of being accosted by a thief, a drug addict, or a police officer.

Further still, many people moved quickly because they were taught—from childhood—to avoid crowds; there was always the threat of being associated with an uprising. It didn't matter if it was an insurgency, a riot, a strike, a march, a peaceful protest, or a candlelit vigil. This fear began decades earlier, when several US states passed laws to limit punishments or even grant full immunity to anyone who rammed their car into a crowd during a protest.

"Why are you with us? This seems like a two-person gig," Cormac said to Aleem.

Aleem waited a beat, and looked to Oakshot.

"Staff has me working with a watchdog for a bit. I got another complaint last week." Oakshot swatted at a bug hovering near his face. "Fuckin' bees."

"Jesus," Cormac said, grabbing Oakshot's wrist. "Would you relax? You've got the mannerisms of a mascot."

"Sorry. I just hate bees."

Aleem quietly put his thumb and index finger to the bridge of his nose and completed a slow, deliberate blink, coupled with a deep but silent breath.

"So this is my guy—my ex-snitch. He did some time, he cleaned up and got off the fentanyl. Got recruited by the Freedom Phonies around that time. And almost immediately, they moved into his property, which in the brief time since, looks to have become the base of their operation. He's been involved for less than a year, but he seems to know everything about their plans, or at least he talks like he does."

"Sounds promising then."

"Yeah but he won't want to be seen with me and Aleem. Uniforms will put him too much on edge."

"Then why are you both here with me? You could have just told me where to meet him."

"Well, it's just, this is my guy, and I didn't feel like checking pulses on limp wrists by the waterfront just yet today."

"Some watchdog." Cormac glanced at Aleem, but only for a moment.

"Okay, here it is. He's squirrelly. Charlie Manson type. He'll know who you are as soon as you walk in. We'll take twenty minutes and walk the area."

Sitting on a barstool in the vestibule, a heavyset woman scanned Cormac's ID—a multipurpose, government-issued smartcard that contained his driving record, healthcare needs, employment information, emergency contact, and more. She then checked his temperature before grunting something indecipherable and motioning for him to enter.

"It's nine o'clock in the morning and you're already too bored to talk?"

"Hm?" she replied, taken aback.

"You can't say one word to someone about to come here and spend his time and his money?"

"Well I just—I said go in—and I just do the temperatures."

Cormac was already two steps away as she spoke. The next words he heard were from the bartender.

"I told you twice already. Do you think you're charming me into it? We don't serve until eleven."

"Then what the fuck are you doing standing back there? Are

you a prop? Are you getting paid? I have a right to voice my complaint!" a bony little man hollered at the bartender.

"Elroy Maitland?" Cormac pointed to the man who was doing the yelling, keeping his hand close to his chest and lifting his eyebrows.

"What?!"

Cormac showed his badge to the bartender. "No trouble here. How about just one for the guy? We'll go to a table in the back and keep quiet. You'll keep quiet, won't you, Elroy?"

"Yeah, sure. Of course."

"And you'll tip the man, won't you, Elroy?"

"I guess, yeah."

"Well okay then."

"Pay first," said the bartender.

After confirming the card payment, the bartender unlocked the topside sliding door of a sparsely stocked cabinet under the bar, keeping his eyes on his patrons through the process. He poured Elroy two fingers of whisky into a lowball glass, pushed it one inch in Elroy's direction, and gave Cormac a dissatisfied, 'here ya go' grin.

Elroy put both hands on the glass, as if it would flip over if he didn't. "Pick a table," he instructed, preoccupied. He waited until Cormac began to move, got a read on which table he was moving toward, and then followed, sliding carefully into Cormac's slipstream. He carried the drink like a small child who had been entrusted with carrying a lidless glass for the first time in his life.

Cormac sat and didn't bother to speak; Elroy would need to be soothed first. Elroy's eyes remained on the whisky, his hands pressed on the table, as he shrunk into the booth. With his shoulders hunched and his neck extended toward the glass, he looked like he needed a booster chair.

He put the glass to his lips and slowly tipped it, letting the liquid lap to and from his mouth, with only trace droplets touching his tongue. He moaned. He took a half-mouthful, and while inhaling slowly, he swished it around his cheeks, between his teeth, and over and under his tongue. He swallowed.

"Ahhhh. Oh." Another deep breath came as he emerged from his euphoria. "It's the worst part, the swallowing. Sometimes I'll spit it back into the glass, if I'm alone."

"Uh huh."

"Okay. Now business. I saw you out the window. Saw you were working with a darky. You like that?"

"Like what?"

"Working with one. What is he, just like a third gen Canadian?"

"I don't know. But I don't mind it."

"It. Ha."

"Him. I don't mind 'it'—working with him. But I don't see him much. He's a know-it-all anyway. He does what he does and I do what I do."

"And what do you do?"

"Criminal investigations."

"I'm gonna cut right to it, okay? We're getting organized too. Not for crime. For salvation. For liberation. And we think it's time to get the cops on our side. The right cops. The ones who are as fed up as us, and the ones who haven't turned into pride queers and ass kissers. The ones who still crack the heads of crackheads."

"I'm listening."

"Good. Because the proud patriots of the National Force of Freedom Fighters want to work with you. You specifically, and others like Oak. No one any darker than him. Too much risk even if they still hold good Canadian values like us—even if they take our oath—because they've got family around them trying to pull them the other way. Oak told me you'd be on board. And we've looked into your… experiences."

"What do you want from me?"

"It's a silent partnership for now, nothing more yet. There's certain influences we want stifled, and we think you want the same thing."

"We?"

"Us. The ones who fight for the freedoms and the history that you cops can't admit you want."

"And who else?"

"There's plenty. We got Lawrence now. The man is a master." Elroy was too proud, too excited. "One. He's ex-US military." His eyes widened as he began grabbing his fingers in an animated counting motion. "Two. He's a former Canadian government food production researcher. And C, he's a damn genius with a capital G." He laughed triumphantly, and Cormac continued to let him talk.

"Besides him and our core group, there's plenty of people who think like we think, but haven't found the balls to come forward yet. But they will, as they continue to see us spreading. That's where you come in. Eventually, they'll start to see legit recognized authority helping out at our functions, supporting our rallies, cuffing the criminals we've been telling you to cuff for years."

"Okay, I see your vision. But this is a big ask, and would be a bold move for me, with my career on the line, silent or not. I'll need to know exactly who I'm partnered with. I need to know who's bankrolling you. I've noticed this increased presence you mentioned."

"Why would you need to know that?"

"There's people with money that I don't like. There's people with money that I don't want to be associated with. If their goals are the same as yours, fine, but that doesn't mean I'm willing to put my name next to theirs."

"Sounds like you've been hanging out with that dark one more than you let on."

"How so?"

"Only a snowflake cares where the money comes from. We don't even care what their goals are or what they've got on the backburner. We just take their money and do what we want. Here's the thing: they think we're the pawns. But we've got our own plans. It's just their money."

"Okay, but if you don't tell me who they are, then I can't be what you want me to be for your cause."

"Then buy me my next drink and go back to dark-man out there. It's your loss, and we'll just find some other muscle-dummy with a badge to help us."

"Good luck, little man." Cormac got up and left without a second glance. Elroy yelled for him to hold on, but Cormac just walked out into the chilled wind of the street. He reconnected with Aleem and Oakshot a few minutes later, when they caught up to him on his way back to The Blade.

"Wait up. How'd it go?" Oakshot hollered.

"Did you tell that fucking bozo that I wanted to work with the Freedom Fighters?"

"Well—"

"Do you know what that does to us when word gets around? Doesn't matter if it's not true. Next time I'm up for a promotion, it'll be the first thing the panel asks me. Keep walking. Snow squalls are coming, so we need to hustle."

"And having this rumour out there won't help our reputation in the poorer communities," Aleem noted.

"Shut up, Naseer. We don't need you to tell us how this was a fuck up. I was the one who was there and met that raving little weasel. I don't need to hear about it from you."

"Sorry, Dawson."

"It was just a waste of time," Cormac resigned as his anger dissipated.

"But they are dangerous," Aleem added.

"Yeah. They won't disappear. We should get into that compound before... whatever it is they're planning."

Pete Canizales sat in a waiting room. It was a stylish space in a modern office rented by his psychologist. With a coffee bar, soft lighting, plush chairs, and pops of colour from fake flowers, it was an inviting location. Anderson Holdings, a subsidiary of Disney, was the company that owned the building; they provided the coffee bar, as well as an iPad, tethered to a massage chair, loaded with pay-for-play games and retail purchasing options for products from Anderson Holdings and its affiliates.

Stockwell Anderson had the building erected six years earlier; it was one of many buildings he owned in the area. His name was quickly becoming ubiquitous in the newer developments in Terrace Bay—on billboards and on skyscrapers and at bus stops and on park benches. He was first an investment specialist heralded by the media as a wunderkind, who then branched out to become a real estate mogul and a self-described professional sports prop-bettor. He was also the heir to a tremendous fortune, with his father, Vance, having made millions in the real estate market, after having himself inherited hundreds of millions of dollars in properties, businesses, and investments made by his own father, Cooper, who was a pioneer in the transition of sports trading cards becoming non-fungible digital files to be traded amongst hedge fund billionaires and fine art aficionados instead of children and sports fans.

Pete didn't know any of that. He just knew the chairs were comfortable and the room was always quiet. Having been waiting for a few minutes, he decided to pull out his phone, and began watching a compilation video of coffees being prepared: the soothing sounds of the pour-overs, the creamy milk froths, the sputtering cappuccino machines, the last droplet of rich, black coffee rippling across the surface.

Ava Gavril opened a door to Pete's left, greeting him as he turned to her while pocketing his phone. "Pete. Please, come in."

"How's the diet been?" Ava asked as the two sat down in her office.

"Good, good. It's not too hard. Limiting sugar is easy for me. I don't really get into sweets much. Caffeine, I don't really miss either. I don't know if any of it is helping, but I guess it's healthy for the long-term anyway."

"And it gives you something new to focus on, when you're home."

"Yeah. Meal-planning I don't mind either."

"And have you found someone at work? Regarding what we talked about last time—someone to confide in?"

Pete hesitated. He turned the thought over in his head, wishing there was a better way to phrase his response. "It's just not really how I operate."

"We've talked about that too though, Pete. It's how you need to operate, if you want to build the tools to overcome your trauma."

"Yeah, I know, but some of these things you're asking me to do—talking to people and finding more people to spend time with outside work and taking those designated break times and—these are all things, or 'problems' that I had before. That was who I was before I found that baby. And further back, that's who I was before I ever had to draw my pistol. I don't understand how changing who I've always been is supposed to help me get over something that happened about a month ago."

"I hear you, Pete. Truly." Ava let her words sink in. "These things you've been told you're supposed to do—told you're supposed to be—tough and silent and strong and insulated and private and enduring and unbreakable… you've been taught wrong, Pete. Someone taught you to spend your adult life engaging in these unhelpful habits. They're mistakes. And you've been encouraged to grip those mistakes so tight. So tight that they hurt you but are hidden from everyone else."

Pete became flush with heat, no longer interested in proving any point.

"It's not that I think I'm right, Ava," he conceded. "It's that I don't think I can do it any other way."

"That's why I'm here for you. I'm not making you into a new person. I'm only trying to show you that you've got the ability. I know that you can. And you've already made some small changes that may feel meaningless to you, but I can assure you that they're not. Those changes are extremely difficult for many people. But your next step really is to find someone who you can confide in. You speak so highly of some of your fellow officers. Why not reach out to one or two of the people who can relate to what you go through?"

"Yeah. Yeah, maybe." He turned to look at the door, and briefly considered walking out. "I found something to relax me a bit, when I force myself into the breaks."

"Good, that's great. What is it?"

"I watch compilation videos. Nothing goofy. And usually not

with music. People making coffee. That's what I like the most. People cooking breakfasts. Painting pictures. Also dominoes falling. Just big clips of people knocking over those dominoes designs. It's stupid, but, yeah."

"It's not stupid, Pete. Whatever helps you cope is useful. It's important."

"I still have the nightmares." He paused, looking at her, gauging her response before deciding whether or not to say more. "I think I'm more irritable than I used to be, but that could be just because I'm thinking about it more, making notes and trying to analyze myself. But the nightmares are real. And the guilt."

"You've got absolutely nothing to feel guilty about, Pete."

"He was just a baby, you know? And they... for someone to... a goddamn little baby." He put his head in his hands, and Ava reached out to touch his knee. He pulled back as though it hurt, like an electric shock. "Sorry, sorry," he said, unsure why he retracted at the touch.

"It's okay, I'm the one who's sorry."

He stood up and took a step to the door, then turned and went back to the chair, stood like a statue for a moment, and then met Ava's eyes. "Can I sit back down?"

"Of course."

He sat, she handed him a tissue, and they didn't exchange another word for several minutes.

Before the snow blew in, Lucian's phone was dinging with notifications. He took the first job he was offered, as he knew that waiting for a bigger job could lead to not getting any job at all. The business of plowing snow was cutthroat, as all operators were unlicensed. Once you could afford to get a bucket or a blade on your truck, you were as good as the next guy. Legitimate contracts were hard to come by. Prices were undercut at every turn, and there was no loyalty from customers, no camaraderie amongst plowers.

Some could buy a plower's time before the snow had settled:

they didn't want to have to wait for the plow to arrive afterwards, so they could pay an hourly rate to have the operator drive out to the site and sit in the truck until there was enough snow to actually do the work.

The winds were fierce and the roads mostly empty as Lucian drove to the job; it was a mere ten minutes from his house, given that he didn't need to have much consideration for traffic. He advertised all over the truck: across the rear window, along the side panels, on the storage boxes in the utility bed, on the tailgate, and even in large white letters across the lowest part of his windshield:

Gavril Plow: Snow, Tow, Contract Work.

He drove an American made quad cab in aquatone blue, with an attached plow blade. There had been a major push in the last twenty years, wherein American car companies began advertising the "Return To Form" with all models available in the popping colours of the 1950s and 60s. Monetary incentives were offered to buyers who were willing to drive off the lot in something coral red, green mist metallic, champagne yellow, or bubble gum pink: old fashioned American optimism.

When Lucian arrived, he was waved down and stopped at the entrance to a fenced-in lot. A man who appeared to have no professional designation instructed him to remain seated, then patted him down with lazy, but rough, flat-handed smacks. Meanwhile, another man hastily looked along the inside panels and under the floor-mat on the passenger side.

Neither man greeted him, looked him in the eyes, or took his temperature. These were not men concerned with germs.

When he was allowed in, he parked along the fence, at the end of the laneway he'd be tasked with clearing foremost. A minute passed, and then Lucian pulled an apple from his coat's inside pocket—a bulging and solid item that the man searching Lucian had ignored. From the truck's glove compartment, Lucian grabbed a folding knife with a yellow plastic handle and a rigid, finely honed blade. He began eating the apple in large, neatly sliced chunks.

His mouth hung open for an extra second, the blade hovering

below his chin, as he watched a man come running out of the closest building on the property, nearly getting swept off his feet by blustering gusts as he ran on his tiptoes toward the truck—he was barefooted, woefully underdressed, and held his hair as he ran, as if it were a hat that would fall off if he let go. It was Elroy Maitland.

"You want to come in? Get out of the cold while you wait!" Elroy shouted through the closed window.

Lucian agreed to go inside, though he would have rather stayed in his truck. He just didn't want to stall to make an excuse, because he felt an obligation to get the man out of the cold.

"What's your name?"

"Lucian."

"What kind of fag name is that?"

"Not any kind. My family is from Romania, lots of generations back."

"Ah. I'm Elroy. Come in. Come in."

Lucian took off his parka while Elroy took a step back, rubbed his hands together, and examined his guest. There were three other men in the small, one-floor office building; all the building's interior doors were closed. The room's centrepiece was a desk with a penholder that contained five small flags: Canada, the United States, the Confederate States, and two that Lucian didn't recognize.

"I don't think I've ever seen a couple of those flags."

"So?" said an alarmingly fat man sitting in a rolling chair in the corner of the room. He had been scrolling on his phone, a pair of glasses teetering on the tip of his nose.

"Well, nothing. I've just always had an interest in flags, so I'm curious."

"Where are you from?" The man removed his reading glasses and rolled his chair a little closer as he spoke.

"Here. I'm fifth gen." He turned to Elroy. "Like I said, I just like flags."

"This one's our flag," Elroy said, holding a flag that was split horizontally: red on the top, navy blue on the bottom. It had a horizontal diamond shape stretching from end to end, and in the middle was the outline of a white bull's head, with two swords crossed behind it. A single word was written in the middle of the bull's head: 'Abwehr'.

Elroy pointed to the other flags: "And that's Canada, the US, the Confederacy, and the UPC. We got our own flag folded up in that display case there too." He pointed to a floating shelf that had two items: a Holy Bible and a triangular wooden box, with the Freedom Fighters' flag folded inside.

"Lord Jesus, Elroy!" The obese man was furious, but calmed himself before he spoke again. "You don't need to give the guy a tour."

"Sorry, ha, yeah. Sorry." Elroy then turned back to Lucian. "Hey listen, you want a cigarette?"

"Sure."

With some strained effort, the fat man grabbed a folding chair from a nearby computer desk, and gestured for Lucian to sit—Lucian obliged him. Without a desk to hide his legs under, Lucian's elongated figure was on full display. A praying mantis in a plastic chair.

The stranger was burly. His beard was overwhelming but well manicured, a tuft of chest hair sprayed out over the v-neck of his t-shirt, and he wore a deeply curved and impossibly faded baseball hat low to his eyes.

"We been looking for someone like you." He waited as Lucian lit his cigarette. "Someone who don't mind hard work, harsh weather. Someone quick to take a call—we noticed you got here in a hurry. Those are the types we like around our compound."

"And we know the struggle, with your line of work," added Elroy. "Trust me on that. We've got lots of extra jobs around here. Lots of things on the go. We could always use a guy with a good truck. Especially someone who looks like he could jump over a ten foot fence if we needed."

Elroy laughed then, though the stranger did little more than let his mouth curl up slightly on one side, noticeable only by the movement of his moustache. He continued to examine Lucian silently for a moment, then sat back in his chair, relaxed his posture, and lit a cigarette of his own.

"The Hatchet-Man cometh," Cst. Oshun Briggs announced in triumph, as he brought a murder suspect before S/Sgt. Canizales to finalize the arrest. Unamused, Canizales stood up from his desk—where he'd been watching an NBA Classics documentary on his phone—sighed, and met Briggs at the doorway to his office to begin the booking process. He pulled his notebook from his vest pocket, and clicked the top of his pen while giving the suspect and Briggs each a once-over.

"And what do you think the first thing I'm going to ask you about is, Briggs?"

Briggs recognized his error before Pete had even finished the sentence. "The cuffing."

"Why are this man's hands cuffed in front instead of behind?"

"I'm sorry, sir. The arrest was completed without incident, and the suspect obeyed all instructions. I cuffed him behind at first, prone position, full search, rights and caution given."

"I assume you did all those things, Briggs. And while I'm glad the process was followed correctly, one major error remains unresolved."

"He said he was uncomfortable, once I sat him in the cruiser. I wouldn't have done it if there was any other concern. He—"

"Say no more, Officer."

"Understood."

Canizales continued with the booking process, first by completing the custody log: he questioned the arrested man about all his biographical information, then used a biometrics scanner to confirm what the sobbing suspect had already told him—name, date of birth, home address, and so on. Briggs stifled his sense of pride in order to answer further follow-up questions—charges laid and place of arrest.

"All right. I'll do the risk assessment, search, property log, and all the rest, and get this man on the phone with counsel. I need one rookie to join me." Three jumped at the opportunity to be involved with a major arrest, and Pete chose the first to approach his desk "Briggs, I can see you want to celebrate this one a bit, and that's why I'm taking over from here. Solid work. Keep your hoorahs quiet."

Briggs was greeted with fist bumps and claps on the back when he re-entered the bullpen with his colleagues. "Another killer off the streets. Now the people can relax, and that sick bastard can rot," he gloated.

"How quickly we forget the dead," Cst. Aleem sat forward at his cubicle, his arms on his desk, looking at his computer screen.

Briggs rolled his eyes and turned dramatically. "What's that you say?"

"Yes, the murderer was caught, it seems. Congratulations on making that arrest, truly. And there is a deserved sense of relief. The public can and should breathe a collective sigh. I'm not just talking about you and this moment, Briggs. Not just this crime and this arrest. People—civilians and officers alike—share the news as though we should feel a genuine happiness. But what about those two people who were murdered? They'll never know that relief. And their families and friends? Many times, even the arresting officer is left haunted: a case solved instead of a crime prevented." Aleem looked to Canizales' office, causing Briggs to briefly do the same. Something gave Briggs pause for a moment, but he remained defensive when he spoke:

"Okay, so I guess I'm sorry? And thanks for shitting on my moment. And now we should just sit here and mope then, yeah?"

"No. I won't tell you how to feel. It's not my place."

"Not your place? Then why not just do us all a favour and go back to saying nothing at all, Alum?"

"You know that's not my name."

"Aleem."

Aleem nodded slightly, then got up and left the room.

The clerk behind the glass was discreet. She waited until another officer passed by out of sight before grabbing a small box, sliding it to Cst. Natalie Ross, and asking, "Why do your deliveries come to the station?"

"I don't like anyone knowing where I live." She took the package. "Have a good day."

Having completed the final shift of her rotation, Natalie kept a brisk pace as she walked to her car. Wet snow fell slowly around her, leaving tiny pockets in the crushed blankets of snow already on the ground. She locked the doors when she entered the car, and with a small pocketknife she kept in the centre console, she carefully opened the package to reveal a voice recorder, this one different from the remarkably tiny clip she used on the job. Designed to be attached to a phone, it was a circular magnet the size of a shirt button. The instruction manual took up far more space within the packaging than the actual product did. She observed it just long enough to ensure it was exactly what she thought it would be, then tucked it back into the box, set it aside, and took a quick look to see if anyone was watching her. Satisfied, she began her drive home.

Her building was not far away, but she always chose to drive, as walking home after seven consecutive days of work without sleep was daunting, and it was vital for her to make the most of her brief forty-eight hours out of uniform. She always avoided taking the final wakefulness pill of her rotation, leaving her drained by the time she was walking to her car—sleep comes first when it's time to go home.

On her brief route, she drove away from the station, which was the east end of The Blade, and through the city's commercial district. These buildings were a continuation of the curtain-wall of The Blade, enhancing the microclimate created by blocking high winds. All the buildings there were tall and ultra-durable, with ballistic glass on the first floors. The district's architecture was essentially disaster-proof, built to withstand both the elements and potential uprisings from the public.

Minutes later, she approached the gates of her apartment complex; it was one of the last large Brutalist buildings before the size of the structures tapered and the value of the real estate plummeted. Recognizing her face, the system granted her entry. She drove down the pathway to the parking garage, nodding to the guards whom she passed along the way.

The cavernous garage was tightly packed with vehicles of varying eye-catching, bright colours—a candy-coated fleet of small, sleek sedans. With understated external features, the cars were a display of neat and refined engineering, expertly parked between hulking support pillars.

As she exited her vehicle, she saw the backlit silhouette of a person who seemed to be watching her from a distance. She watched a tiny flame flicker and the cherry of a cigarette begin to burn. The person may have been watching her, but hiding did not appear to be a concern. As Natalie continued to walk, she indexed her tools—moving the fingers of her left hand over the softy holstered along the inside of her right forearm, then tracing her left middle finger along the burner implanted in her left palm, feeling its dull heat. She chose the staircase rather than the elevator.

Upon entering her apartment, Natalie locked the door and spoke:

"Laura, turn the lights down low and play the song, Stilted Austerity by Cold Weather Curators."

"Okay, just a moment," came the reply.

"Thank you."

Natalie's apartment was small, sparsely furnished, and clean. Everything had its place, and nothing seemed hung haphazardly or tossed aside in a rush. She removed her coat, hung it on one of the two hooks on the wall beside the door, and placed her shoes neatly on a small rubber mat. She lit a candle on the desk at her window. The desk was a relic from a public school that had boarded up in the twenties—an immobile chair with a folding desktop barely bigger than a sheet of paper. She sat at the tiny desk, folded the tabletop down, and attached her new recording device to her phone screen; a magnetic snapping sound confirmed the connection.

With heavy eyes, she read the back-cover of the instruction manual: 'Concerned with privacy? Say no more. The Incognito's specialized technology and near-limitless memory allow you to attach and detach the memory card without concern for time or space. No set-up. No configurations. No concern for adaptability. No need to save. No extra steps. Simply stick it to your phone's screen and tap to begin recording your reminders, your notes, your song, your diary, your journal, your thoughts, your stories, your memoir, your conversation. Then, without a moment's notice, take it off and slip it into your pocket. If you've got phone numbers, photos, and videos you want kept off the cloud and out of the hands of potential thieves, the Incognito is your best option! Further, a single droplet of water will wipe the memory but not ruin the Incognito's future recording capability. In today's society, your privacy is paramount. Enjoy it with the Incognito.'

Before using the device, Natalie rethought her position, and moved to rest comfortably on her bed instead. She began recording:

I don't like my little desk. I thought about putting in a floating desk to save space, but I didn't want to be bothered with the installation and with removing my current desk. Those are just menial tasks, I know, but all the same... I don't want to do them.

She paused, lingering in the satisfied silence that followed expressing herself without concern for judgment.

My job. No matter who you are, the job is hard. But it's harder still because I'm a woman. Thank god I'm tall. At least that keeps the runts at bay. There are lots of people looking for a chance to bully. And these are just the people I work with. I'm 5'11" and-a-half. I won't say I'm six feet because I'm not. I'm 5'11" and-a-half. So all the guys that are two or three inches shorter than me try to tell me that I'm 6'1". It's like 5'10" is this cut-off point, and no man in the western world is comfortable admitting he's shorter than that.

There's nothing I can do to make these guys want to partner with me. Not that I care, but regardless of my size, my marksmanship, my track record of avoiding fatalities—which means less paperwork—and the fact that I don't like to talk, these guys still don't want to work any cases or take any calls with me.

They had me out of uniform for a while. I focused mostly on interrogations of suspects and undercover work in the cells for a couple years. That's where my skill set allowed me to stand out. But they just put me back on the street because they knew there'd be fewer police-caused casualties that way. They could let some other officer strong-arm witnesses and slap around suspects; that stuff is safer inside the walls of the station. Better for the service to have me work a beat, and self-sacrifice is what the job's all about. In a way, it's been like this for over a century, I know, but the demands are different now. Self-sacrifice for a community or a cause, sure. But the cause isn't clear anymore.

I can put up with everyone on the job, despite all the grating personalities. It's not that hard. Calculated restraint comes naturally to me. I'm not talkative, but I'm good with people. All kinds of people.

The only guy I actually like at work is Pete, my staff sergeant. He's battle-hardened, a former combat engineer who served overseas. He has a deep antipathy toward people who speak sarcastically or passive-aggressively—it's a matter of principle. Pete despises visible weakness, and he's skeptical of everyone he meets. He's short, but he doesn't care. He's bald, but he doesn't care. He has deep pockets on his face and wears a permanent scowl. He's tight-fisted, but he's a good person. He organizes our pantry fund and does our monthly lottery ticket purchase.

Our platoon goes in on the lottery at the end of every month; we call it our Way Out. A jackpot winning ticket hasn't been claimed in several years. The pot just keeps growing.

It's been a win/lose for the government, as they let the largest and most powerful corporations buy in on and control the lottery. These corporations still operate separately, but their group name, strictly for the lottery, is The Association. I guess they couldn't think of anything more sinister. The Association is a sub-group from the UPC, which is an organization that has a lot of pull in Canada and the US. So anyway, now Canada and the States share the lotto, with each country's government getting 12.5% of the profits from every ticket sold, and The Association getting 33%. It used to be just 25% for The Association, but they raised it twice recently. They didn't lower the amount the governments get though; they just don't give out as much prize money now. But, though the major jackpot hasn't been claimed, there are still people winning—enough to keep everyone buying tickets anyway. And the governments try to put their shares back into the communities, but it gets harder and harder to find something to do with the money that doesn't feel like just throwing it away.

We even got some civilian employees on our shift—data entry clerks, *admin assistants, custodians, and a coroner—to join in with our lotto purchases. If we win the Way Out, there's plenty for all of us—enough to retire comfortably. People talk about quitting the service right away and moving into the Landfill Lofts, where it's safer. I wouldn't want to stay in Terrace Bay, personally. I'd probably move farther north; Nunavut has enough water and a lot of land, or uninhabited Ontario is where it's truly safe—no one to bother you.*

A balmy breeze swept over Terrace Bay as dusk fell on the city. There came a rare instance of the night air feeling like a snug blanket. Within hours, desolate, snow-covered streets turned heavy with slushy puddles as hundreds emerged from their homes, sensing the moment, looking to take advantage in whatever way they could: some desperately began collecting the snow, stockpiling water for home-use; others sat on their porches, enjoying the paradoxical feeling of sitting outside in complete comfort while looking over a winter night; some started immediately into outdoor exercise routines, unconcerned with the hour—walking or jogging with joyous disregard for puddles and ice; and others knew that it was time to loot. To exploit. To seek the vulnerable person who ran out the door unprotected or the house that had been left unattended.

Ava Gavril woke before dawn, as if by a sixth sense, and set to work with exhaustive discretion for all possible scenarios: by sunrise, she'd filled four large buckets with melting snow and placed them carefully in a locked cabinet, cleaned the basement in preparation for flooding, and then replaced the full bowls and damp towels in the attic at the usual leaky spots in the roof.

Because of their house's weak and aging structure, the Gavril family had focused on reinforcing their basement, in particular, to fight flooding. They had salvaged old car batteries and 12V water pumps from abandoned motorhomes, rigging the batteries to power the pumps, which would send flood water back out the basement windows; they had applied beads of caulking across the floor to funnel the last of the excess water into a floor drain; they had re-plumbed their hot water tank and elevated it with cinderblocks. Ava examined the handiwork in the basement, giving the hoses one more tiny turn to tighten and giving the cinderblocks a little push, as if touching them ensured their existence.

Out of necessity, people living in The Junk neighbourhoods that began around the west-end of The Blade developed the ingenuity and the practical skills to endure, and occasionally they would save enough money to improve some aspect of their home's security system, plumbing, or air flow efficiency. However, the plight of those same people was that they would never have the ability to move out of The Junk and into somewhere more desirable: the newer houses in The Blade's shadow, the apartments in the commercial district, studio apartments inside The Blade itself, or the lofts along the shores of Lake Superior, near the landfill.

The new builds were unattainable daydream-talk for the Gavrils. Lofts or Blade studios weren't even worth dreaming about.

The Gavrils had managed to fortify some key aspects of their home, installing impact-resistant windows and pressure-rated doors to defend against the strong winds and potential flying debris. Further, their waste-powered energy distribution system was brand new, meaning they could now use some supremely efficient garbage fuel and limit their reliance on heavily-taxed biofuels; however, the fact remained that the structure and foundation of the house were always at risk from the harsh winters, forceful winds, and especially the continued water damage.

During her preparations, Ava saw Lucian was already awake, sitting in the basement with his headphones on. She wasn't sure if he knew she was busying herself nearby, but she saw no reason to stop to find out. She was accustomed to the routine of readying for a rapid thaw, and she completed her duties in specific steps—to stop and do something else would shake her from the elevated state required to complete everything expeditiously. To veer from the process would be to run the risk of forgetting something vital.

When all was finished, Ava readied her weekly tea. Compared to the rest of her morning's activities, the tea was not as much a ritual, but just as much a careful process. Ava allowed herself one cup on any day of her choosing each week—she almost always chose the day in which she felt she was at her greatest deficit. The day when she felt there was a good chance her world would disappear: the roof might cave in, someone who still owns a gun could kick in the door, a man on the street might think she looks a little too close to Aboriginal, David will get caught in a tornado on his way home from school, Lucian isn't going to wake up, that tickle in her throat will be a life-sucking virus by day's end.

When the adrenaline crash came in the aftermath of her preparation, she felt like her entire existence was easy prey for anyone who might want to inflict some pain. She measured 150mL of water and peered out the front window while the kettle heated.

The day's first rays of sun began to sparkle off the slushy water on the street when the kettle was ready. As easily as she could hear the kettle click off behind her, she could also hear the water rushing into the sewers, like the rapids of a rocky stream.

Appearing as though he had just emerged from hypnosis, Lucian entered the room behind Ava. His eyes were bloodshot and his posture was hunched.

"It always did take you a while to straighten up in the morning," Ava quipped, smiling.

"Yuh." He straightened up a bit, flexed his legs, locked his knees, grunted. "Got some follow-up work from a job a couple days ago." He rubbed his face and then finally looked at Ava, waiting for her response.

"Good. That's great. Where is it? What's the job?"

"Little compound across town. I did a plow there last heavy snowfall. And they were odd folks, but… it's cash in hand. A weird guy invited me inside before I started. They seemed standoffish at first, but as they warmed up, they just kept finding reasons to put a little more money on my account, finding odd jobs and saying they could just pay me ahead of time. Some on the account, some cash. Some of the stuff was so simple, I can't believe they don't just do it themselves."

Ava enjoyed hearing Lucian speak for so long. She only nodded and continued to give space for him to keep talking.

"Yeah, there's eight or twelve people hanging around the place, but from my guess, none of them can hammer two boards together. Or they just don't want to bother, and somehow have the money to pay me. I'm not asking too many questions, but with plowing season nearly finished, it's good to know there's some repeat work there. They want me to build scaffolds today, and install this fancy new security camera system they just got. And they said when I'm finished this, they're going to pre-pay me to put up a new roof and build them a second bunkhouse in the spring."

"Great news, definitely."

"This'll keep David in school until June, for sure. With that pre-payment, we can probably put him up to three days a week for the rest of the year."

Cautiously optimistic, Ava's smile broadened as she touched a hand to Lucian's shoulder. He returned the smile in kind, and right there, they both remembered what they were working for, and why it was worthwhile.

"I'm gonna get out there now. You know what an early rise and a strong back gets you?" He waited a moment and she smiled in anticipation of the answer, which she already knew. "An extra hour's work."

With Lucian out the door, Ava took a deep breath, felt her muscles relaxing as she let the smile fall from her face, and put her mug of steaming tea to her lips just as David spoke.

"Mom? Can I have toast today?" He was dragging a full sized blanket the way a toddler might drag a teddy bear. "And can you bring this blanket back to my room?"

"Why did you bring—" she stopped short, knowing it was a pointless question. "Yes, baby. Just a second."

"I'm not a baby."

"Oh you're not? What? Yes you are!" She put her mug down

and ran to David, scooping him up with a laugh and cradling him like an infant, cooing and tickling and making kissing sounds while David giggled.

When he settled down on the floor to watch a cartoon, she readied his breakfast, his clothes, his snacks, and his backpack while her tea cooled to room temperature. And when she sent him off for the three-block walk to his school, she half sat, half fell onto the couch. She picked up her tea but then sighed and put it back down after confirming there was no longer any heat hovering over the cup. Exhausted, but with her mind racing, she curled up on the couch, hugging a pillow between her knees.

She closed her eyes and thought about all the horrible things that might happen to her and her family that day or the next.

Pete sat down in the office of Insp. Hunter Gilchrist, who studied him for a moment. A smile crept onto Gilchrist's face.

"I never see you wearing a hat, Canizales. How do you keep that cue ball head of yours warm all winter?"

"By minding my own business, sir."

Gilchrist sighed, chuckled, and moved on. "Well listen, as per your request... It's just not in the budget. We don't have the resources to keep sending people off the beat and down these rabbit-holes, trying to uncover some cloak-and-dagger conspiracy that only feels true under black light."

"Listen, Hunter. We've got good leads, not just consp—"

"Three officers! One detective and two in uniform, walking down the street together to do the job one guy could do. A job that should never have been signed off on in the first place. We could have used all three bodies at The Blade at that time. Did you know that a security guard got arrested for excessive force on a civilian? The whole debacle was humiliating. Videos are all over the internet. People laughing at us."

"That was a mistake, I agree. And yes, I heard about the arrest."

"And you should have had my approval before you placed Oakshot with another officer. He's not a recruit. Just because he's made a couple mistakes doesn't mean he needs a coach officer. He's fine on his own, and now I've got administrators breathing down my neck about one bloated salary placing two other bloated salaries together to do one job. You know oversight's cracking down on the budget for the new fiscal."

"Sorry I didn't clear that with you. It was due to some unjust search complaints, and I thought Oakshot could learn from an experienced and even-handed officer. I didn't want to bother you with something I knew I could handle myself."

"Well... okay. But put Oakshot back on his own beat. And I mean it: stop barking up this tree, Pete. Seriously. This isn't just coming from me. Deputy Chief Crawford, The Oversight Committee, the people that write the cheques. The 'they'. I'm serious. They told me what to tell you: forget who is funding these low-life losers. I'll give you a little slack, okay? Go ahead and keep an eye on the Freedom Fighters' facility for a while. But no separate operations—just send your beat guys to cruise past there now and then. If there's drug dealing or water hoarding or something, those idiots can't hide it for long."

Pete nodded. "I read you. Understood."

"But that's it. Focus on maintaining good presence around The Blade. Keep it simple. Protect the property, calm the unrest, keep foot-traffic flowing, make people feel safe. There's nothing wrong with old-fashioned policing, Pete."

"You won't get an argument from me there, sir."

With his facial expressions muted, shoulders back, and stride purposeful, Pete left Gilchrist's office and returned to his own, where Cormac was waiting for him. Cormac leaned on the top of the divider at a cubicle outside the office, his fingers clasped and his posture relaxed, and when he saw Pete, he straightened up firmly.

"Staff."

"Mac."

"Verdict?"

"Not good."

"Thought so. No money in the budget to fight crimes?"

"More or less."

"I'll find a way."

"Seems like we're hurting some feelings up high. Lots of push back. I know this is important to you, but—"

"Pete. Say no more. I will find a way."

"Send the new guy out to do the pickup. That's the easiest way," explained Zach, one of the Freedom Fighters. Zach was clean-shaven, and his hair was short on the sides and long on top, neat and tidy, with a military gloss. He wore a slim fitting jacket with an oversized collar. Zach's cosmopolitan style stood in stark contrast to his bearded friend, seated in his usual rolling chair against the wall in the Freedom Fighters' office; a hulking mess of a man, his beard had grown unkempt, appearing more like something that happened out of neglect than something he had allowed to grow. He sat forward, pulling his loose-fitting jeans up a bit on his quads, exposing his socks as he continued to listen to Zach.

"If that psycho Vickshaw—and I know he's family to me and I know he's a patriot, but the fact remains that he is crazy. So if that psycho Vickshaw won't leave his precious scrapyard and the UPC has eyes on us all the time, then the only one they won't bother tailing is the maintenance man, with his company vehicle, with his obligations elsewhere, with his minimal time spent on our grounds, with his nonexistent connections to our cause. He's just a contract man who comes and goes. Plus, no cop will suspect anything about the load when it's a contractor's truck. So he'll come, with the gear, and drop it off like he might on any other day, and we'll give him another beggar's task to do while he's here."

"UPC won't know a damn thing. The plot will officially be ours—reclaimed," the fat man added. Out of breath, the man still managed to heave himself off his chair, giving a stiff Nazi salute to his peers.

"The Abwehr strives on!" Elroy hollered in agreement, and all the others in the room stood up too. Zach offered a soft smile, chin held high, and a showy salute.

Lucian had just finished raking up muddy leaves to clear drains around the grounds of the compound. He went inside and grabbed some dry soap to clean his hands.

"Just put another twenty-five in your account for that one, buddy," Elroy said.

"Thanks. But hey, let me ask you something." He looked both ways and took a step toward Elroy before continuing, "Why don't you get one of these guys to do some of this grunt work? Don't get me wrong: I'm happy to be paid to do stuff like this. But I count at least ten guys lingering around, not doing much. Sometimes I catch people looking at me. Guys whose names I don't even know."

"You don't need to know their names and you don't need to know how many of us there are," the burly stranger said, emerging from a back room as though he'd been listening and waiting for the moment. "If you're ungrateful, you can piss off." He awkwardly reached an arm behind, tapping at his own lower back. It was the first time Lucian had seen him standing. His belly poured over his belt and his knees seemed to buckle under his own weight with each step, but he was nearly as tall as Lucian.

"I made it clear already," Lucian said, quietly but firmly. "I appreciate the compensation you folks have given me. Truly. And I'm not trying to get anyone else to take my place. I just feel strange because most of this is not skilled labour."

"You're on the books, my man," Elroy jumped back in. "We run a tight operation here, as you can see. You're our maintenance guy now. That's what you do for us when you're here. Everyone here has a purpose. You see it's always the same people working entrance security. That's what those two do. You see I'm doing the community outreach. That's what I do."

"And I decide if people are worth having around. If they can be trusted," the stranger finished.

"I'd like to know your name." Lucian was steadfast.

"Why?"

"I think I've proven myself committed and capable here. I can't trust you if you won't even tell me your name."

"Mickey."

"Mickey?"

"Mickey Mouse. Now I've got somewhere to be, and Elroy has another task for a mop-and-bucket man like you. If you don't take it, I'll suck all that money back out of your account. And if you keep whining and snooping, maybe I'll just put a b—put my fist through your skull." He was trying to get out the door before his final sentence was finished, but his movements were so cumbersome and his speaking miscue seemed to rattle him into slowing down. The words spurted out in stunted bellows. He pulled the door to slam it shut, and a photo fell from the wall.

Elroy waited, dumbfounded. Lucian's fists were clenched. He turned to Elroy and exhaled. He didn't realize he'd been holding his breath.

Elroy started, "Sorry, I—"

"Just give me the job. I don't care. I just want the job, and I want the money up front. Cash this time."

"Cash?"

"Cash."

"Okay… it's just a delivery. A pick up and drop off. Simple as that." He moved behind the counter and began rearranging paper, pretending he needed to look under the shelves for something. He then grabbed his phone and began typing. "I'll text you the address." He then tossed his phone so that it twisted in the air and spun in circles on the desk when it landed. "Ugh. Better, I'll just write it down here. There you go."

Lucian took the paper, looked at it for a split second, folded it once, and stuffed it in his pocket.

"You will want to check that address though," Elroy reasoned. "It's out pretty far beyond The Blade."

"I been there before. It's a scrapyard. I bought plow parts from the guy. Big old bulked up juicer living in the woods. A hard guy to forget."

"Okay, good. And I know this sounds odd, but I'll need you to make a couple stops along the way. Charge your vehicle, get a snack. Just little things so you can look around and see if anyone's following you. If you think someone's following, abort."

Lucian only looked at him, knowing there was more to be said. Elroy continued, "So we've got some materials we need. Out there in The Wilderness. He's a good guy though. Solid. He's a patriot. You'll have no problem there. Oh and here." Elroy reached under the counter and produced two framed photos, one of an elderly couple and one of a young family of four. "Take these and give them to him. Do not say anything or ask anything about the photos. Do not. Just give them to him. Don't even look him in the eye when you give them to him. It's... it's unrelated. Then you pick up our stuff, only saying as much as needs to be said. Bring it back straight to the compound. No stops on the way back. And that's all you need to know. Any questions?"

"If that's all I need to know, then no, I don't have any questions about the job."

"What else would you have questions about?"

"My money. How much and where is it?"

"You just sit tight and I'll be back. We can count it together."

Natalie Ross slept for eight hours. When she woke, she pressed her hand to her heart, soothed by the slow and steady beat. She then bit her lip and briefly held back a sudden urge to cry.

Composing herself almost instantly, she manually checked her resting heart rate, rolled onto the floor, and held a plank position for several minutes, without a timer. She transitioned seamlessly to a set of push-ups. Without counting, she did as many as she could until her arms trembled and her pace slowed. She stood up, shook out her arms, and walked to her treadmill to complete a five-kilometre run. Despite her aging body, almost every movement was like something seen in a tutorial video—nearly perfect form and balance during all exercises.

She stretched, set up her sandbag on an extra chair that was tucked between her school desk and the sandbag's usual spot in the corner of the room, and then began her softy practice. She focused on quick draw, short and mid-range accuracy, sometimes while moving. With small pivots and side steps, she fully maximized the little space she had in which to work.

As she cooled down, Natalie began rearranging her apartment from a workout space into a living space, but continued to exercise while doing so: she picked up her sandbag and completed a set of squats before placing it back into the corner; she folded her bed back down from the wall, but dropped down herself as she set it, completing a set of push-ups; she pushed the chair back beside the sandbag, but not before using the chair to do a set of triceps dips.

Before long, the sandbag was the only thing that might seem out of place to a visitor. Natalie pulled back the curtains to reveal a bright, economical space. It was tidy, from the clean laminate floor to the single potted snake plant and small collection of books neatly stacked on the windowsill.

She sprayed a single, carefully aimed mist of water at the snake plant, then cleaned her hair, hands, and face with dry soap and shampoo. Finally, she spoke:

"Laura, play yesterday's episode of Three Pipe Problems."

"Okay, just a moment."

As the podcast began, Natalie drank a cup of water, then warmed a second cup in the microwave and sipped it like it was coffee, while preparing breakfast: a single slice of rye toast with peanut butter. She folded the toast in half and devoured it in three bites while standing up at the counter of her kitchenette.

With the peanut butter jar nearly empty, she scraped what she could out of it, then placed the butter knife carefully over the edge of the sink. With some effort, she cut the jar into two jagged halves with a large kitchen knife; she used a baking spatula to clean out both halves until the plastic looked as though it had never had anything in it at all. She then poured a spoonful of water into the bottom half, swished it around, and drank it. Next, she screwed the lid back onto the top half, and repeated the same process with the spoonful of water, before licking the butter knife and the spatula clean. She briefly examined the large kitchen knife, but decided it wasn't worth trying to lick any peanut butter from it.

Natalie had the habit of cleaning up her space while still cooking and eating. By the time she had licked the last remnants of peanut butter from her gums, the kitchenette appeared unused.

Her morning routine completed, Natalie began walking on her treadmill while continuing to listen to her podcast. She listened a little more attentively as she began her walk: *And as we've seen, when people are fighting for water, they turn their thirst into hatred—other religions, cultures, countries, languages, occupations, generations. It's an uninformed hatred that gets groomed for political gain. Then when the violence starts, the suppression of the poor or Black or Indigenous cannot be hidden anymore. People will pick sides.*

When the podcast finished, she moved swiftly to her desk, retrieving the recording device she'd recently purchased for herself. Her movements were pre-meditated; it appeared as though the recording device was just another longstanding part of her morning ritual. After re-attaching the device to her phone, she held the phone instinctively to her left shoulder, but then pulled it close to her mouth and began quietly speaking:

I won an award once: special recognition for bravery in the line of duty. The chief gave me a challenge coin at a banquet at the end of the year that year. I pulled over a reckless driver and found a little girl in his trunk. Some footage of it went viral—surveillance cameras from a nearby store. That's how the service was more or less forced into rewarding me for the 'act of courage'.

The guy got too close to me because he knew I was going to pop the trunk, so I kneed him in his balls. It's the same mistake half a dozen male perps have made with me over the years—they all think that if they crowd me I won't be able to operate. That's why I commit so much time to grappling and hard hands-on training. I don't care how big they are—and most of them aren't as big as they pretend to be—if they try to get on me, I'll just throw them off or choke them unconscious. I'm aware of my limitations, but I also know what I'm capable of.

Next thing I know I'm on the internet, and there was a week there where people wanted to take pictures with me.

Then a few days after the video went up, I was offered a bonus of two days off and a chance to go to a dinner at an upscale restaurant with some politicians and businesspeople who had flown in for some conference. When the chief told me it was going to be at Juteux, I didn't want to go because I thought I would have to wear a dress. They have an extremely old-fashioned dress code there. It's part of their high society appeal. But the chief told me that they'd make an exception for me and I could wear a pantsuit.

When we got there, I immediately wished I'd just worn a dress. It was like showing up to a gala where the theme was to wear white, but no one told you to wear white so you wore black. These people were dressed like they were at the Oscars and it was 1950. The place was the picture of decadence. The first thing I saw was a waiter doing that thing where they pop and pour the champagne and just let it spill out to other glasses below. And so much of it is wasted, fizzing out of the bottle and then dripping over the tops of the glasses. I wanted to strangle the guy for how wasteful and stupid the whole charade was.

Anyway, I have to assume the invite came because someone somewhere thought I would fit well into their mould—that I could be a showpiece puppet to bolster the power structures in place. I don't pretend to be pretty, but I have a slender figure, and back then I was only twenty-seven and I looked younger than that. And I'm white. And I'm educated. And the only thing anyone knew about me was that I had recently foiled a kidnapping. I think it also helped that the child in question was also female, white, and the closest thing to objectively beautiful that you can imagine, even at only six years old.

But they figured out pretty quickly that I wasn't going to fit. It wasn't that I didn't want to. I wish I did, so that I could giggle my way through the dinner and avoid the awkwardness. I've always been jealous of people who have that type of social skill. But I can't glad-hand and I don't have charming anecdotes to throw into conversations.

An American diplomat was there. He was tall and bloated and I think his skin was bleached. He tried to be cute with me. I was polite in my distant sort of way, but he just advanced on me so quickly and without any sort of consideration for... anything. These men just assume they can put their hands on anyone. I reflexively pulled his hand off my leg as soon as he touched me. It rattled the champagne flutes on the table and some people looked. Not a lot. But a few. He started backtracking, but I didn't care, as long as he didn't touch me anymore and my food came quickly. He didn't talk to me much after that, but I still had to sit beside him through the meal. He put his napkin on top and pushed the plate away when he still had a quarter of the food left to eat. Then he ordered dessert. It was a disgrace.

Enough about that guy though. The whole point of the night was this: the chief told me afterwards that the mayor's campaign manager wanted to groom me to run for public office. But he told me in this sort of defeated way, like he just felt an obligation to let me know that was the failed experiment I'd just been put through. He knew they weren't going to ever contact me again. I was thankful, to be honest. Even the meal was shit.

I was legitimately excited to eat there. It's the kind of place that you just hear rumours about. It's like no one actually knows anyone who has eaten there. You just hear about friends of friends who know someone important enough to have been invited, or just wealthy enough to reserve a table there on an off-peak night.

I'd never seen a menu like that before. It wasn't a large menu, and everything sounded so delicate and refined. It really didn't appeal to my specific tastes. Honestly, eating in public doesn't appeal to me at all, anywhere. It's because I don't like to take small bites of anything. Even when I was a teenager, I remember people telling me I should savour things, or that smaller bites would help me better appreciate the flavours. I never felt that way. I like to mix my foods together. I like to take huge heaping mouthfuls because I want it to take longer to chew, because the flavour comes from the food being in your mouth, not your stomach. It's not rocket science. You can barely taste it if you take a little tiny forkful of whatever it is you're eating. I never use teaspoons either. They're too small. I don't get it. And I never like my food too hot. I'd rather it be cold in the middle, just as long as I can shovel it into my mouth and not burn my tongue.

More about Juteux… You hear the rumours, but it's still staggering to see real meat on the menu. They didn't serve anything that had the word 'faux' in it. The words on the page were elegant and intimidating to a layman like me: saffron risotto, Tahitian vanilla, romesco sauce, black truffles, mozzarella di bufala, pomegranate poached pears, black gold Iranian beluga caviar. Some of it didn't sound real.

They had veal, which I'd never even heard of before that night. I ordered a blackened fish. The menu said 'charred', which as it turns out means they literally burn your food before they serve it to you. I would have ordered something else if I knew they were going to ruin a perfectly good piece of fish.

It was my first time eating any real animal since I was a little kid. And it was not worth it. That's probably the one day in my entire adult life that I'd like to relive, just so I could order something else.

I prefer to eat at movie theatres. Most people go to the movies on a date or with friends, and they get popcorn, but I'll go by myself and eat a feast in the dark. When I was a teenager they still sold pop too. That was great. I'll get nachos, a slice of pizza, and popcorn, and I'll sneak in a bag of candies or chocolates and my little flask of water. Chocolate covered peanuts—that is my favourite. Especially eating them with popcorn. Sometimes I get extra butter with the popcorn. Nostalgic people around my age will say they don't like the faux butter, but they're just looking for any reason to pretend like past times— when we were young—were better. The bygone era. But I love the chocolate peanuts and the buttery popcorn—that mix of salty, sweet, and savoury. I don't know if other people would call that savoury, but it's savoury to me. Yeah, I could live off chocolate covered peanuts.

The first time I felt brave enough to just go to the movies by myself, it was so freeing. Once the lights are out, no one is looking at you anyway. I was maybe nineteen at the time. I didn't eat as much in the theatre back then, but still I always said my favourite part about going to the movies was going to the bulk food store first.

All junk food aside, going to the movies is the only thing I like doing outside my apartment. I may sound extremely lonely, but I'm not. I'll never go see something like a romantic comedy. Those movies are for lonely people. Same with love songs. They don't have the same appeal if you're truly happy in a relationship. I don't consider myself a happy person, but even though I'm alone, I almost never feel lonely. I like to go see movies that have substance. That maybe sounds arrogant… I just mean, the stranger and less linear the narrative, the better. I like to see a film where it's obvious the director does not give a shit whether or not you like it. They're just making their own art, and you can call it what you want. I have a great respect for that kind of self-belief.

Sometimes if I'm lucky, I'll go to a matinee and I'll be the only person there. That is bliss for me. And when I finish all my food thirty minutes into the movie, then I just sit there in complete, undivided silence. In a big, empty, black room. When I'm alone and I'm engaged in something—most often a movie—sometimes it feels like I don't even exist. And it doesn't bother me.

The Freedom Fighters' compound was entirely fenced in, with a security booth at the only entrance. There was a small house—converted to an office building years earlier—in the centre of the square lot, flanked by a bunkhouse and a midsized warehouse that doubled as a garage. Before it became their headquarters, Elroy had lived there with his ex-wife, and they ran a truck and trailer rental business. They went out of business after a couple of lean years, and she left a few months later—she couldn't handle his drinking and the way it amplified his bitterness and contempt. He joined in with the Freedom Fighters seven weeks after she was gone, just when he was on the brink of having to sell the property.

Outside the buildings, the area was a mix of patchy grass and fresh, level concrete. In a far corner of the lot, there was an old and weather-beaten 16-foot camping trailer, and beside it, an outdoor gym area, with a basketball hoop and various mismatched dumbbells, plates, barbells, and weight machines. A single, ancient, rock-solid, water-damaged, brown leather punching bag hung from a sturdy metal support.

With the snow completely melted, the grass of the compound was sopping and overflowing, water spilling out and running in a thin layer across much of the pavement. There was a woman on the grounds, using a push broom to sweep the water toward a sewer. Elroy, Zach, Mickey, and a new recruit, Danny, were seated around a folding table, playing cards outside of the office when Elroy's cellphone rang. He saw who was calling and perked up, but didn't move from his chair. He glanced up to see if the others were watching him, a sly smile betraying an attempted poker face.

"Freedom Fighters," he greeted.

"Elroy. It's Sofia."

"Yes I know." Then he pulled the phone away from his face and whispered to the other men, "It's Amanita Virosa."

"I can hear you."

"Oh sorry. Yeah, yeah I know you can. Remind me again

why you don't text?"

"That's not important, Elroy. I'm just calling to ensure you've got everything you need for any upcoming events, as the UPC financing department is empathetic to your cause."

"All upcoming events? Or just the one?"

"Discretion, Elroy. Any events, any at all."

"We're all set on our end."

"You know we truly do love supporting tremendous community initiatives such as yours."

"Uh—"

"And any organization that believes in supporting people's freedoms is a friend to the UPC. Please remember that."

"Yes, ma'am. Yes, indeed. I assure you, we know that."

"Good. I'll be in touch again in the near future. God bless you!"

"Yeah, you too."

Elroy hung up and snorted a laugh while the others waited to hear his summary of the phone call.

"She has no idea," Elroy explained, continuing to laugh at his own deception.

"What did she want?" Mickey questioned.

"Just to make sure we were ready for the bombing."

"Did she say that?" Zach asked.

"Of course not. But she wanted to know if we were good. I said we were good. We all know what she means."

"Blame the poor." Mickey began what appeared to be a rehearsed refrain.

"Blame the non-whites," said Zach.

"Blame the left-extreme," said Elroy.

"Blame the elected ones," said Danny.

And the four Freedom Fighters all nodded in agreement while Elroy concluded, "As if we'd ever let all of them get credit for our work."

People don't ask me about dating anymore.

Natalie was walking on her treadmill as she spoke into her

phone.

When I was in my twenties and thirties, people would ask. Even though I never wore makeup and occasionally cut all my hair off, people would ask, or they would try to set me up with someone. Well, the setups stopped when I was around twenty-six. Then there was also a strange shift where people started asking me about if I wanted to have kids. Like they stopped trying to find me a boyfriend and they started putting it on me instead. 'If you want a kid, you gotta find a guy'. I always thought I was too selfish for kids though. I value my time alone too much.

I'm not saying I'd be unhappy if I had a partner. I might be happy. But I found out early that having another person wouldn't bring me the same joy it seemed to bring all my friends. We turned thirteen and then suddenly having someone else was the priority, and that switch in my mind just never flipped. I once heard an adult call me a late-bloomer, even though I was five inches taller than half the boys; even people in their forties and fifties didn't think I could be fully developed if I didn't obsess over a boy.

I've actually had three lovers. That fact would probably shock everyone at work. I hear them talk about me. All false-alphas are incapable of lowering their voices. They just can't do it. They call me bull dyke, they say I'm a virgin, and in the next breath, they joke that I'm secretly an insatiable whore. They don't say 'insatiable' though. They might say 'total' or 'disgusting' or 'cock-hungry'.

But yes, I did have three lovers. When I was in my early twenties, I had a girlfriend who was a few years older, Camila, who was supremely confident, had a lot of sexual experience, and was simply never afraid to explore her desires, or even indulge the desires of others to her own benefit. She was always very much in control, and I admired that about her. She said she fucked the boys. They didn't fuck her.

I think of her as one of these 'just a little' people: her hair seemed just a little longer and thicker; her eyes were just a little bigger and darker; her skin glowed just a little brighter.

And she seduced me, I guess. Or it felt like seduction… but in a good way, without any pretence. And she knew how to touch me and how to guide me, and she said all that she wanted was to make me feel pleasure. No one had ever touched me before, not like that. And really, not since then either.

I'd never even found myself in any of those horror situations with men who never miss the chance to corner a young girl in a dark place. I think men, *maybe even the worst of men more than others, have a keen instinct for when a girl is someone who you're better off not bothering to corner. You might get what you want out of it, in the end, but it won't be worth the risk or the damage incurred. I know I was never the beauty that some of the other girls grew to be, but either way, men knew I was not the one to try.*

So there was that time with my girlfriend, Camila. And I told her, in so many words, that I would like it if we had another night like that. But although she was gentle with my feelings and didn't gaslight me or lie to me, she made it clear right away that she wasn't interested. She was a tourist, in that regard.

And then years went by without even a glimpse of a sexual encounter. And more and more, I found my attempts at dating to be wasteful. Someone might show an interest, but I always found a way out of it. At first I told myself various lies to avoid dates or kisses. Then I stopped lying and just allowed myself to realize I wasn't really attracted to anyone. Not in the way that other people seemed to be attracted. I was never overwhelmed. I never looked at anyone that made me ache.

Then when I was in training at the police college, it just happened one night. I'd done some studying with a pair of boys who were both... good guys. Side-note: it's not the job that turns these men into false-alphas. Most of them have their competitive, impatient, self-conscious, showy, aggressive, Type-A personality before they even dream of applying for the job. But just like with Pete, there are always examples of other 'types' who get into the career.

These two guys were different too. Marco was very funny, very goofy but self-aware. He could always use humour to ease tension. And Saul was also funny, but in this understated, charming way. Marco was also obsessed with working out, which didn't seem to fit the rest of his personality. But yeah, his body was hard. And Saul had a handsome smile that matched his charm. He was very tall, his teeth were straight, and he seemed to have his hair cut twice a week. He was polished; that's a simple way to put it.

I can see why people say different lovers help them meet different needs. Like I appreciated how Marco could always make me laugh. But again, my needs didn't extend the way other people's needs do. I didn't need anything in bed. Or maybe I was never sure what I wanted, or if I wanted anything at all.

Those two didn't seduce me the way Camila's romance felt like a seduction. It just sort of happened. You get closed off from the world when you're in training. Even more so when the harsh weather hits. Your group gets even smaller when you figure out whom you are comfortable with. Especially small when you're a woman who doesn't get along with many other women and doesn't desire male attention. So I spent hours with those two guys. Eventually, I was with Marco for a night. He was considerate, though a little too excited. He talked to me about if I liked it, but not in a creepy way. It was different.

And I think Saul found out and was jealous. I'll never understand why. Because I never had any inclination that he was attracted to me like that before he found out his friend had slept with me. And soon I had a night with Saul too. He was slower but somehow more forceful. Didn't say as much once we were naked. I didn't really enjoy it, because it didn't feel like as much something I was doing as something that was being done to me. It was okay though. Just okay.

Then soon those two didn't like each other, or didn't both want to be around me at the same time. And other people started to talk and influence how Marco and Saul treated me, and how comfortable they were around me, and the types of moments they were willing to share with me. It all became so different so quickly. Marco still wanted to be close with me, at least as a friend, maybe more too, but I could see he was far too concerned with how everyone else viewed him and our relationship. So it was never the same.

I think the reason two men can't cope with both having slept with the same woman is they can't come to terms with the fact that she now knows something about both of them that they don't know about each other.

Saul found a moment alone with me once more when training was almost finished. I think he wanted to have me again and knew there wouldn't be any backlash because we were deploying soon and wouldn't see each other. Despite everything we had gone through together to that point—which was a lot, because training is nearly unbearable at times—he was by then just another horny asshole who just happened to be near a girl, so figured he could sleep with her. He said some stupid shit. He didn't have me doubting myself, not even for a split second. But I let him talk at me. Just to see how much of a snake he would turn into. He kept saying he was 'trying'. He said things like 'I'm just trying to show you I care about you,' and 'I'm trying to tell you that I haven't stopped thinking about you since that night,' and eventually he was just tripping all over himself because I didn't bite, and it was so pathetic and *infuriating, so I put my hand up to get him to stop. And then I started talking while he was sucking in a breath, because I knew he wasn't actually going to stop.*

I said, 'I know what you're trying to do. You're trying to exploit my insecurities. But now you found out that I don't have any.'

And we never spoke again.

"I got our Way Out." Pete showed Cormac the lottery ticket as he spoke. His expression didn't change. "Don't tell people on different squads. These other jack-offs can buy their own tickets."

"Check."

"Good answer."

"I've got a home follow-up with an officer who's off for psych eval. I'll be back in less than an hour."

"Okay, but let's talk about how you want to move on the Freedom Fighters. Because I've got good news: Briggs' perp from yesterday said he got his fentanyl from the Fighters, so we've got evidence of narcotics checked off. With the right judge, we can turn that into a warrant no problem."

"Great, I'll get Oak to write it up. He's been itching to get involved more."

"Christ no, not him. Some of these judges will deny searches if they don't like the goddamn font you use. I don't want him half-assing it and then us getting denied. This has to be done right. I don't like the way Gilchrist was talking to me. I don't like being talked to like that by anyone, of any rank. And I know it's because there's people that want us to forget this whole situation is even happening. Though I have no idea why. Now, I'm with you—I want these guys out of our city. But it has to be done properly. All red tape, all logistics, all evidence gathering, all the paperwork, everything needs to be perfect."

"Okay, check. But let's ease your mind a bit here, Staff, because I've got good news too. I've got a CI who told me today that Danny Atkins, *the* wanted sex-offender Danny Atkins, is staying in the bunkhouse on the Fighters' compound. So we've got that, plus we've got the intel on drugs, we've got sufficient evidence of a recent influx of funds, we've got the weasel telling me all about their big plans that sounded like full-on anarchy. There's clearly a grow-op, which is another piece I gathered from Elroy running his mouth about his associate, Lawrence, the ex-government researcher. That, *and* proceeds of crime *and* potentially a wanted criminal on the property. Plus don't forget we already know they've got two repeat violent offenders in their ranks.

"I've done the research, Pete. This is easy work. We're serving prime rib to this judge. This is a fresh cut of real beef, a bottle of wine, and a filled-to-the-brim pint of water in a chilled glass. It can't be squashed—I don't care which judge sees it. And I'll get Aleem to do the search grounds paperwork. That dude knows how to pick a font."

Canizales smiled with his eyes, but fought to keep his mouth from moving. "Okay. And when it comes time to get this over and done—it's no half-measures. We're taking our time and making sure everything is in place and we have all the manpower and expertise we need. Me and you can scout, with the tactical team on if a raid is required. Aleem can lead the search, and let Oakshot be exhibit officer. That way you can tell him he's got a job to do."

Detective Cormac Dawson, he him, GLR Police. Currently on duty out of our Terrace Bay detachment, en route to a fellow officer's private residence for a follow-up since she's been off on stress leave for a while. I already explained about my outreach position, and I thought—while I'm on the road here—it might be good for this project to tell you all about our recruiting and training.

It was something I was well prepared for... actually excited for. I was like a starving wolf that knew the leash was about to come off. Honestly, the initial training—at least the physical aspect—I knew it would be excruciating. 'Hard' or 'difficult' are words that don't do it justice, and I knew that before I even experienced it.

The stress levels there are incomparable. The physical training is taxing, but the mental strain is debilitating too. I had some horrible days there, but...

in other ways I was very much in my element. It's not that I thought I would enjoy it—it's that I wanted to be able to say that I'd gone through it. And that's the mentality I want all the rookies to bring now. When I did a stint instructing at the college, I put my recruits through a blast furnace. And if they don't make it out, they don't make it out.

I ran lots of PT sessions, use-of-force scenarios, and defensive tactics training. Mostly they wanted me to take the lead for straight physical training. I ran them into the ground, and I loved it. But don't get me wrong, I was right there with them. I went to the college in peak physical condition, ready to tear my own body to shreds, right down on the floor beside the recruits. My eyes don't drip and my heart doesn't bleed.

It sounds cruel to the outsider, I think. But it serves a purpose. The ones who don't make it, they weren't meant to be there. They're better off now. Because it's not like you graduate and get the badge and then the next twenty years get easier. You might not have to do push-ups before sunrise anymore, but that doesn't make your load any lighter. If you can't hang at the college, you learn from the experience and you go find something else to do for a career.

But the ones who do make it through, now they have a better understanding of what they're in for, and more importantly, what they're capable of. And we are bonded for life after that experience. Some of my best friends are people I myself tossed into a vice for months at the college. Like Oakshot. He was one of my rookies, and I was his coach officer in the field afterwards, and we've stayed tight ever since.

Oak is selfish in training, and at first he was a bully in the locker room, but when you're in the field, no one has your back like he does. And I know he's not perfect, but when it's time to fight, imperfections can be talents too. When we trained kickboxing at the college, that's when I really saw Oak's potential. He had never been in a fight before, never trained any striking. But the man chucks rocks. He's got a special capacity for taking punishment. I think of him like a video game villain from an arcade a hundred years ago: he throws hammers at you, and he has a limitless supply. And you might hit him or knock him down or dodge a hammer, but he'll just keep throwing them. When we got our tools on and he started working scenarios where he had to choose whether or not to draw his firearm, that was when he made plenty of mistakes. But like I said, he's not perfect.

The golf course had been Terrace Bay's greatest point of contention for decades. Its continued existence was polarizing, with the emerging city's wealthier citizens enjoying access to one of the few remaining utter wastes of space in the country. As other courses closed and were converted to designated green spaces or affordable housing, Terrace Bay's course stood firm in defiance. Club members savoured their involvement in what had become the world's leading leisure activity in terms of consuming time, space, and resources.

Cst. Naseer Aleem sped up a bit as he approached the golf course, resisting the urge to soak in its surreal green grandeur. Back on a beat without a partner, Naseer was in the area in response to a call for a domestic dispute at a private residence along Lake Superior.

Shortly after speeding by the golf course, Naseer passed the landfill, receiving expressionless nods from a handful of guards on patrol. Unlike the golf course, the landfill was primarily a point of pride in Terrace Bay. The facility was a leader in biotechnology, green energy, and scientific innovation. The landfill's only negative aspect to the citizens was the danger involved with being near it. Such a facility was under constant threat of terrorist attacks, both domestic and international. Armed attacks from militant extremists and covert theft of scientific data from foreign operatives were often discussed by politicians and media pundits, but there had never been concrete evidence of any such occurrence. However, protests that blocked the entrance, attempted break-ins, acts of vandalism, and other such disruptions were near-daily experiences around the landfill, and punishments were served indiscriminately, sometimes with lethal consequences.

The grounds had become more dangerous in recent months, after the billionaire father-son duo of Vance and Stockwell Anderson began spreading a pair of conflicting rumours: first, that the painstaking complexity of the process of refining trash into clean energy was a government-funded lie, and that the process could be done anywhere if the simplified truth of the science was revealed to the public. In the next breath, the pair would claim that the process wasn't real at all—rather, even after paying for retrofitting, new systems and software, and the more expensive waste-based energy forms, citizens were still having their homes powered exclusively with biofuels, using the same decades-old process of converting methane gas. There was no way to tell the difference, and the people had been tricked by big government.

Just one week earlier, Stockwell announced that he would be running for public office. At the same press conference, he distanced himself from his father, who had recently suggested that impoverished families should be allowed to rent their children out to the labour market, since so many adults were refusing employment in worker-starved industries, like shipping warehouses and fast-food restaurants.

The lie that had gripped the public was that the process was simple and could be done at home. Compounded by the false hope it provided, the misinformation spread and mutated. People became convinced that the process could be replicated if only they had enough garbage. Desperate citizens began attempting to steal from the landfill—they wanted to stockpile at home. People stopped leaving trash bins out for pickup. Homes became overrun with heaps of garbage. Streets stunk of putrid, rotting waste.

Still, Vance Anderson led the charge: "Keep going," he said during a video conference from his palatial summer home in Barcelona. "The government will produce at-home energy conversion kits if we continue to apply the pressure. The landfill laboratories should fall like the Berlin Wall, and the government's grip on us will loosen with it. No more government overreach! Stop telling us what to do with our garbage!"

Closing in on the property to which he was called, Naseer rolled slowly up a long, sloping driveway to a sprawling lakeside mansion with a detached five-car garage. He exhaled smoothly, wide-eyed, as he scanned the property's lush green grass, tennis court, pool, and outbuildings: a greenhouse, guesthouse, pool house, and servants' quarters.

It was the property of Cannon and Constance Slayback, long-time associates of the Anderson empire: the Slayback family owned the local golf course and the property upon which the landfill was built. Renting land to the government had proven lucrative when it became clear that the energy produced from the landfill would be powering homes for the foreseeable future. There had been many offers to purchase or rent the golf course's land over the years: opportunities for government-backed low-income housing, sale to ultra-wealthy American land developers, or expansion of the landfill's refineries and research laboratories. There was a deal in place for the Slaybacks to sell the course to a prominent heiress turned divisive politician a few years earlier, but Cannon balked before the papers were signed.

With a measure of caution, Cst. Aleem approached the guard standing at attention at the mansion's front door. The guard had a weak chin, but compensated with an enormous beard. Aleem scanned the man's duty belt, noting cuffs, pepper-spray, an electroshock baton, a flashlight, and a dubious badge, emblazoned with the Slayback family crest: the outline of a Viking helmet inside an othala rune. Beneath the crest was the family's adopted slogan: Blood And Soil.

"What?" The guard stood eye-level with Naseer.

"Good morning. I'm here because Mrs. Slayback called about a dispute with her husband."

Maintaining eye contact with Naseer, the guard held a brief radio correspondence with someone inside the mansion.

"Okay, go in," he said, but didn't move out of the way.

Naseer sidestepped and angled his shoulders to get around him. As he entered the foyer, he saw Constance Slayback, wearing a silk, floor-length robe, hurriedly approaching with the dainty tip-toed gait of a gymnast building toward a great leap. The entrance area had an open-concept floor plan and minimalist aesthetic; Naseer checked his watch and adjusted his belt as he waited for Constance.

"It was all a dreadful misunderstanding, Officer. I'm terribly sorry to've wasted your time." She spoke in a practised, charm-school cadence, masking the accent she'd developed from her childhood home, wherein she was a first-generation Canadian.

"Yes, ma'am. I understand, but I'll need to take a statement. It was you who called, correct?"

"Well—"

"If you phoned in because of that cat, just tell the guy it's dealt with," called Cannon from an indoor balcony overlooking the foyer. He was holding an open book in one hand. He wore a dress-shirt with the sleeves partially rolled up, and his hair was finely combed, but with a noticeable tussling in one spot.

Without waiting for a reply, Cannon slammed the book shut and replaced it on a large bookshelf before making his way to the staircase. Naseer stood still and Constance busied herself, smoothing her robe and running her hands underneath her eyes, then checking for makeup on her fingers as she sniffled. They waited, listening to Cannon's approaching footsteps.

"Listen, I'm Cannon Slayback. Can we get you a drink, Officer?"

"No, thank you. I'll just need a statement for my report."

"Oh, reports? Statements?" Cannon laughed. "Shootouts and bad guys? Listen, I'm a lawyer, so I think we've got everything under control here." He gestured toward the door.

Naseer stood stiff as Cannon placed a hand on his shoulder to try to guide him to the door. And when Cannon felt the resistance, he first began pushing harder, then thought better of it, stopped, and looked at his wife with contempt. Naseer let the silence hang for a moment.

"I'll take a statement from each of you and then I'll be on my way."

Cannon had thrown his wife's cat out a window. They both claimed it landed on its feet and scampered off. Cst. Aleem knew the same thing had happened a year or so earlier—different cat. A brief spat; he's just a passionate person; women and their pets; never happened before; oh this mark? It's nothing; he'd never hurt me; you know how the ladies can be, eh?

Naseer was accustomed to the common responses. He could

have written both statements without even speaking to the Slaybacks. He was back in his cruiser ten minutes later, and sped up again as he passed the golf course.

Are we really better off? That's what I always ask myself.

Natalie was reading an e-book, In The Country of Last Things, but had closed the file and then synced her Incognito to her phone. She continued:

The scientific and technological advances are amazing. But we didn't get to start with a blank slate.

Food production is done almost exclusively indoors. Anticipating the potential land scarcity as people continue to move north, it's all vertical farming—growing food in skyscrapers through controlled environment agriculture with no sunlight, no soil. It's truly something to marvel at. I admire the ability of those who work in the field: they maintain precisely calibrated growing environments where they can manipulate air temperature, humidity, carbon dioxide levels, light wavelength, growth cycles, and more.

And even beyond that, other food production facilities aren't indoor farms, but labs, where they create food catered to the exact calorie and nutrition needs of particular citizens. As of now, it's exclusive to the elites. Scientific engineers combine the lab-work with wearable technology, so a person's smart-watch can monitor their activity and needs, and even predict future health concerns, which are then mitigated by adjusting the nutrients or specific minerals added to their food. I've heard steroids and anti-aging medicines are involved too.

The sustenance from those labs is just gelatinous, created through automation. Textures, colours, and flavours are all added after the fact, but mostly those ultra-wealthy people survive off the goo during the day and then dine at one of the exclusive clubs or restaurants at night.

The labs and vertical farms have taken a huge strain off both the water crisis—since agriculture demanded so much of our fresh water—and the food production crisis, as the new ways make for inexpensive, fast, sustainable production.

Traditional farming is obsolete, so now there's more space, less pollution, and very little slaughtering of animals. And automation has expanded to the point where there are very few valuable jobs remaining. No need. Machines can do it. People in engineering can do all right for themselves if they have the money to get graduate degrees, and if they're willing to work a ton of overtime. Doctors and nurses are needed everywhere, but again, it's not just about being smart: there's no public education here anymore, and the more advanced the degree, the more expensive it gets. And being a doctor of medicine, psychiatry, or psychology has to be a burdensome job. We get a lot of service-calls for suicides.

That may seem surprising: doctors taking their own lives even though they seem to have it so good. But with poorer communities, there's an expectation that life is going to be hard. That this is just how it is. You have to bear it. With people who were somehow able to afford all that education to move up in the world, there's got to be an expectation that life will go easy on you. And then it doesn't. And not just doctors and nurses, but a lot of other people who would have been considered middle class or upper-middle class in the last century—their place in this world is no longer secure.

Other than that—science, engineering, healthcare—there aren't too many decent careers out there. In the trades, unions have all been stamped out. And between that and the expansion of automation, it's become hard to make a living even if you've mastered multiple skills like carpentry, welding, and plumbing.

Some government work can be okay, and like I said, law enforcement comes with good job security and guaranteed time off. Most other people either work in mines, where the wages are terrible, or they get support jobs doing laundry, cleaning houses, walking dogs, or getting groceries for some wealthy person in a loft or an estate on the water.

Post-secondary education is profitable for the administration in the few universities that are left, because it's just so expensive to be a student. My neighbour's son did a double major in Fresh Water Plumbing and Food Genetics; he works privately for one family along Lake Michigan. And he's doing okay, by today's standards. The pay is brutal, but he gets a room on the estate, plus food. There's an engineer who works for the same family; he maintains their energy systems. And all that garbage burns clean. They've found a way—the chemists and biotechnologists, many of the brightest minds across the planet—they were able to work together when the fate of humanity was on the line.

The process began with a tiny organism they found, called a methanotroph, which consumes methane gas. From there came the conversion of that energy into biofuel. Then decades later came the mass production and engineering of synthetic organisms, designing them to consume the methane. Then eventually, the biggest breakthrough came when those synthetic organisms could be programmed to literally start consuming the garbage. It's a long process, but it means there's eventually more space for more garbage, while the organisms can be liquefied and transported—via armoured car or drone—to homes for clean energy. Large quantities of the organisms are also converted to gas, and sent down the existing lines to paying customers, but it's the liquid that is the most efficient. And there's still traditional biofuels too, but the good stuff—the premium stuff—comes from what is ultimately garbage consumed, then the consumers liquefied.

So there are many improvements, but the changes haven't helped most of us, in terms of... living fulfilling and happy lives. No more gasoline either. Not much of anything except the... liquid trash... erasing the mess past generations left for us. Everything is better now. That's what we tell each other.

We want to be concerned with the world we leave behind. Many of those before us were not. The governments—and the banks and businesses that control them—waited until the last possible moment to finally ditch fossil fuels. I suppose both the people 'then' and the people 'now' were and are concerned with the present. It's just that before, it was greed, ignorance, or disregard for consequences. Whereas now, we focus on the present because if you don't, you'll be lucky to survive the day. We live life by the drop. We have to.

Pausing, Natalie was silent for a time. She ran her hand through her hair, keeping her eyes closed as she gently massaged her scalp. She squeezed her hand, tugging the hair just a bit, then continued running her fingers through it for a few more seconds.

"I should cut it all off again," she whispered to herself, though her hair was already only a few inches long. She ran her hand down her cheek, cupping her face like someone would to comfort a sad child. She had high cheekbones and a narrow, angular jawline. She let the tip of her middle finger run down and off her chin, then slapped her hand down onto the bed. After an audible breath, she moved to continue reading the novel, but changed her mind almost instantly; instead, she continued to record:

The layout of the city and its surroundings are like this: everything is based on The Blade, and there is a stark contrast between life north of The Blade and life south of The Blade. There are four types of real estate, and with that, there are basically four classes of people, socio-economically. Three groups live south of The Blade, or we just say 'within The Blade'. There are mansions across the street from The Blade, where some elites live. Most of the wealthy people have only moved into town in the last decade, at the start of the ongoing expansion. So some live in those mansions, and other elites live very close to Lake Superior, either in the Landfill Lofts or in one of the few lakeside properties. And there's also some elites who have those studio apartments inside The Blade. I've heard there are some people who have both a landfill loft and a Blade studio, which is baffling to me.

Living in a loft or lakeside property puts people a little farther from all the amenities of The Blade, but a hospital, the landfill and its adjoining refineries, and the laboratories are all down there, which provides an incalculable comfort for those in the area: should society collapse—which is always a possibility—they have the best access to the water and the energy, and they live in the area that is most likely to be protected by those in power. Just like having a second home, a cabin, a helicopter, a security team, it's that back-up plan that allows people to live happily, ignoring all that is wrong with the daily lives of most people around them.

So all those people make up the first-class citizens. And those citizens—I know this for a fact—consider everyone else to be the poor. I mean that literally, like they refer to everyone else as 'a poor': 'Don't go near him, he's a poor.'

Anyway, still south of The Blade, there's what I would call second and third-class citizens, but they live in the suburbs and housing projects between the lofts and the mansions. Most call it The Junk, as in the junk that gets produced off the edges of a plow blade, where the snow and ice have mixed with dirt and trash. They benefit from their location, for sure, but there's a lot of struggle in those areas too, as I've been saying. And even from block to block or neighbourhood to neighbourhood, there are huge gaps in quality of life. That large area is where desperation is at a near constant, and desperation and crime go hand-in-hand. Though changes in the weather definitely influence the volume and type of crime being committed.

I consider myself to be one of the second-class citizens. I'm in the best possible housing outside of the wealthiest areas, and I have a career that offers me steady pay. From the moment I got my badge, then moved into this apartment, I've never lost sight of how good I have it, compared to most.

And then there's the fourth-class citizens—the only ones who do not benefit from the curtain that is The Blade. It surprises me every day, but there are still plenty of people who live in The Wilderness. And it extends quite far north. The farther you go, the more space there is between properties. It's only when I drive up that way, maybe a hundred kilometres, that I'm reminded that Canada still has sweeping landscapes—places where the nature feels infinite, like water when you're in the middle of the ocean.

The people out there... some are there by choice. They want to live a life outside of normal civilization, and they've adapted. They manage, somehow. Others are there because they can't afford to live anywhere else. There are plenty of immigrants still finding their way to Canada—millions of people who lived in coastal zones or on small islands have had to relocate in the last few decades, displaced by rising sea levels. But it's not just people who lost their homes to the sea who come here. People come to Canada for many reasons.

They want to be close to the water because the fresh water in their home country has dried up or been overtaken by private enterprise. They want to escape religious or cultural persecution. They want to return to a place that still has visible nature, to get steady work in food production or the energy sector, to reunite with family, to live in a place where they can survive. They might cram eight people into a house in The Junk for a few weeks or months, but eventually, most end up on the street, and then often in The Wilderness.

I remember last year, I was on patrol in The Junk. I was in a neighbourhood that was relatively poor, lots of theft, lots of addiction. Always people hanging out in the streets at night. Frustration and depression used to lead to alcoholism, but booze is too hard to come by for most these days, so that's not so prevalent, but I still see it. So, with poverty comes theft, assaults, drinking, drugs, domestic abuse, self-harm. And everyone hates the police.

So I was on patrol, and I was questioning this swarthy-looking little man who was reported to be walking up and down the same block over and over, when Pete came by in one of the hulking SUV cruisers the staff sergeants drive. He told me to make sure to be on high alert that day, as there had been some panic around the landfill. He said to keep my softy drawn whenever I left my cruiser.

One hand at twelve o'clock on the wheel, he looked forward for a moment. But instead of driving off as he usually would, he turned back to me, and he said, 'Tomorrow's the day.'

The Super Max would be announced. Pete always counts down the days. I can't imagine he thinks we'll actually win, but maybe he just likes to have something to look forward to.

Then he left. The little man was moving his mouth around, as if he were chewing gum. His lips were cracked and dry, even a bit bloodied. No moisture in his mouth, but he retained a soft, kind look in his eyes. He had no priors, and he said he was just looking for a cat, so I sent him on his way. Just then, I saw a latchkey kid staring at me from the front window in the weather-beaten bungalow his family lived in.

I had trouble placing his look. Fear? Longing? Sadness? The heat was choking the area, and a thick, orange haze limited my vision. That's from the forest fires blotting out the brightness of the sun, but it doesn't make it any cooler. I was already sweating from having rolled down the window. I grabbed a water from the glove box—we've got coolers installed. I drew my softy, and put the bottle in my support-side pocket. Anyone who saw me was probably more intrigued by the bottle than the gun.

I approached the house carefully. The boy jolted back a bit when he realized I was coming to his door. I saw him holler over his shoulder as he climbed off the couch at the window. I knocked. He opened the door slowly, looking like he thought he was in trouble. When I greeted him, he started by saying that his mom would be home soon. I asked if anyone else was home, but he didn't seem to want to answer. I waited. Then he pointed to an old dog asleep on the floor. I think he said its name was Frank.

I walked inside. It was nearly as hot as it was outside. On such still days, the houses couldn't be cooled by a cross breeze. And very few families in that area would be able to afford the cost of cooling a house properly and consistently.

The boy didn't say anything. I saw a box fan was on high in the living room, with an air-filter taped to the back of it. This family was one of many who had learned to be creative and vigilant, in order to maintain a liveable space. I walked to the stairs and moved toward the lower level. I looked back up—the boy was at the threshold, watching me. I knew he was worried I'd find something.

The basement door was closed. I felt a cool draft. I knocked. I announced myself. No reply.

Down three cold concrete steps, I watched him come into view. Sitting on a lawn chair in the middle of the room, with a beer in his hand and bottles strewn across the floor: the boy's dad.

"Sir, are you awake?"

"Yuh."

He didn't look up.

"Is this home retrofitted for waste-powered energy distribution?"

"Naw. But I traded for this space cooler."

"Traded what?"

"Not your business."

"And why don't you have your son down here?"

"He home?"

"School's been out for about three hours I think."

"Oh you think, huh?"

"Yes, I do. I'll give you a few minutes to clean up, and when your wife gets home, I'll send the two of them down."

I waited, but he didn't respond. I turned back as I got to the top of the stairs, and I saw he was looking at me. He looked down again when I met his gaze.

I reached the main floor just as the mother walked in the door. She had a look of shock on her face.

"It's okay, ma'am. I was just checking in after I saw your son at the window."

"Lucian in the basement again? Drinking this time?" *Her tone matched the quick change in her facial expression.*

I nodded once in response. The boy was looking at me.

"Can you go up to your room for a few minutes, buddy?"

He looked to his mother to be sure, then did as I asked.

"Does Lucian do this every day?"

"No, no. He's been better lately. When he has a bad day, it's just that he needs time alone, and even on those reclusive days, he doesn't usually get drunk. It used to be much worse, him needing all this time by himself. He'd gone back to school for mechanical engineering—had a cousin who was going to get him in with one of the car plants. But he couldn't handle it. Flunked out. It was too many years since he'd been in school. We lost a lot of money. After that, he fell off for a while."

"Does he work now?"

"He does. What he can get. He's on a shovel crew at the lofts for when the squalls come. Strong back, thank goodness. Can't do any shovelling in a heat wave though. And we finally just saved enough to get a used plow blade installed on his truck. He did the auxiliary lighting and the hitch himself. It's in the shop for the blade right now. He picked it up for cheap at a scrapyard in The Wilderness. So… better times ahead, but I figured I'd come home to find him drunk one of these days. We got a small collection of beer and liquor through my uncle's will when he passed. We sold most of it, but Lucian insisted on keeping some."

"So you don't feel there's a safety concern here?"

"No, no way. We're okay. Thanks."

I see the recidivist addicts pretty often. It's usually a single old guy or a young father. The fathers are the ones to worry about. They have people they can hurt. That 'Oh no, we're fine, no problem' is a familiar refrain from mothers like her. I believed this one though; her delivery was unpractised and her tone was even, almost dismissive, but without being defensive or curt. Those that have been victimized still seem frantic, nervous, scared, or angry—some kind of elevated mood—when they try to assure me they don't need help.

When I left, I was hit by the heat wave as soon as I stepped onto the porch. It had been hot in the house, as I said, but then with the sun hitting me, even as it was beginning to set, the heat was soul-sapping. I took the water bottle out of my pocket—forgot to give it to the kid. I took a drink, and noticed two guys standing at my cruiser. One had his hands cupped around the passenger window, peering in. The other was looking directly at me. No admiration, no respect, no fear. I looked away from him. I glanced skyward and found the moon: it was a sliver over a melting grey-blue sky that was giving way to the darkness of dusk.

Looking back down, I observed the rest of the area. The near-barren park across the street resembled a stockyard. The little man was sitting on a bench, a cat now perched on his lap. It was small, but I still wondered how he could afford to feed the thing. I took a deep breath and looked back at the strangers by my vehicle. Still there. Both looking at me by then. I kept my body language relaxed as I began walking toward them.

"Hi gentlemen."

Nothing.

"There's nothing in my vehicle for you, and I'd appreciate if you didn't touch it or lean on it."

"Or else what? Whadaya gonna do?"

"Nothing. I'm only making a request. Now I'll be back in thirty seconds, and I'll be driving away, whether you're leaning on my vehicle or not. So, the choice is yours."

I walked to the bench and gave the rest of the water to the old man and his little, shorthaired cat. His hair was slicked back, jet-black, shining and pressed like it was a helmet. I'm surprised it didn't have a blue-tinge, like a comic book character.

He thanked me, took a quick sip, and then poured some drops into the cap, which the cat licked up feverishly.

I offered him a ride. I knew the two pricks would steal his water, and probably kick his cat, if I didn't drive them home. You can never just do something nice for people. And you can't just mail it in at the end of a shift. Opportunistic thieves are everywhere. Deprivation makes for conflict, and its influence is universal. A chance opportunity for more water will often lead to a bad decision, even for someone who usually obeys the law. So every act of kindness has to be a two-part plan, or it will result in another theft or something worse.

The inspector did later ask Pete why his officers were giving away water unnecessarily, but they can transfer me back out of uniform if they don't like it. I take their pills, I keep the peace, and I don't question the agenda. I'm as close to the ideal as they have.

And that's what a normal day is like for me. I can't even remember why I wanted to talk about that day. It's a touchstone memory for me. And in my mind, it blends with several other days. The shifts go on for so long that all the days become one. And so, I guess I wish people knew that those are the types of interactions I have. In case they think I'm a hero. For the people who think it's something else—that's the job.

There are depressing family dynamics, suspicious people on the streets, and potentially dangerous situations that I work hard to curb by maintaining emotional detachment. The only thing missing from that day was a struggle through a sudden change in the weather. There probably was one hours earlier, actually—maybe a dust storm. I don't really remember. Better not to bother recollecting anyway, as the effort would probably just lead to me remembering some sad detail about that latchkey kid's face. It's better to let it be.

People like to talk about the past. Some people are old enough to remember what it was like before: before the wealth gap became astronomical, before the virus and the lockdowns, before all the businesses and the money they generate were controlled by a dozen people, before they shipped in the garbage from China and India to fill the new landfills opposite the lakes, before checking the weather forecast gave us anxiety, before people would murder each other for water.

So we ask each other questions about the past. Some people like to listen. Other people can't shut up about the glory of what's gone. And the question that always stands out for me is this: if you could go back to any time in your life and relive those moments, when would you choose?

People bring up their childhoods: a basketball game and a drink from the hose or a spring in full bloom. They talk about being pregnant back when it was a joy instead of something that caused crippling anxiety. Used to be that pregnancy was more of a celebration. Now people are concerned that they won't get the urgent care they may need for childbirth, and parents are worried about the kid's general livelihood before they're even born. Will we be able to afford to put the kid in school? What if the kid has something that limits them from being a labourer?

My older colleagues talk about their parents' memories as if those memories belong to them. Like their own lives weren't good enough, and they want to go back even farther to a time they didn't live through. Or other officers talk about what life was like before they were cops. Most of them wish they never had this job. They talk about screwing girls in private school or getting wasted in Europe.

I'm okay with where I'm at now. That's what I say. But when I think about the people I see on shift—the miserable families, the addicts in the alleys, or the unhinged lunatics fighting for garbage—I think to myself, what about these people? What about the people who don't have any good memories to relive?

I didn't ask to be anyone's hero.

Cormac got dressed quickly, having just finished showering while on shift. Sweat continued to bead on his forehead as he busied himself in front of the mirror—trimming his fingernails, shaving with an electric razor, and moisturizing his face. His pace slowed considerably once he was dressed and began his routine at the mirror, and he continued to record, paying no mind to the other officers moving in and out of the locker room.

There's a lot of outside pressure. From the media, the public, the service itself. I understand we have to be held to a high standard, but the idea that I have to be everyone's personal hero, that I'm supposed to be best friends with everyone else that has a badge, or that I have to be Mr. Nice Guy, or that I need to be filmed doing something heroic every day... it's impossible. And even if I do attain all that, there are millions of people that it will just never satisfy. It can never be enough because their minds are already made up. And here it is: They. Fucking. Hate us. And there are dangers present for us daily, which are related to these people who don't care to understand anything else about you, because as long as you wear the uniform, you are an enemy. That's something we in law enforcement have to deal with constantly, and it's something that doesn't get talked about much.

All right, so I just finished my workout and took a shower, which are normal parts of my routine on shift. My showers are always too hot, so I keep sweating after. Funny how people can keep making the same mistake, and you know you have the solution—you know you can correct the problem—but you just keep doing it anyway.

The workouts on shift are really important to me, as they keep me sane. And for the showers we're only allowed three minutes every forty-eight hours, so it's tough to enjoy it. We try to get the number of minutes increased whenever there's contract negotiations, but it never works. Otherwise, it's dry soaps and hand sanitizers. The water treatment system in-house is extremely efficient, and the service is always bragging about it in our newsletter emails and in public relations puff pieces. That's why I don't get why they can't give us a few extra minutes.

Anyway, for my workouts, I don't listen to music or talk to anyone. I don't let my mind drift. I focus only on the pain and building up my capacity to endure it. And I start hard, no matter what I'm doing. Overload the weights for the first set. Make the first hundred metres the fastest of them all.

Forget trying to save your energy. Why? To me, it's first lap, fifth gear. My pace is my weapon. I don't worry about saving anything because anyone trying to match my pace will concede mentally well before my lungs give out on me.

Satisfied, Cormac put the pin into his pocket. Wearing a white dress shirt and a light grey suit jacket, he commanded space as he walked through the halls, with a brisk pace and a long stride. Although his next destination was his own workspace to complete a simple arrest report, he moved with purpose. But when he passed the front desk, he was halted by Cst. Aleem.

"Dawson."

Cormac stopped short and his dress shoes squeaked on the waxed floor. "What is it?"

"We received some new intel from an outside agency, about one of the Freedom Fighters and his associations. One Zach Marten, who has been seen at the compound more and more often lately, is the brother-in-law of ex B&E artist, Daryl Vickshaw," he explained, reading from his notes. "Doesn't sound like much at a glance, but Vickshaw's travel history tells us he's made multiple two and three week trips to Estonia and Latvia, where he's assumed to have been training with far-right movements. In the past three years, he's been detained, searched, found to be in possession of hate-material and propaganda from the Abwehr Reborn, and has been spotted in and around the main camp of the Feuer und Rauch Division. He's always able to quickly make bail. He's done a bit of soft time, but got early release."

"So you might say these morons are a little more capable that we originally thought?"

"Yes. And I think their operation wouldn't have interested you at all in the first place if you didn't already think so too—before I even gave you this information, I mean. I think we spend a little too much time poking fun at them, and ignoring what they're capable of, what they have access to, and maybe what they've literally been training to do for a long time. These people might have something in place, ready for us, even if we

contact and get the desired arrests before the search

eck. That's good. Good to know. Thanks Aleem. But I don't underestimate any threats, and I'm prepared for anything, trust me. It ain't that kind of movie."

Lucian woke before dawn. Although his movements were methodical, he didn't rub his eyes or yawn or stretch or sigh. It was as though he had been awake all night. His knees cracked as he rose from the bed, but it was an otherwise silent scene as he put on the jeans that were strewn at his bedside, then shuffled to his closet and took the first shirt he saw, tossing it over his hunched back as he moved toward the door.

Moving slowly but never breaking his stride, he put the shirt on over his head, stretching his spine and fully extending his arms for the first time since he'd been laying flat on the bed. A tired "grmph" finally emerged from his throat.

"You need to eat something," he heard from behind him, and he waved backward as if to say 'I'm fine', but there was no one there. He stopped and turned, realizing the voice had been in his head, but was unshaken, and then wedged his feet into his untied shoes and was out the door at the break of day.

In his truck, he sat still, like he had forgotten why he was there. Then with shocking force, he pulled and pushed at the steering wheel, like a frustrated child who wanted to break something but was unsure how to do it. The wheel remained unmoved, and Lucian screamed as visible veins emerged in his neck and head.

He stopped as suddenly as he'd started. He took one deep, heaving breath. Then three that were short and panicked, like someone breathing into a paper bag. He pushed a button to start the truck, removed the yellow folding knife from the dash and put it in his pocket, and then craned his neck toward to the passenger side of his windshield, scanning slowly from the far side back to the driver's side, reading the words—backwards—printed there. Gavril Plow: Snow, Tow, Contract Work.

Then he laughed, like it was all an act for a camera, and began his drive to The Wilderness.

He didn't stop, as Elroy had instructed, but he looked frequently into his mirrors—short, quick checks. Side-view and rear-view. Then again. And over his shoulder. And again, like he wasn't really looking for anything at all. Regardless, his hands never wavered, and he handled the vehicle expertly as he drove north, up the wet and winding back roads, well past the airport, far from the Trans-Canada Highway, passing nothing man-made, save for a single automated vehicle charging station.

Several kilometres past the charging station, Lucian saw a large piece of plywood with some writing spray-painted onto it, propped against a tree by the side of the road. The writing was upside down, but he slowed his truck so that he could read the words: 'July 17→ All Systems Off.'

It was nearly two hours before he arrived at the scrapyard. A tall gate with loose chains wrapped around it was already wide open upon his arrival. He drove in and navigated confidently around various indistinct piles of rotting metal, as though he'd been there a thousand times. There were several barren vehicles, some aged over a hundred years—ancient chunks of American steel.

He parked out front of a small office building, constructed with poured concrete. He exited the vehicle promptly; squaring his shoulders and stretching out to his full height, he appeared inconceivably tall, as though he had folded to fit into the truck. It was Lucian's overall length, not just his considerable height, which gave him the look of something alien—a sort of imposter. His gangly arms and spindly skeletal fingers, his stilt legs further accentuated by his tiny waist, and his prominent jaw, which stood out amidst his subdued facial expressions. Physically, he was a paradox: you might just be able to shove him over with one hand, but what if you were wrong?

The scrapyard owner, Daryl Vickshaw, sat inside the building, his feet up on a desk, in front of a window that faced the property's entrance. The interior of the building was a withered museum of Americana: walls lined by posters that advertised Coca-Cola, McDonald's, Levi's, Civil War recruitment, tent revivals, ice cream parlours, barbershops, old timey concerts, diners, Disneyland, dance contests, defense bonds, Winchester rifles, classic cars, minstrel shows, silent films, gas stations, football games, cigarettes, and moonshine. A large black binder of baseball cards rested beside Daryl's feet, with dozens of other cards strewn across the desk. A hanging display case, housing numerous unopened bubble gum packages, was nailed to the wall beside the desk. The wall opposite the front entrance was the outlier, as it was filled with framed family photos, floor to ceiling, with each picture showcasing a different family.

Lucian was still in his car when Daryl burst the office door open, ready for war as much as he was ready for a business exchange. When Lucian stepped out and around the car, into Daryl's unobstructed view, Daryl took a short step back, rethinking his strategy. He kept a hand on the open door as he spoke:

"What uh, what do you want?"

"Do you remember me?"

"Why—"

"You sold me this." Lucian punched the plow blade with the underside of his fist, never breaking eye contact with Daryl.

"Ah. Yeah, I sell a lot of those. If there's something wrong with it, it's not my issue."

"Nothing wrong with it. I use it a lot. There's never been a problem. I'm here to pick up for my people—the Freedom Fighters."

"Well shit man, you should have started with that. I didn't realize you were a patriot. You've got to be clear when you come here. Wear the hat next time. You pull your truck up the lane to the warehouse and we'll load the barrels together."

Daryl was medium height with a shaved head and a top-heavy, barrel-chested physique. He walked at *his* pace—unbothered—as though inviting others to ask him to hurry up. He was nearing the warehouse when Lucian slowly passed by him and backed his truck up to the garage door.

The warehouse was well maintained, organized, and clean. The concrete floor was spotless, dry, and free of any cracks. Sturdy metal shelving units held plastic storage boxes of varying sizes and understated colours. A pair of side-by-side orange shipping containers—closed, chained, and padlocked—took up much of the space at the rear of the building. Based on the stocked items that were visible, the warehouse was a cross between a bomb shelter and an army surplus store: tents, gas masks, sacks of rice and grain, canned food, water jugs, bowie knives, bars of soap, blankets, coats, rubber boots, bottles of rubbing alcohol and peroxide, and bug-out bags. Some items were ready for immediate sale, with visible price tags. The room smelled of gasoline, but there were no jerry cans in sight. Lucian noted two large boxes of ammunition, clearly labelled: .40 calibre and 9mm.

Together and without speaking, the two men heaved four 55-gallon plastic drums into the bed of the truck. After hauling the first drum together, Daryl hopped onto the truck bed while Lucian put the next drum onto a steel hand-truck, without so much as a glance in search of approval to use the hand-truck. Daryl was noticeably careful as he set the barrels down, sliding each to make room for the next. The drums were heavy, packed with multiple solid items, shifting and clanging as Lucian continued the work with the deft assuredness of someone who had done that sort of labour since he was old enough to walk.

With the barrels in place, Lucian broke the silence: "That it?"

"That's it that's all."

"Let me get one of those bug-out bags."

"You want a forty-eight, a seventy-two, or a ninety-six?"

"Ninety-six."

"That's 500. Cash only for warehouse gear."

Lucian handed Daryl the cash from a thin stack of bills folded in his back pocket. He then gave Daryl the photos, as Elroy instructed. After offering a short nod, Lucian took the bag and moved to the driver's side door of the truck. He reached the handle and opened the door before Daryl spoke again. "And why do you need all the smoke bombs? Why don't we just keep burning their houses down? It's easier."

At that, Lucian flinched like a robot with an internal glitch. As he closed the door and turned to face Daryl, the colour drained from his face so quickly that it was difficult for Daryl to tell if Lucian's complexion had actually been that pale all along.

"I said why don't we just keep burning?" Daryl clarified, since Lucian wasn't speaking. "It's easier. It's efficient. Gets the point across in a big way. And far less room for human error—I just think it's better."

"Yeah." Lucian tried to gather himself. "I prefer it too. But this is what Mickey and Elroy want."

"Is it what Amanita Virosa wants?"

"I don't know. I'm new. I just do what I'm told… support the cause."

Daryl squinted, nodded, and let out a reflective "Hmm" as he pondered Lucian's point. "Good… good. That's important." He reached out his hand to shake Lucian's. Lucian looked at it first, then clapped hold of it for a firm shake before the two men parted ways.

Lucian began his drive in silence, but after a few kilometres, he gagged violently and slammed on the brakes, dry heaving momentarily on the side of the road then letting out an ear-piercing scream, a sound so visceral and high-pitched, it didn't seem possible for a man to have produced it. But he did, all the same. A pool of blood appeared on the white of one of his eyes—a popped vessel. He saw it as he glanced into the rear-view mirror, and studied it for a moment. He found himself hyperventilating, tasting blood in his mouth.

Without giving himself time to calm, he returned to driving. Unsoothed, his composure came only as a result of sheer exhaustion. His eyes watered and his nose began to run. After twenty minutes of silence and several wipes of his eyes and nose, Lucian looked no different than he had when he left his house hours earlier, save for the popped blood vessel in his eye.

He turned the radio on and listened:

It's been a busy day in federal politics, with some major shifts in the political landscape and some new players entering the race as party leaders get set to start on the campaign trail.

Top story today is the result of this morning's Supreme Court of Canada session in regards to the forthcoming federal election. The court has ruled against the injunction that would force political advertising campaigns—those produced in-house and by lobbyists—to, as the complainants wrote, "advertise responsibly". Had the injunction passed, campaigners would have been forced to eliminate any disinformation from their advertisements, including—amongst other things—photo-shopped images, cherry-picked statistics, and quotes used out of context.

The case was first filed shortly after the Elections Modernization Act was replaced with a simplified set of best practice guidelines just five years ago. Since then, it was discovered that political ads from the last federal election were tampered with, as an ashamed editing-room whistleblower admitted that he was told to darken the skin of multiple political candidates for the ad. He also said he was told to use his editing software to make certain candidates appear shorter and heavier, and even adjust some of their hairlines and jawlines.

The tactic of misinforming voters has been a successful one for multiple political parties in several high profile elections both at home and around the world in recent decades, and it appears the problem may be about to get worse, as the decision could, according to former Member of Parliament Brooke Zavek, embolden parties to increase the amount of alternative facts included on the campaign trail.

According to the presiding judge, Chief Justice Connor Whitmore, the court's ruling was that it is up to the people to decipher truth from propaganda, and that while politicians should be fair, forthright, and truthful at all times, those same politicians should have faith in the knowledge and critical thinking skills of the people.

Still with politics, the federal government also announced today that there is officially no longer a cap on political fundraising, as any mention of fundraising has been removed from the aforementioned best practice guidelines. Coinciding with the announcement, Anderson Holdings held a press conference to proclaim that they are about to make the largest political donation in history, and the donation will be going to the newly formed Free Patriots Party, which has recently gained traction after the United People's Conglomerate endorsed the FPP's new leader—

Lucian turned off the radio, closed his eyes for a beat, and continued the rest of the drive in silence.

Natalie was on her last day of rest before returning to work. Having just woken up, she went immediately to her desk to begin another recording on her phone. Without a plan, she simply began talking about the first memory that came to her mind.

Is this the world we deserve? That's what I was thinking when Pete came by to talk to me a couple weeks ago.

I was writing up an arrest report after having picked up two strung out addicts breaking into a house in the north end. They told me they'd been chased away from the lake, so they were trying to get some water. You can't drink straight from the lake—you have to pay, you have to be registered, and you have to get your pipes set up proper. It's all regulated. So the addicts need to steal water first, so they have the energy to go score. It's easier for them in the winter, when they can harvest snow. It all sounds bizarre, I know. But it's not scarcity that leads to violence and crime. It's the power imbalance. It starts with water becoming a privilege instead of a right.

Anyway, Pete pulled his phone out to check the results of the Super Max draw. He asked if I had plans for my days of rest. I could tell he was feeling eager; the lottery made him chattier than usual.

"No real plans for the DRs. Maybe go see a movie." *He wasn't listening—too focused on the task with his phone.*

"Ah man." *He was looking at the screen.* "Bad news. No luck for us. Just a few smaller prizes claimed. Here."

He showed me a video clip of the elderly couple that had won $2.5 million. It's always nice to see the winners' faces. Their smiles aren't fake.

"No Super Max winner sold though. Pot's up another 1.4 million now. It's huge. But you know what else I heard? They're gonna raise The Association's cut to 33%. Like they need it. It's just the rich getting richer."

"Seems they've got carte blanche."

"Carte what?"

"Total control."

"Yeah, carte blush is right."

Another increase for the big companies. It didn't surprise me. I don't see a point in buying the tickets, but I just keep pitching in because it's good for morale; it's good for people to have a little bit of hope. Plus, if I stopped pitching in, someone would ask me why, and I don't want to have to explain it.

I sleep decently. When my days off come, I take full advantage. But it's not exciting; it's just getting the natural rest that I need. I try to make a habit of going to the movies, just to do something outside my apartment.

I like to go to matinees, when there are fewer people there. I used to read books more often, but it just made me fall back asleep. So yeah, I get my sleep, I exercise and do some combat training, I go see a movie.

They don't play indie films anymore, but they play old movies sometimes. I don't like most of the big budget stuff. We don't need to see another reboot of the beautiful billionaire who solves all the crimes the cops can't solve. Popular movies are too often about a better world that doesn't exist, a glamourized version of the past we can't go back to, or a future that's too far down the line for me to ever see. It's all white saviours and wishful thinking.

Maybe we'll turn things around enough before civilization falls apart. I doubt it though. I just focus on making it through my shifts and getting the sleep I need whenever I get the chance. I'm just trying to survive, like everyone else.

"We can tell him about the plan. Short-term then long-term. See how he reacts to the cleansing project. See if he is really willing to sacrifice to save God's country," Elroy said, pacing anxiously, and audibly grinding his teeth while awaiting Lucian's return to the compound.

"He doesn't need to hear all that yet," Mickey replied. "Maybe he's one of us—the foundation has been laid—but the details can reveal themselves in time."

"But then maybe he's not with us, and we'll know soon," the third man in the room, Zach, spoke up. "We still don't know if he's committed. Picking up the equipment for us is one thing, but he's getting paid, and he still doesn't even know what he's bringing us. We should make him burn one of the houses, or actually help us follow through with smoking the sheep out of The Blade."

"That'll be the acid test, Zachary," Mickey was calm in response. "When he gets here, we'll tell him what he's done for us. We'll tell him we're proud of him. We'll tell him it's time to become a Freedom Fighter. Depending on how he reacts, maybe—just maybe—we'll show him one of the carbines or the AR-15. Then we'll see if he's got God's glory in his eyes, when he reacts to the look of it."

Zach smirked, but capped his giddiness before he replied, "But I don't think it matters how he reacts, once we've told him all that. We'll be celebrating a new patriot or we'll be eliminating a threat. Either way, we'll be showing him the AR."

"Where's Dad?" David asked his mother, Ava.

"He had another job today. I know it's strange not having him around as much these past couple weeks, but it's nice for us. When dad's working, we're all doing well."

"Why?"

"That's just how it is, David. Mom and Dad make money, and money buys us things."

"Like food."

"That's right. Like food, and clothes."

"And… dinosaurs!" David pointed to his toys in a small beach bucket on the floor.

"Exactly right. Dinosaurs too. I *was* expecting dad to come home by now though. He should be here aaaany second, and we can surprise him with a BOO!" Ava spoke to her son in the slow, upbeat, singsong cadence to which young parents become accustomed. But her mind lingered on the idea of it just being the two of them: her and David, in this world, with no one else.

"I miss him."

"Well, you should tell him that when he gets here. And remember, when Mom and Dad leave, we always come home. Daddy *always* comes home."

"I never saw an animal that felt sorry for itself," said S/Sgt. Canizales.

"How do you mean?"

"I mean it how I said it."

"Yeah…"

"I saw a squirrel once, had been run over by a car. The back half of her body was crushed flat. But she kept crawling. Front paws working as hard as they could. She didn't have it in her to feel sad or cry or quit. Her only thought was to get off that road and keep going 'til she found some food or got back to her babies or died. That's what I mean. And that's how you need to be when you're on shift out here. Bad things happen to good officers who get lazy, get feeling sorry for themselves, get thinking that all civilians are good people. The people you get response calls for, they know what you got. They want the car, they want the water, they want your pistol, and they don't care if they take your life with it. So when I see you out here complaining that your belt don't fit just right, or giggling by the coffee pot—refilling your cup when you know damn well it's one cup a day—I get thinking you're not ready for what this district has coming to you. I get the feeling like you don't appreciate what you got here."

"No, sir. I do appreciate it, sir."

"Show me. Don't tell me. And tie your boots, for Christ's sake."

Pete moved on. With shift briefing finished, he commenced his meticulous and critical inspection of his staff, a daily ritual while they prepared for the day's tasks. They knew he was watching from before briefing began to the time when they were out of the building. He approached Det. Cormac Dawson.

"What's that new transfer's name again?" Pete asked.

"Not sure."

"Just as well."

"I'll ask."

"No, don't. Doesn't matter."

"Why do you make it so obvious that you're watching everyone after briefing?"

"Heightens their senses before they're on the streets. You ready for today?"

"I'm ready for anything."

"Good. We need this done efficiently. Whisky-neat."

"I'm telling you, I'm dialled in."

"Perfect. Just a second." He turned to Natalie, who was nearing the exit. "Ross?"

She stopped and turned: "Yes, Staff?"

"Anything to add before you start your patrol?"

"No issues."

"About today's operation, I mean."

"Why would she——" Cormac started, but was silenced by a glance and partially raised hand from Pete.

"For today, I know you said it in the briefing already, sir, but it's worth repeating: you've got the skills and training to trump their tenacity, should any confrontation arise, so just use that and stay above their level."

"We hear you. It's understood. You're concerned about optics," said Cormac.

"Not optics. I'm talking about the lives at stake. The men in there are pretty well-insulated, hence why we haven't learned much about what they're doing in that place, despite their growing presence around town. It gives me the feeling that, when it comes to protecting their interests, they're not playing. Violence is first."

"Check," replied Cormac. He didn't look at Natalie when he spoke.

"So long as the weather holds out, we'll assemble in place at the compound in half an hour, and reassess with the team," said Pete. "And forget about the pin, Mac. I don't need you distracted en route. You're done with the recordings. Ross, you can stick with the recording project for one more day—today—while you're on routine patrol. Now let's get to work."

"Work!" Cormac barked with enthusiasm.

Outside the Freedom Fighters' compound, with specialized combat medics on stand-by and the tactical team containing all doors and windows, Cormac and Pete sat in an unmarked cruiser, monitoring the compound, mere minutes before their raid was slated to begin.

"How much longer until you make contact?" Cormac was eager.

"Take a breath, brother. Four minutes left until I make the call to this owner, Elroy. Starting early might leave an officer off guard if someone makes a move to a window. Remember, we're doing it right."

"Check... I'm just excited."

"Well don't be." Pete managed a short laugh then. "This'll play out satin smooth, Mac. Make the contact, get this coward out and detained. The rest of his minions will follow quietly. We know how these types are. Thorough search leads to some hands in cuffs—behind the back, like we do—and the sun shines a little brighter this afternoon. That is that."

Just then, a voice came over the radio: "Dispatch to Staff Sergeant Canizales. Do you copy?"

"Copy. Two minutes out from making contact."

"Abort. Repeat: abort. The project is off."

"What?"

"There's something wrong with the warrant. Judge came back with an edit."

"An edit? In sixteen years on the job, I've never heard of an edit to a warrant."

"Well, hopefully this is the only time you hear it, but that's what happened. Something about the proof of residence that was submitted. Judge said it was out-dated. The bill is too old. The warrant has been adjusted and is only valid from 1900 hours to 0700 hours, pending you provide a more recent proof of residence."

"Why not approve the warrant for a full twenty-four hours starting tomorrow or the next day?"

"I'm not here to argue that point, and I don't disagree. But this is what came down from the judge. Call it off now."

"Base to Constable Ross. There's been a report of a missing person at 384 Heinrich Street. It's out of your zone's patrol, but Oladosu is busy on a call. We need someone to complete the report with the immediate family."

"Ross to base. I'm on my way there now."

Natalie arrived at the Gavril residence, where Ava had recently called to report that her husband hadn't come home from work the night before. Ava answered the door; masking her anxiety with a practised confidence, she greeted Natalie with a polite smile.

Natalie watched as Ava guided her to their kitchen table. She planted her feet firmly and stood up straight; she was dressed as though she was ready to leave the house immediately if needed.

"I'll be writing while we talk, just to fill out the report and keep notes on anything that might be important."

"Sure, of course. I feel ridiculous to even call this in. I'm sure he'll be home any minute now. It's likely just that he keeps getting more good work he doesn't want to pass up. Really, it's good for us."

"But he hasn't been in contact since when?"

"I wasn't awake when he left the house yesterday morning. Likely around six o'clock."

"And is it typical for him to be gone for such lengths? What does he do for work?"

"It's not typical, no... never really. But he's been so busy lately. Repeat work with the same clients. He has a plow, but he can do anything. Lucian can fix anything, build anything, maintain anything. So he takes whatever comes."

"And you work as well?"

"Yes, I'm a psychologist, but my clinical hours are restricted at the office—we're underfunded, and it's a shared space, so even though there are dozens of people lining up for appointments, I have to limit my hours. I try to make up for it with virtual appointments, when possible."

"I see. It's such a shame when you aren't allowed to give people the help they need. And you have a child, don't you? Is he here?"

"Yes, but he's at school right now."

"Okay, let's start with you giving me a list of places your husband might be."

"First though... I just want to tell you about the fire. Lucian's demeanor has changed since the fire. And that is what I'm worried about here. It's the only thing that has me concerned. He... he saved a child earlier this year, from that burning house a couple blocks away. He saved the sleeping boy, but he didn't know there was a girl too. It's... he hasn't been the same since then."

When the call came in for a missing person out in The Junk, I wasn't all that close by, but dispatch called me out of my zone to go do it because, well honestly, they know I won't come back to the detachment and complain about it. All the false-alphas want to wait for better action, or in this case they were probably praying to get a last-minute call to join the raid. I don't mind these types of calls because it's a chance to get off the regular beat, out of the vehicle, and just talk to someone. Yes there are added risks based on neighbourhood, time of day, or any number of other variables, but there's always risk when you're on duty, and the shifts are so long, so arduous, you reach a breaking point where it's preferable to have some contact and some challenge to stimulate your mind, even amidst increased risk.

I arrived at the house, and I recalled it from when I was there once during patrol a while ago; I remember it as the house with the latchkey kid in the window. I had a bad feeling, based on what I remembered, and some educated guessing: mother works all day. Family holding on by a string. One kid who has a sense that something's wrong in their family picture, but has an ingrained loyalty and doesn't know the dangers inherent in being loyal to a lost cause.

I don't mean to give myself any credit. After all, I already knew it was a missing person case. But my mind generally goes toward the worst outcome: mom's beaten body stuffed in the freezer after too hard of a push sent her tumbling down the stairs, or boy's body dumped haphazardly in the woods after dad's misplaced rage. Neither was the case here, thankfully.

The wife, who I won't call by name for this project, told me something like this: 'husband's been gone for a day and a half. He's been increasingly reclusive, and he had a traumatic incident with a house-fire a couple months ago, saving one child but not saving the other.' I can't properly imitate the voice, the dramatic inflections, and the panicky cadence, but essentially she was afraid for her husband's life because of how much his solitary behaviour had increased since that horrible accident.

A lot of people here, myself included, have survivalist tendencies that can be mistaken as neurotic. I don't have it as bad as she does, because I have this career and my apartment doesn't need the kind of care and attention her house requires. But we are definitely both ascetic people... because we have to be. It was written all over that woman and her home—the care she took to preserve something with a flawed core, not quite built for this time and place. The way she carried herself as someone ready to move, ready to speak, ready to stand, ready to flee, ready to defend. Yet she maintained self-control. There's people who are always anxious... but that's not what she is. It's different.

The people who live in the unprotected parts of this city have a blood simple mindset. This woman was the perfect example of it. After years of prolonged exposure to this society without the many layers of protection that wealthier citizens have, these less fortunate citizens develop a perennially fearful outlook. I'm not doubting her stance. Obviously her husband is missing. But the way she trailed off, the way her mind wandered, the way she assumed the worst, the way she tried so hard to maintain composure despite clearly crumbling on the inside... these are all symptoms of the Terrace Bay blood simple mentality.

For these people, their world is an echo chamber. Struggle, sleep, repeat. And try to smile for your kids and be supportive of your spouse while you're at it. And it builds. Each day begins to feel worse than the one that preceded it, even if it is just the same. Something might even be incrementally better, but it's impossible to tell in that chamber.

Your daily struggles are amplified by the continuity of them. How can you feel better if you don't have an escape to look forward to? My first thought is that's what led to her husband's disappearance. We get these calls two or three times a day, and with almost all of them, the missing person is found alive within a day. A person whose struggles are ceaseless finds a way, whether they intended to or not, to forget the struggles for a fleeting moment.

They're usually people with untreated mental health illnesses or *psychological disorders. With the former, it's often young parents. The repetitive mental stress overtakes them and they wander off, go on a bender, skip town for a day or two, or get found in a junk-house or alleyway somewhere. Her husband has a history of binge drinking, has recently been behaving erratically, and is under constant blood simple stress. 'Constant' is a word that gets overused, so I want to be clear that I used it with specific intent: constant stress.*

The only difference here is that he had been getting lucrative work lately, and the best way to briefly escape the shadow-flicker of a life in this town is to have a topped up bank account. But as the wife told me, he's been getting repeat work at a place that is under recent police surveillance. Lots of criminals there. Likely some addicts amongst them. Could be trouble for the husband. I'll be informing Staff Seargant Canizales as a precaution, as I begin my search for the man.

In the briefing room at the Terrace Bay detachment, Pete gathered his officers.

"We got judge's approval—it's official. And we don't have time to complain about it. We can whine all day, but it won't make any difference. This is what we've got: twelve hours, starting at 1900, to get this job done. Management says if we want to apply for a new twenty-four hours, it has to be all new grounds. Nobody above us thinks this is worth our resources, so it's just up to us to get the job done and prove them wrong. Also, tac team has been pulled. It's not in the budget to keep paying them their OT and travel assistance if they have to stay overnight."

"Fuckin' hell. Such bullshit. All over the price of some breakfasts," said Oakshot.

"Enough!" Pete yelled. "As I said, it's not going to make any difference if we spend time breaking down all the ways we're getting railed on this. We still have a job to finish. There's a serious time restriction, we're going to have to get this done without the tactical team, it's going to be done in the dark, and the combat medics have been pulled too—budget concerns." He motioned to Oakshot. "Don't say a word on it. It's done.

"Now, I've consulted with Aleem and Mac here, and we've got our bases covered to still work this thing right. Intel says the only two guys who stick around after sundown are the owner, Elroy, and the kiddy toucher, Danny Atkins. No idea why, but the CI says these two go by the names 'Paul and Evan'. Shouldn't make any difference to us. Now, Atkins has a big fucking dog, trained to attack. But we know with certainty that he walks that mutt every night at 2100 hours, weather permitting. And if we're lucky, Elroy will be with him. He wears a balaclava, but a CI confirmed just today that it's him because he knows the dog. It's confirmed as best as it's going to be. We make the arrest for the sexual assault, dog is controlled and out of the picture, and Elroy is detained too. If Elroy's not out for the walk, we can contact him in the house, when he's by himself—no friends, no dog. Get his ass out of there, and pop this thing off just like we were supposed to this morning. Questions? Good. We'll brief here again at 1845, but for now, keep your minds on your day-to-day. This is locked up until it's time to move in."

"You want someone watching the compound until then?"

"Gilchrist says no. All officers are to continue normal duties until our scheduled raid, and if the Oversight Committee catches anyone setting up shop to stake out anywhere, it will be viewed as mismanagement of funds, with sweeping punishments rolled out immediately. Those are his words. Do not post up at the compound, but passing by on occasion is just a normal part of the routine for those of you assigned to that zone, so just keep an eye for bodies leaving the facility.

"On that note, Ross has a report of a missing person from The Junk, a man named Lucian Gavril, who may be at the compound. He is not one of them—as far as we know—but he's been doing contract work there recently and has gone missing as of yesterday. Likely he's there shooting dope with the couple fiends who linger on the premises. This is a problem for us, because we want to go and check to see if he's there, but this is our shot with the search, and we don't want the Freedom Fighters spooked before the raid happens, so Ross is exhausting all other avenues to give us this chance. So in zone three, watch for a very tall, very thin man, early forties, drives a truck with a plow, and decals reading 'Gavril Plow'.

"And Mac, it's unrelated, but I already told you to take that pin off your shirt. No more recordings. Dismissed."

Detective Constable Cormac Dawson, he him, making one last recording en route to a raid this fine evening. I thought I'd tell you about the one time I got in a bit of trouble in my first year on the job. It's just… it's a good story, and I feel like I haven't said anything all that interesting on this recording project yet.

So at the Terrace Bay detachment, we have a directive that we don't chase. If there's a pursuit, well, there isn't a pursuit, because if we light up the cherries and the vehicle speeds away, we just let them. The new areas are all designed with pedestrians in mind. It's a walker's community. You can talk to city planners about that. But that's how it is, so pursuits are dangerous. So we get the information we need—plate number, make, model, colour—and we just let them go because we don't want some pedestrian getting crushed when we're chasing someone we know we'll just pick up without incident in an hour anyway.

But, I got a little excited the first time someone tried to flee when I was going to pull them over. It was just for an expired plate, but the drivers know you're going to run them, and then if they've got conditions or a warrant, they're getting hauled in. He didn't hesitate when he saw my lights, and then I don't know if it's just in my nature or what, but I floored it. I buried the needle and was on his ass like white on rice.

Before long, he totalled his vehicle. Lost a hubcap, blew a tire, his muffler dangling, sparks flying. The man was not afraid to run his little box over some curbs, that's for sure. I believe he was dragging a street sign by the time he just pulled over and started running.

He was better off quitting there, obviously. Because I can run. People see the way I'm built and they figure I'm not a guy with speed. But I'm built for these short burst moments, and it's not like the chase is going to last 5K. So I lit every match I had, running his ass down.

And I remember vividly that he did give up. He gave up before I got him. He wasn't really running for the last few paces. Obviously he was still moving, but it was more like he was just waiting to be tackled. We were moving so slowly, I just stuck my foot out and tripped him over. I didn't even touch him after that. He just fell and proned himself out. He'd been arrested before, plenty of times. He knew what to do.

That guy was a nightcrawler—breaking into the landfill to smash windows or try to burn the garbage on multiple occasions. That was what his warrant was for. Those bozo landfill cops couldn't catch a cold. I did what they'd failed to do three or four times. And no credit! Well, the boys were proud of me. But I got a slap on the wrist for that one. But even the administration that warned me not to do it again… they were happy about what I'd done and what they knew I could do for them and the service. I know it.

A chilled breeze blew through Terrace Bay as Cormac hopped over a cold puddle on the pavement, making his way to Pete's unmarked cruiser parked half a block up the road from the Freedom Fighters' compound. It was a fully overcast, starless evening, especially dark for the time of night.

Cormac tapped once on the passenger side window and opened the door before Pete was even aware who he was.

"Fuckin' cold out there."

"Hmph," Pete replied.

"Only two left inside?"

"Hassan spotted a mass exodus around dinner time. Five or six people. Should be just the two remaining, as expected."

Together, they drove slowly up the street with the lights turned off, parking nearby the compound. Cormac studied the compound's razor wire along the chain-link fence on the nearside, and the glass shards embedded atop the cold concrete wall on the far side.

"I'm just thinking about those losers in there," Cormac said, breaking the silence.

"What of them?"

"Just the things they've done. What we know about and what we don't know about. I think the Hatchet-Man murders shook me a bit. I looked over the case file yesterday. It's chilling stuff, what desperate people do. And that pedo in that building." He pointed to emphasize. "Right in there with the Fighters, I read his file too: assaulting his niece and nephew, and the way he did it and the way he hid it for so long... How could someone do that?"

"The longer I work in policing, the more I hear people say that. It's one of the most common phrases: people always say, 'How could someone do this?' You just have to come to terms with the fact that... there is no limit to human cruelty. There is no limit to what people are willing to do to other people. It's disgusting, but it's the truth.

"And that's one incident with one guy. There's a dozen milling around in there in the daytime. A few I've booked. Fiends with kitchen knives walking into random houses, looking for any trinket to steal to go get a hit... every day is just addled fear of becoming dope-sick for those junkies. And now they're in here? In this place with that child molester, with their god-complex basket-case leader, with some hapless underachievers whose lives didn't quite turn out the way they wanted and now they're angry about it, with these other life-long, small-time criminals trying to become revolutionaries. They're likely building bombs, planning to lynch someone, rallying every other white, unemployed, unloved loner with no other support or brotherhood in his life. I'm not sure what we're going to find in there, but I've never been as confident that a raid will result in something major as I am about this."

"It's intimidating."

Pete turned his neck to Cormac without moving his shoulders. "I never thought I would live to hear Cormac Dawson say he felt intimidated."

"Looking at that place, thinking about what might be going on in there every day. It feels like standing in front of a skyscraper, even though it's just a little half-ass base."

"Lotta windows to break though."

"What's that?"

"With a skyscraper. They're tall, sure. But they'll crumble just like the rest of them. 'The harder they fall', they used to say in the fight-sports world, way back."

Cormac ruminated for a moment. He smirked and then

quietly—almost whispering—repeated, "Lotta windows to break."

With Briggs, Aleem, Oakshot, and Hassan standing by, Cormac and Pete waited for the dog-walkers. Hours passed.

Pete radioed his team: "We've got eyes on two men exiting the front entrance of the compound with a large dog. Must be our guys—'Paul and Evan', AKA Elroy and Danny. We are moving in."

Surgical and swift, Cormac and Pete approached the men, softies drawn and pointed to the ground as they moved in a practised, covert, tactical fashion. These were officers accustomed to high-risk arrests.

Cormac confirmed the guardhouse empty before the dog-walkers knew they were being followed.

"Hands up. Danny Atkins, you are under arrest. Control that dog or I will shoot it dead in the street." Pete commanded, tossing a muzzle to Danny.

With the muzzle applied and the dog calmed, Cormac cuffed Danny and frisked him. Danny resorted to crying almost immediately; he was sobbing and sniffling, like a toddler who had just come down from a fit, as Cormac escorted him to Pete's cruiser. Meanwhile, Pete allowed Elroy to take the dog's leash, and Elroy guided the dog to a nearby streetlamp, tying him properly, until Pete was satisfied.

Pete told Elroy he was being detained and showed him the search warrant. With the learned ease of a consummate professional, Pete frisked Elroy, promptly finding a serrated spring-release knife. He announced the arrest for the prohibited, concealed weapon, then cuffed Elroy and placed him into the back of the car with Danny, whose sniffling had by then erupted into pleads to the gods for mercy.

"Come on man, at least put my cuffs to the front so I don't have to sit on my hands while I try to console my friend here."

"No."

While surveying the compound's grounds, the other officers

moved in and listened to Pete. Scanning the buildings, Aleem focused on windows, awaiting lights being turned on, silhouettes passing by, or blinds being moved. There was nothing.

"Is there anyone else in that building? Or the trailer or any other spot on your property?" Pete asked Elroy.

"Don't think so."

"What do you mean, you don't think so? It's a yes or no. That your residence?"

"Uh huh."

"And who else is in there right now?"

"No one."

"You sure?"

"Yes."

Pete waited just outside the gated entrance while the other five officers began their search. Sweeping the grounds with flashlights in hand and firearms drawn, the men moved in silence: along the fence-line, across the scattered exercise equipment, around the exteriors of the office building, bunkhouse, and trailer, and over a small berm that held a few thin, withered, long-forgotten trees.

Pete couldn't bear to listen to Danny's pleading any longer, and was further infuriated by how Elroy did nothing to calm him. Elroy sat in smug silence, appearing completely unbothered, as though he enjoyed the whining.

Pete moved to the guardhouse, busying himself with examining the hastily constructed concrete box. Exposed wires led him to a single computer screen and separate touch-pad, where he was able to swipe his fingers across to change the picture on the screen: first, a screensaver of a naked woman, then split-screen views of the compound and the rooms in the office building. He swiped through them with haste until he was alarmed at the sight of four men and one woman crammed into a small, windowless room. They were smoking, talking, laughing. One was standing up, moving his hands in the animated way a maestro might conduct an orchestra. He was telling a story that was constantly being interrupted by laughter, shaking heads, and pointing fingers. Pete's mouth dropped.

He radioed to his team: "There are people in there somewhere. I can't tell where. I think there's a basement. Five people."

While Pete continued to speak, Briggs was already in the process of rushing to the entrance of the trailer. As if pushed on by an unseen force, he burst into the trailer with Cormac close behind. Via a mixture of his own voice and the overwhelming rush of adrenaline, he couldn't hear Pete's continued communication.

"They're unaware of our presence. Stop now and return to the entrance with me. Now!"

In the trailer, Briggs screamed, "Police! Everybody get on the ground!"

Cormac shouted over Briggs' voice, but to no avail.

Briggs turned on the light. His last thought was a recognition that the switch was heavy, hard to use, like it was designed to make you think twice before flipping it. The trailer exploded. Cormac's body flew backward onto the pavement.

Pete turned at the sound and looked on in horror. The explosion produced ear-piercing metallic screams, blinding flashes of light, and intermittent popping sounds as other smaller chargers burst through fiery ashes. Pete moved to leave the guardhouse, but stopped when he saw, out of the corner of his eye, the five people on the screen reacting frantically to the sound.

"Stay low! Prepare to make arrests! I see no weapons. Repeat: no weapons! But be ready! They're off-screen now. Move! Move! Move!" Pete moved too, toward the office entrance as he drew his firearm.

Aleem, Hassan, Oakshot, and Pete all moved in near the entrance, but left the space free for what their instincts told them to expect: the five people came running out the door, though with a surprising amount of space between each. And one by one, they fell to the ground in fear as the officers shouted out warnings, instructions, arrests.

The trailer had already been reduced to flaming rubble as

Pete radioed in for paramedics, a fire crew, and back-up officers. He hustled to Cormac and dragged him a few metres away from the flames, shocked at how far he already was from the blast site.

Pete heard a gunshot ring out, and when he turned to check on his other officers, he saw Oakshot mounted on one of the Freedom Fighters, beating on him with both fists, like a gorilla raining down blows. Aleem tackled Oakshot.

"Fuck," Pete said in a whispered sigh. His mind raced and his heart pounded through his chest—because of what he saw from Oakshot, because of the stuttered, choked breaths and bleeding ears of Cormac, because of the heat scorching his face, because of the hopelessness of the situation. Still, somehow, he deftly applied a tourniquet to Cormac's severely damaged left leg.

The fire was extinguished, all parties were interviewed, Briggs was confirmed dead, and Cormac was taken from the scene, clinging to life. With no hope for assistance from the tactical team, the search continued with four new officers at the helm.

"We bleed for this," exclaimed one officer as he fist-bumped another.

"But not from our hearts," came the response.

"Don't drip, don't bleed!" And they entered the office building together to begin searching.

Natalie arrived amidst the chaos, while dozens of flashing red and blue lights backlit the scene, forming dancing shadows of the frenzied responders, who worked tirelessly into the early morning.

"Your man wasn't in there," Pete called to Natalie, with his feet dangling off the rear of the ambulance, holding a cold-pack to the back of his neck.

"Lucian?"

"Yup. He wasn't in there… thankfully. I'm sure he'll turn up soon elsewhere."

"Are you hurt?"

"No, just using this to slow my heart-rate, calm my nerves." He pulled the cold-pack from his neck, placing it in his lap.

"Briggs though. He's gone. Maybe Cormac too—he's in intensive by now. We'll see." He couldn't meet Natalie's eyes.

"I'm so sorry, Pete."

"Not your fault."

"I know, but... what happened?"

"Briggs didn't listen. Didn't fall back. Tripped a wire or something. Mac was caught in the explosion too. The other boys got everyone, only one round fired. It was Oakshot—an accident while he tried to holster his gun. Lucky he didn't shoot himself. I think his own shot spooked him though, because he beat the shit out of someone, no reason and no need to have done it. Laid into him hard with his burner too." He paused briefly, then added, "We likely lost a lot of evidence in that fire."

Natalie only continued to look at him, giving him time to gather himself. He seemed very much in his own head, thinking out loud.

"Paul and Evan was a code, maybe... I think Paul and Evan was a code, to make it seem like they weren't hiding anyone. Like no one else lived there. Maybe Paul and Evan was a term for the whole team."

"But didn't most of them leave earlier?"

"We thought so. But it was more like half of them. Half the group still there overnight. If Paul and Evan are really just two guys, then why doesn't anyone there actually have those names? It's... it doesn't matter now. But that's how we got duped."

"I don't see it that way—getting duped. We suffered losses because you have false-alpha officers who don't listen and are here doing a job they're not fully and properly trained to do, because you have management siphoning your resources. This is not you missing a link or going in blind, Pete. This is you getting stripped of specialized assistance, and left with a pack of rabid bloodhounds to do the tac team's job."

Natalie stopped herself, thinking she was ranting, wanting to maintain her reputation for silence, perennially petrified of being labelled emotional.

"Sorry for that, Pete. Are you okay, really? Is there anything I can do?"

"Get your ass back on the beat and away from this crime scene," called Insp. Gilchrist as he walked toward them. "I don't know how many times I need to explain to your squad, Canizales, that I don't want gawkers, neck-craners, procrastinators, fake heroes, and lazy *girls* wasting the service's money on standing around, fishing for gossip, trying to avoid the beat, or whatever the hell else is going on here."

Natalie looked at him with a furrowed brow and held her hand to her heart.

"Are you gonna cry, kid? Do not cry here. Jesus."

"I'm not fucking crying!" Natalie screamed loud enough for anyone nearby to hear, livid at the accusation. With Gilchrist shocked into silence, Natalie turned and rushed away, in the opposite direction of her vehicle. She recognized her error immediately, but didn't want to have to turn and face Gilchrist again, so she walked around the block and back to her vehicle, fuming and muttering to herself the entire time. She felt sick to her stomach as she drove away, directionless.

"Oakshot," Gilchrist called out, and Oakshot approached. "Looks like you went Scattershot again. Firing a round into the ground? With your finger on the trigger while you tried to holster? This your first day in the field? And the kicker: sitting on an unarmed man's chest and pounding him unconscious. Did I hear that correctly?"

"Yes, sir."

"I didn't actually want an answer, Scatter. I know what you did. Maybe this is the—" he paused, changing his tone mid-sentence, letting the next word emerge in a soft, slow exhale: "*teachable* moment you needed."

Gilchrist slowed down, stripped the rhetorical condescension from his tone, and finished his reprimand sotto voce: "Listen, I like you, but this can't stand. You need something concrete to help you comprehend the significance of your actions. Administrative leave, unpaid. Someone from the Oversight Committee will likely contact you within a few hours. I'll be in touch in a couple days. Your job is on the line here, Oak. You better hope these Freedom Fighter folks come up dirty as a dog in a mud-pit."

Gilchrist turned to Pete, but didn't say anything. After a beat, Pete looked up at him, then hopped down from the ambulance and threw the cold-pack aside as he arched to stretch his back and shoulders. He stood face-to-face with Gilchrist, looking at him squarely. He made like he was going to speak, but then walked away, leaving Gilchrist in puzzled silence. Pete drove to the hospital.

Inside the Freedom Fighters' compound, the main room of the office held various lockboxes and a large locked filing cabinet. The two laptop computers bolted to the front desk were found to have intricate coding systems to login, requiring voice, retina, and fingerprint identification. The software had been designed and installed with significant expertise, but most of the search of the property was as simple as opening doors, cutting locks, and sifting through boxes.

A utility room revealed surprising complexity and detail to the security systems and records-keeping on the premises, including thorough written logs of everyone who had visited, with times and dates, as well as an expensive full scale video surveillance system with recently updated hardware.

The lone bathroom was a toilet behind a pocket door with a pull-cord light switch. The kitchenette was cramped, with most of the walking space cut off by rows and stacks of collapsible 5-gallon water containers, some full and some empty.

A locked door to a backroom revealed piles of chairs stacked on top of each other and cardboard boxes half-broken down and then left to collect dust. Totes and closet shelves were full, but without any discernible filing or packing system. The rest of the building wasn't filthy, but that backroom looked like the early stages of a hoarding scenario. Despite the clutter throughout the room, there remained a clear walking path from the entranceway to a full-length mirror on the wall.

There was also a set of two doors between the kitchenette and the cluttered backroom, with a setup like side-by-side hotel rooms: opening one door revealed a small, empty space, just one step away from another door, which led to the next room. Within that small space was a floor-door, leading to a bomb shelter with a bunk unit.

At first, the shelter space appeared to be shotgun-style, as the ladder led down to a reinforced shipping container. There, searching officers found the space well equipped, with weeks' worth of non-perishable food and bottled water, as well as emergency cooking supplies, board games, tools, and communication equipment. Everything was stored on shelves along the walls of the container. In contrast with the building upstairs, the shelter was systematically organized.

At the far end of the container, a steel door led to the rest of the shelter: it was a mostly open-concept living space, quite comparable to a small house. There was a fully stocked kitchen and a common room with a sectional couch, a poker-style table, a television, and a treadmill. There was a bathroom, plumbed with a wastewater pump for the toilet, sink, and shower. Further, there were two bedrooms, both with multiple bunk beds, footlockers, and wall-mounted desks.

Finally, off the kitchen, was a room fully dedicated to an LED-lit, hydroponic growing operation: beans, spinach, lettuce and other quick-yield vegetables were growing. There were several grow-tents, each with water filtration and ventilation systems.

"Water testing kit, found on the table in the garden-room of the bunker," one of the searching officers listed to his exhibit officer, explaining what he had found.

"Did you hear that?" the exhibit officer replied.

"Focus, man. There's a ton of stuff here to itemize."

"I know, but I think one of the guys just called down to us. He yelled, 'GUN.'"

Pete was in the shared staff sergeants' office, reading an email regarding his position as the US-Canada collaboration liaison—a role Chief Calvin Till had encouraged Pete into taking on, wherein he had to maintain consistent communication with other liaison officers from all around the Great Lakes, with the goal of helping make the GLRPS a perfectly aligned team "not despite," Till had said, "no, no, *because* of" the fact that the service crossed international borders. The GLRPS included detachments with officers all across Ontario, as well as in Quebec. As far northeast as Quebec City, GLRPS officers had a joint project with the Canadian Coast Guard, tasked with controlling, defending, and maintaining the traffic, the invaluable ecosystem, and the flow of fresh water along the St. Lawrence River.

It was easy for officers deployed in Canada to forget about their brothers and sisters stateside, with numerous detachments across seven US states, spread out over hundreds of kilometres on the US-side of the lakes. Ohio was the outlier, refusing to sign on when the new service was created in 2061.

Before long, Pete's duties were expanded to include communication with police officials in Toledo, Sandusky, and Cleveland. Next the liaison role was re-designed to include the handling of complaints and requests from constables. Despite his many years with the service, Pete was shocked by the variety and volume of complaints from employees: their treatment by other officers, their denied training requests, their denied or abruptly adjusted travel-time, overtime, and vacation-time, their incorrect pay cheques, their various required work modifications regarding tools, desk chairs, nightshifts, uniforms, and vehicle use.

Pete's own request for paid leave due to his shock and mental strain from the raid had been denied. He simply returned to the Terrace Bay detachment and threw himself into another task. A sergeant from Sandusky had written in a complaint about Michigan GLRPS officers patrolling "too close" to his district.

"What the fuck am I supposed to do with this?" Pete muttered to himself, rubbing his forehead. Aleem knocked and entered the room. "Your leave got denied too, eh?"

"I didn't bother requesting it," Aleem replied. "Did you get the findings report from the search?"

"Yes, I haven't looked at it yet. I can't bring myself to. They brought Elroy in though. The arrogant detective from Schreiber brought him to me with his hands cuffed to the front. What is it with these pricks? Cuffing to the front?

"They told me they got him on multiple charges: water-hoarding, a full-scale gardening operation without a permit, and some huge weapons charges. Let me pull up the report on my email: they found a loaded Sig Sauer P320 inside a fake bible. And right beside it on a shelf, there was a Glock 19 with a separate 33 round magazine hidden inside a flag display case. Then they found the real stash—a mirror cut into the wall, with a keycard sitting right on top of it. The officers told me about that part: swipe the card across the mirror, and 'click', it unlocks, slides open to show them six pistol calibre carbines and an AR-15. All loaded. Multiple magazines, thousands of rounds of ammunition. Bricks of cash. Fake IDs, passports, and vaccination papers. Hate literature and propaganda material from the Neo-Nazi group, Feuer und Rauch Division, based primarily out of Latvia, Estonia, and the US. This is real, Aleem."

"I didn't think it would go that far. Yes, I thought maybe a gun... or homemade bombs."

"There's that too. Homemade bombs. They found acetone peroxide. Large quantities. Now those carbines are old, hidden somewhere over the decades. But that AR-15 is a ghost-gun: 3D printed and completely untraceable. They didn't have the ability to make it in-house, so someone else is doing it." He paused, sighed, rubbed his forehead again. "Somewhere."

Aleem sat down, collecting his thoughts. "And that trailer—there must have been flashbombs, gunpowder smoke—between the sounds and intensity of the light, I couldn't bear it. When that billow of smoke came blooming out, then I could hold my gaze there for a bit, but it didn't matter."

"No, it didn't." There was a long pause. "I hate admitting this, but I don't know what to do with myself right now."

"Because you should be at home. We both should."

"Or at the hospital. Cormac might be dead by now. And I feel like an idiot saying it with Briggs dead and Cormac halfway there, but I'm worried about Natalie."

"Ross? Why?"

"It's... it doesn't matter."

The men sat in mutual disorientation—a heavy silence.

"Hey what do you think it feels like to die? Like if you knew it was coming." Pete looked at his desk while he spoke, but flicked his eyes up to look at Aleem when he was finished asking the question.

Aleem was taken aback, and even moved his upper body backward slightly. "Like nothing? Or... I don't know."

"I think it would feel like struggling to stay awake when you're laying in bed and you're fully exhausted. You know that feeling? When you don't want to let yourself fall into that sleep but you just can't fight it any longer? Just focusing all your energy on lifting your eyelids, but failing. Maybe it's not so bad."

Ava sat in her living room, peering out the window through the partially closed blinds. David was on the floor, drawing pictures with markers. He gripped the markers like he was trying to crush them, and pushed on the paper as if his goal was to bleed the markers dry.

He was keenly focused on the task: piecing together multiple sheets of paper to form a map, with a story playing out across the pages. Orca and dolphin characters appeared multiple times on different pages, with their facial expressions varying, but the same distinct markings of pink and orange dots on their backs. The pages formed one big picture, but also seemed to be acting as separate panels, like a comic book. The story played out mostly in David's movements and narration as he poured himself over the drawings while talking out the terms of the fantasy. It was a tale of the good guys teaming up to defeat the bad guys, working together and having fun too, all over a choppy expanse of ocean blue.

Ava looked down toward him, biting her lip to hold back a laugh at some silly part of the story that David had just expressed. And as she stopped herself from expressing her joy and interrupting his play, she returned to peering out the window, the smile fading from her face like a wave lapping back into the sea.

Natalie knocked on the door, and Ava sprung up to answer. Natalie knew what Ava was expecting, so she skipped the greeting: "I haven't found him yet. I'm sorry. Is this an okay time to come in and talk some more?"

"Yes. Yes, come in. David, this is my police officer friend."

"Hello! Can you show me your sirens?"

"Hello David. How are you? Yes, I will show you when I'm leaving."

With a quick nod, David was right back to pressing his markers, swiping a long line of midnight blue across his multi-page vista.

"Let's go to the kitchen. Would you like anything?"

"No, I'm fine, thank you."

"I hope you don't mind me saying this, but are you okay? You look like you haven't slept."

"I haven't. We don't sleep on shift. But yes, no, I understand what you mean. It's been a long night. I think I might be getting sick. That's why I've got my mask on."

"Were you at that explosion? I haven't slept either, honestly. I just kept waiting for you to call and tell me Lucian is gone forever."

"Please, try not to think that way. I know it's hard. But yes, I was there after the explosion, though not when it happened. And it's been confirmed that Lucian was not there. Not in the fire, not on the grounds. He wasn't there."

"Good... good. And what now?"

"First I want to clarify a couple things, since we now know there was some serious criminal activity happening at the residence where Lucian had been getting the repeat work. I want to know if you think, at all, that Lucian might have been too deeply tied in with those men? Like a debt? Or he knew a secret? Or if maybe—maybe—he was recruited to join them?"

"It's embarrassing for me to say, as his wife, that I'm really not going to be much help with those kinds of questions. It's been two months since that house-fire, and Lucian just hasn't been the same person. Like there's a clear split. There was Lucian before and Lucian after. And the two men look the same, but they're not the same. He can come out of it, out of the rut or hole or depression or whatever you want to call it. I've seen glimpses where he can be in a good mood and talk to me, and laugh with me, and play with David. But it's always fleeting. It's ten minutes or a few hours, or sometimes a whole day if we're lucky. Otherwise, he's the new Lucian. He doesn't talk. He stays in the basement and works on his projects. He… he broods. And he lies beside me in bed, but I feel like he's never sleeping. Like he's just waiting for me to fall asleep so that he can leave. And I think he goes back to the basement. More and more frequently now, that's just the feeling I have.

"I've wanted to get him help. I have excellent colleagues who I know could support him through his trauma, but we can't afford it. It's absurd to think a psychologist's family can't afford psychological help, but that's the truth.

"So those men, that place, I don't know. I can't see Lucian falling for any schemes or pressure. He has never been all that social or eager to please people, even before the fire. He didn't like those guys though. He did tell me they were weird. But he knew there was lots of money to be had for easy jobs there. School's not cheap. Maintaining this house isn't easy."

"I understand. Trust me there. I am not judging. I know how valuable consistent work is for everyone these days. And I see you do a tremendous job maintaining this house, and taking care of that boy out there."

"How can you tell?"

"I've been in a lot of houses in this area and others like it. I don't think you need me to say much else. I see all types. I know a good mother when I see one."

"Thank you." Ava began to cry. "I'm sorry, it's not the compliment making me cry. It's like it was the tipping point. All these big feelings I've had lately. And I'm trying so hard to control them and shield David from them. It's so hard."

"It's okay to cry here now, Ava. We all need that occasionally.

I need it too sometimes." She waited, reaching her hand out to hold Ava's. "Now if you will allow it, I would like to go downstairs to look at this workspace where Lucian has been spending so much time. Can I do that?"

"Of course, just right down those stairs, and down the next little set around the corner. Go ahead. Take your time. I should check on David anyway."

Without looking up, David felt his mother approaching, and continued colouring as he spoke: "Why do they call water 'blue gold'?"

"Well—"

"It's not blue. It's clear."

"Yes, you're right, David."

"I miss Frank."

"Me too." Ava wiped her eyes and sat at the edge of the couch, offering a half-hearted smile when David stopped to look at her directly.

Natalie had vague memories of the cool concrete basement. The workbench with a vice grip, the chest freezer, the laundry tub. At the far end of the room was a little makeshift enclave. Boxes built up for privacy, in an L-shape around a small table with a chair on either side of it. A laptop, a microphone, and a headset were on the desk. There was an Incognito recording device attached to the laptop screen. Natalie opened the laptop. No password required. She searched the browser history and the recently used documents and applications. Nothing of note. The icon for one of the desktop files appeared to be a photo of a burning house. Natalie opened it to find Lucian had saved an article about the fire that Ava had mentioned:

One dead after house-fire in Terrace Bay
Neighbours suspect foul play

Emergency responders were called to the scene on Memorial Street late last night, as a blaze tore through a local residence. Irene Lancaster, who is running for deputy mayor in the upcoming local election, is the owner of the home. A neighbour (who requested to remain nameless) said that Lancaster was at work for a nightshift while her two children, ages 5 and 11, were asleep inside.

The same neighbour expressed deep sympathy, stating, "Some of us around knew her kids stayed alone some nights, and we didn't blame her for that, because plenty of us are in the same situation, where we have to leave the kids alone sometimes so we can provide for them. That's just how it is. I can't believe someone would do this."

Several neighbours crowded around the scene, talking amongst themselves and arguing while the fire still burned. Arson was mentioned as a likely cause of the fire, and one man screamed obscenities about Lancaster's aggressively left-leaning politics dooming her, but refused to answer this reporter's direct questions.

Onlookers said another Terrace Bay resident was walking by with his dog when he saw the house aflame, and ran inside without hesitation, eventually emerging with the elder child, Richard. Both were later taken to hospital due to excessive smoke inhalation, and as of the time of this publication, are expected to make full recoveries.

The younger child, Alyssa, could not be saved in time.

This article will be updated when more information becomes available.

Natalie stood up and walked around the room, hoping something might spring to her as a clue. She struggled to focus, however, as an illness was washing over her, its presence quickly becoming unavoidable. She felt herself beginning to perspire. Her thoughts drifted to Cormac, to Pete, to Briggs, to that clown Gilchrist. She turned back to the desk, swiped the Incognito off the screen, stuck it in her vest pocket, and hurried up the stairs and out the door, offering a half-hearted goodbye to Ava.

She was almost in her vehicle when she shouted, "I'll be in touch soon." It was all she could offer as her eyes became heavy and sweat started to drip down her cheeks.

Pete was called to the cyber crimes unit office to review what Cst. Emily Girard had found on the laptops confiscated from the Freedom Fighters' compound. Girard was a veteran officer, one who looked older than she really was. She had been off sick—cancer—and had recently returned to work after several months of treatment. With a gaunt face and bags under her eyes, she looked as though she was still sick. Her skin hung off her arms, and her breathing was laboured.

Here was a woman only in the earliest stages of regaining her strength, who was posted to desk-duty daily, searching through phones and flash drives and laptops and tablets, finding texts and emails and photo after photo and video after video of kids at parks being spied on, child luring plots being planned, human trafficking rings being expanded, children being exploited, women being threatened, people being coerced, blackmailed, exposed, drugged, humiliated, extorted, beaten, raped, killed.

"There's a lot to see here," she said. She sounded like she was on the verge of falling asleep.

"Okay. Give me a summary version." Pete looked at her, then at the computer screen. "Please."

"Emails reveal a significant amount of contact with various far-right movements. Globally. Not just ultra-conservatives. Some of these groups I'd never even heard of before. These are the furthest of the alt-right I've ever seen. In Poland, Ukraine, Estonia, Latvia, Germany, Russia, the US, and Canada too. Looks like it's a couple groups; one started in Estonia and the other in Ukraine, and then spread across the world, before splintering into various factions and offshoots with similar but sometimes competing goals. In the beginning, it was about whiteness, but then that wasn't enough. After reviewing all the correspondence and all the files, my partner and I have done fact checking and background investigation work—that's how we've learned about the timelines, origins, and leadership of these groups.

"As I said, it started out as being about preserving whiteness.

But lately Elroy's got emails arguing with chapter presidents from across the world, talking about the differences in certain kinds of whiteness, what types of Christianity are acceptable, what languages should be banned, whether women should be allowed to join.

"But they're sharing tactics, resources, and ideas. How to make bombs, poison water supplies, dates and times when there should be global attacks on government officials. Dark web open-source material on 3D printing firearms. Specific instructions for barrels, lower receivers... every part of an assault rifle. Paramilitary hate groups troubleshooting issues with firing pins on homemade guns. That's some of what we've found. But it gets deeper.

"He's got hundreds of bots on social media, spreading fake news—not even just misquoted or out-of-context—it's fully fabricated: The LGBTQ+ is now including pedophiles as part of their 'group'. The conservative politician whose views are closer to central is wearing socks that have jihadist Muslim codes stitches into them. The white prime minister is actually Asian and she had advanced plastic surgery to look white. The Jews and Hollywood elite delayed their plan from the twenties and are now starting the great economic reset. These fake news items that we've seen re-shared hundreds of thousands of times started from this computer, or this computer was the first to receive them from a private email source outside of North America. Then this computer began spreading the news with bots.

"This Elroy has a video file saved here, which he has shared to dozens of people on their own dark web email server, where he reads his entire manifesto: saving the race, the war-on-whiteness, the brilliance of this idea of 'sundown towns'. He talks constantly about the need to convert every town into a sundown town. He's recruiting, and he's been successful. In his email correspondence a few months ago, he began using "Smoke out the masses" as his closing salutation. And before long, I've seen others here start saying it back to him, in videos and emails and on message boards. Now they capitalize the first letter of each word, like it's a proper title. Some kind of prophecy or oath.

"This man is backed by some powerful, influential groups. After about three hours of reviewing this material and two other hours of outside research, my hypothesis is that he's a figurehead—a fall-man—for some smarter people who want what Elroy wants, but aren't willing to die or go to jail for it. But it appears to me, Elroy and those closest to him are committed to dying for this cause. These men are not conflicted."

"What do you mean, he's being released? There's not even bail court hearings today." Pete was enraged.

"The judge got called in special, for some reason. They did it on a video conference. She set the bail pretty high, but said he's not a flight risk. No conditions, just a promise to appear. A confidant posted the bail almost as soon as it was set," the officer working cells explained.

"Confidant? We don't know who posted it?"

"I think you remember the new rule, sir." The officer treaded carefully. "This is the first time we've seen it locally, but those posting bail no longer need to have their cash-source named in release forms, if they choose to remain anonymous. That's all we have to go on. The one person who knows is a clerk in Ottawa, who has to take an oath of secrecy. They make a big deal out of it every time. So I hear."

"So they're all out… passports not revoked, no time-warning for a chance for us to review… has a court date even been set?"

"They're working on it."

"Who?"

"I'm not sure, sir."

The virus had sapped Natalie's energy. Lethargic, she hobbled to her tiny kitchen, and opened her fridge. She wanted to rifle through it, but knew it wouldn't do her any good, so she focused, found what she wanted with her eyes first, then grabbed it: a carton of orange juice. She drank straight from the carton, but didn't let it touch her lips. Some juice spilled to the floor, and she wiped it with her sock, grunting quietly, unable to fully commit to her anger at her own wasteful mistake.

She moved back to her bed, swallowed her multivitamins dry, pulled her phone from her pocket, and fell back onto her pillow. She pressed her hand to her heart, feeling its rhythm as she slowed her breathing.

I used to take my wakefulness pills even on my days off. It was extremely easy to get extra pills. No one asks why—no one cares. They're not addictive. And they don't make you feel good. They just give your body what it needs to remain in a steady state of wakefulness. They're not uppers. They don't make you jitter. You don't have to compensate for the sleep later. You just don't need to sleep when they're in your system. The continued advances in medicine are extraordinary. Some great mind came up with this pill. Keeps the economy moving, I guess. I wonder what that scientist could have done if allowed to pursue their passion? Maybe instead of removing sleep, they could have removed some disease. Maybe.

So I would take them on my days off. After a while, I did find they made me feel a little less. So there was a long-term effect, but even that one effect was hard to notice. I could have been fooling myself too.

The first time I took one during my rest days was after I read an article about a rare condition called chromosome 6 deletion, and an extremely rare form of that condition can lead to unbelievable effects: you don't feel pain, and you don't feel the need to eat or sleep, so you never develop a sense of fear. Maybe I wanted that. To want for nothing. Not the way an ultra-wealthy person wants for nothing. Those people want everything. They can just afford to have someone else go get it for them. I mean if you really don't have any urges to satisfy, and can afford to disregard the threats this world imposes on you. It doesn't make you superhuman the way most men fantasize about, but I think it's the kind of extraordinary-human feeling I wanted to experience.

I don't mean to say it would solve anyone's problems. Being special doesn't necessarily make things easy; those people actually have a much harder life… it just intrigued me. I stopped with the pills eventually. I just went back to taking them for work. There was no thought process for stopping. I just stopped. But I do remember something else that happened on the same day that I stopped: I had this old box of my grandpa's photos and news-clippings and letters. Things he'd saved over the decades. And I'd looked through all of it before. But that day, I looked again, and I opened this little pocketbook, and there, planted between two random pages, flattened to the point that it was almost one with the page, was a handwritten note. On one side was a list of songs, and on the other was a poem. It was Grandpa's writing. It said

1. *Without a Map by Sam Roberts*
2. *Butcher's Breakfast by The Rail Splitters*
3. *State of The Union by Public Enemy*
4. *Brave Man's Death by J. Roddy Walston & The Business*
5. *List of Demands by Saul Williams*

and the other side said

On the bus to the fields
There was laughter, for I
Know that it's the season
Not the reason
That we're after

Natalie felt the rush of sleep, and resisted at first, forcing her lulling eyes back open. However, in the next moment, she pulled the corner of her blanket over top of herself as she rolled to her side. She was asleep in seconds.

Elroy Maitland was in his bunkhouse, streaming a movie called Blade Carves Time. Its premise was typical of major motion pictures of the last hundred years, though with a few aspects that made it specific to the year it was filmed, 2078: it was about the search for a way to regain lost time, fix humanity's countless mistakes from the past two centuries, and build a better timeline for the present day. Someone—a hero—would have to time-hop through the decades, disrupting various major historical moments in order to create a future favourable to the masses.

Fade in on a bleak housing project in rural Maine, where we

find a gifted medical doctor and decorated soldier living in solitude. A powerfully built, square jawed man who had lost his family in a shootout years before. He is shockingly youthful and handsome for a man whose experiences have been so arduous. The man lives a lonesome life: listening to old records, lifting weights, mastering multiple martial arts disciplines, and abstaining from love despite recently gaining the affection of a stunningly beautiful dream girl, named Pixie, who is half his age and seems to have no goals or interests besides helping the protagonist achieve his inner greatness.

The protagonist's name: Blade. He is eventually recruited by a brilliant team of rogue scientists who operate underground because their goals run counter to those of the tyrannical government. The scientists need a brave subject to test a time-travel experiment. With no hopes or loved ones, Blade agrees, though Pixie begs him to reconsider. The bulk of the movie is Blade travelling through time to save humankind from its own destruction. And he does it. And he kisses Pixie.

Slumped into his two-seat couch, Elroy watched the movie in silence, never looking at his phone or letting his mind wander. He watched the end credits too. At the film's completion, he let out a single scoff, muttered the words "So dumb," and climbed the ladder up to the loft bedroom.

Elroy lifted the mattress to reveal a trapdoor in the solid wooden bedframe. With a key dangling from his necklace, he unlocked the door; using the key to gently lift the door, he revealed a space no bigger than a shoebox, with a stash of two bottles of single malt Scotch whisky, stored side-by-side, neck-to-base to conserve space. A dishtowel had been wedged between them. He removed both and held them to the light, checking which had less liquid left in the bottle. He chose the one that was nearly empty, poured what was left of it into a lowball glass, and held the bottle overtop of the glass, completely upside-down, for fifty seconds. His hand was surprisingly steady. Every drop. Almost three fingers.

After placing the partially full bottle and towel back as they were, he looked at the empty bottle longingly for a moment, then wrapped it in another dishtowel and placed it inside a backpack. Even when it was empty, he handled the bottle with utmost care, like it was a kitten.

Finally, he sat down on one of the two chairs in the loft space, placing the glass on the lamp-table before sitting. He looked at the glass for a few seconds, amber light glistening off it. He picked it up and held it close to his face, seeing his reflection. For a moment, he was deceived by the fault in his depth perception, unsure whether he was looking at the wall through the glass, at the liquor, at the glass, or at himself.

He poured it into his mouth, swished it around, spit it back into the glass, leaned back, and sighed as his saliva oozed. After a few seconds, he poured the drink into his mouth again, swished it around, and swallowed it. He basked in ecstasy until he could no longer lick any precious liquid from the inside of his mouth. He then used a medicine dropper to drip five droplets of water into the same glass, swirled the glass gently, and drank the water mixed with the imperceptible amount of whisky.

He then received a video call from his father. He answered.

"Hey Dad, how are you?"

"The hell are you doing at home in the middle of the day?"

"I… you called me."

"I didn't think you'd answer. Thought you'd have a job by now."

"Times are tough for chemical engineers too, dad. You know I've still got lots left over from the lotto."

"I don't want to hear about that stupid lotto money anymore. It makes me cringe when you even mention it. As far as I'm concerned, you should come back south and join the military if you're not gonna do anything else."

"Okay Dad."

"Okay what?"

"I'll think about it."

"No you won't. I don't know why I bother." And he hung up.

Dumbfounded, Elroy hung up too, tossing his phone a few inches away and letting out another scoff. He then sat, unmoving, for fifteen seconds, eventually grinding his teeth and fighting off frustrated tears. He touched a finger to his molars, feeling their blunt and flattened surfaces.

Moments later, with the backpack on both shoulders, he was out the door. He wore a black and white skeleton-print handkerchief across his nose and mouth, with his shifty eyes peering out overtop. He moved in anxious toe-striking leaps, crossing properties, peering over his shoulder, hopping fences, falling into crowds, ducking around corners, tucking his face to his chest. A diligent effort from a sore thumb of a man, like a rodeo clown trying to avoid detection. Eventually, he made his way to a storage garage behind an automotive repair shop, where he joined his fellow Freedom Fighters.

"Gentlemen," he said.

"Elroy," replied Mickey.

"Okay boys, the plan stays the same for us," Elroy continued.

"We're on orders from Amanita Virosa," replied Zach.

"Elroy takes lead," Mickey quipped, then continued, "Zach stands firm in defiance. How will our comrades resolve this dilemma?"

Elroy peered at him, side-eye, considering the severity of the moment. "Okay, out with it, Zachary, my brother. What do you have to say?"

"The plow-man has to go." He turned to Mickey. "Elroy here has been running off at the mouth, giving away far too much information to far too many outside parties." Back to Elroy. "Do you not think the UPC has people on the inside of the GLRPS? Do you forget that *we*, in fact, have a man inside?"

"Yeah, I—"

"Let me finish. Your intentions are often good, Elroy. But it's the vainglorious way you go about your business. Too concerned with getting liquor. Too quick to give away information. Did you not think I would find out about your attempts at radio and podcast promotion?" He watched as Elroy shrunk, completely shocked that Zach would have found him out. "So certain of your own judgment that you don't even seem to recognize its failures even after you've played your hand and lost. You didn't get that detective to run with us, but you sure told him a lot.

You've convinced an unreliable seven-foot-tall psycho to do our bidding, leaked information to him to try to impress him too. All because you're too proud. Too weak to admit that Amanita Virosa, a woman, is calling your shots."

"I run this organization. I communicate with all our most important contacts. I keep the information flowing. I do the recruiting. And it's my compound. It's my ideas!"

"Listen to him now, stuttering and shouting. We appreciate your compound, and we still want you involved, Elroy. But you're small-minded. You're a child of God. You're from a backwoods, podunk, dead-end, nothing-town, and you moved here when you stumbled into money—of course I know about you winning one of the small-pots from the Super Max, because you tell anyone who will listen. And that's the only reason you're here. And the only reason you had the cash to buy a place and start a business that went nowhere, and then eventually build a shelter. A good shelter, I know. And that's why me and Daryl started to work with you. And that's the reason why you're useful."

Elroy stared, fury in his eyes.

"Don't look at me like that, brother. Did I say you're out? You're not out. I know you're a true patriot." He turned to Mickey again for a moment, a caring smile on his face as he quietly finished, "A child of God, this one."

"Okay. So what then?"

"So we take out the plow-man, we link up with Daryl at the yard, and the plan goes on just like you wanted. See, you were actually right this time. The plan continues. But with some new additions. And with two things you need to remember: number one, you're not in charge. I am. And Amanita must continue to think she's in charge for the time being. And two, keep your fucking mouth shut, little man."

At the start, disappearing is easy. With a full belly and a stubborn resolve, drifting in and out of rundown areas, and staying only long enough to get what is needed. All with the memories of the people you care about still fresh in your mind. The details of their faces and voices, a recent conversation you had, the last time you touched them.

First, Lucian was in an abandoned house northwest of his own neighbourhood. It was a new build, but only partially completed before the owner's life fell into turmoil when he lost all his savings in a stock market scam, subsequently losing his family and moving farther north himself.

Lucian waited there for less than twenty-four hours. He laid out and took mental note of all the supplies in his bug-out bag: a tent, a tarp, a multi-tool, a compass, a reusable water bottle, a roll of duct tape, a camouflage balaclava, an air-filtration mask, a fire-starter rod, a folding shovel, a first aid kit, flashlights, food bars, pepper spray, hand-sanitizer, hard-knuckle gloves, water purification tablets, and a solar power bank. He left the power bank, the air mask, and the compass in the abandoned house.

By night, he moved to a shantytown to the north. He wore his hood up, held one elbow with his other hand like he was covering a wound, and carried himself with the shifty broken rhythm of an addict. He hunched himself at his shoulders and spoke in grumbly whispers. It was too risky to stay there long, as the area was known for violence and police intervention. He warmed his hands by a fire and traded three food bars for a refill of his water bottle, then moved on.

He spent a night in the forest, far outside of town. He lit a small fire, ate a food bar, sipped his water like it was boiling hot coffee, and slept in his tent.

Farther north, he broke into a rural cabin and raided the cabinets. The wealthiest people, sheltered in the secure confines of the top floors of The Blade, still had their own escape plans. They were the least prepared for nightmare emergency scenarios, but if they had the means to get away—the helicopter or armoured car on standby with capable servicemen prepared to make haste at any moment—they would suddenly move from the least prepared to the most capable. Whisked away into a stocked cabin, prepared to wait out the disaster for weeks.

Breaking in when no one is around—that's easy too. The

alarms are triggered, but who is coming? When? There's time. For the elites who own the cabins, it's not even worth the trouble to go check on the intrusion until the next day—send your man out to re-stock what the thieves took, and be done with it.

Lucian allowed himself a half-night's rest on a bed. He pulled back his water bottle and downed it to the last drop, then filled it twice more and repeated the indulgence. He'd never drunk so much water at once in his life. He filled the bottle again, to the brim, licking the droplets that spilled over the bottle's neck as he twisted the cap back on.

Then again, he was gone into the night.

Aleem leaned on the counter of the evidence room, talking to Martin Chan, the Terrace Bay detachment's property manager.

"So I spoke at the conference, and it went pretty well overall," Chan was explaining while Aleem listened. "But there's always at least one guy. Usually two guys sitting together, actually. I can spot them three minutes into my talk, sitting in the audience, just fuming, slouching in their chairs like teenagers—arms crossed, with a scowl—or sometimes their faces look like they're stuck in this just-about-to-roll-their-eyes position. And they typically jump in pretty early during the Q and A.

"They start in with how my viewpoint is slanted by my own life… as if anyone's viewpoint isn't? That being the son of immigrants, not being white, being a police employee, that all these things combine to make my opinion invalid. And not just my opinion—also my research, my experiences, everything that happens to me."

"All your research would be permissible if only this or that. If only you weren't you. Some such circular nonsense. I understand," said Aleem. His voice remained steady, calm, as though he'd heard this conversation in his own head beforehand, and had planned his response.

"Some of them will point to my status as a first-generation Canadian, and the advantages I've been afforded as a result. They'll say it point blank."

"People love to talk about the advantages other people are afforded. But never the ones from which they themselves benefit."

"Right? Thanks Naseer. I can't really talk openly like this with anyone else here."

"Me too."

"Have you been taking care of yourself, since the raid?"

"I'm fine, thank you. I just can't believe the way it's all happened. And how nothing good seems to be coming from it. A lost life, and another officer who'll never be back on the job. Solid officers too. Men who made significant arrests. Men who did good police work. They'd be shocked to hear me say that, as most here assume that I don't like any of them. And really… I didn't like Briggs. But that doesn't mean he wasn't a valuable officer. So, the raid wasn't worth the effort—and I hate that phrase, but it's true here—even if a life hadn't been lost, it wouldn't have been worth it. Those Freedom Fighters are protected by some powerful affiliation, so I don't think there will be any justice here. Between this and the slew of overdoses and the unsolved arsons, well, the GLRPS has been failing. And I'm not blaming a faceless agency or the administration. I'm a part of this failure."

Chan contemplated Aleem's words. He waited, plotting how he wanted to phrase what came next. Aleem went to speak again, but Chan stopped him: "Just a second, sorry. I want to tell you something, but I'm unsure how to start. I'm just thinking about… how we could use a win. And how, officers working major crimes have been blocked at every turn lately. Besides the Hatchet-Man. Okay, I'll just say it and we'll see if what I'm thinking makes any sense: Inspector Gilchrist was weird when he brought some of the evidence down to be logged, relating to one of the recent arsons.

"He doesn't like me. He's usually a dick. Most of his disdain toward me comes from his lack—the lack of eye contact, the lack of talking. He comes down here pretty often, but he never looks at me. He doesn't engage in small-talk. He doesn't give me any instructions. He sometimes doesn't say anything at all. He just gives me stuff and I figure it out.

"But with that arson evidence, he gave me a flash drive that had copies of neighbours' security footage, and he said something like, 'This has already been reviewed. Just log it like usual.' Then he started to walk away, but turned back and blurted out, 'Deputy chief's orders.' Then he left. It felt like the dumbest, bumbling criminal mistake. If it wasn't so strange and obvious, I would have assumed he was hiding something. But how obvious it was, coupled with how intimidating the guy is and how much he hates me, I guess those things combined to make me gloss it over in my mind. 'He's just weird today,' I thought. The words came out funny. Whatever. So I logged it and forgot about it."

"I don't think you're reading into it too much. I think that's worth investigating. What's the worst that could come of it? Let's look at the recordings."

Chan looked up at the camera outside his workspace, then turned and looked at another camera behind him. Disheartened, he looked back at Aleem.

Shivering, Natalie woke from a long but fitful sleep. She couldn't remember when, but at some point she had adjusted and got completely under the blankets. As she opened her eyes, she realized she was drenched in sweat and freezing cold. She got out of bed, dried her entire body with a towel, changed her clothes, removed her soaked bed sheets, and put down a fresh bath towel to sleep on. In the morning, she woke again, soaked and freezing, but even the simple act of getting up and towel drying made her uncomfortably hot. Every action was a futile labour.

Lying down on another bath towel and on the unfamiliar side of the bed, she sifted through the few photos she kept on her phone. Between painful coughing fits, she began purging old emails, and eventually came across one from Justine, a former friend of hers from high school. It was a message that surprised her when she first received it, as they hadn't spoken in several years, and it surprised her almost as much seeing it again, having forgotten about the previous correspondence. It was a simple note: 'How are you? What's new? Oh my God it's been so long!' And Natalie had replied promptly, but that was the last she'd heard from Justine. She considered writing her again, and began to do so, but only got as far as 'Hi Justine' before deleting the words, discarding the email, and moving on.

Natalie then connected her Incognito to her laptop, and began speaking.

There was a day when the monsters came.

From age sixteen onward, I was always a disappointment to my mom. We endured a lot together back then. And now I still think about her often. She's probably the only person whose approval I would care to have anymore, but she's gone now, so...

My dad was a deadbeat—left when I was a baby. Mum told me he said I was too much to handle. But she never told me that until I was sixteen. Before that, she thought I was special. Not just in the way parents always say that. I mean, she really thought I was special.

'You've got the spark of Joan of Arc. Marie Curie, it was meant to be,' she'd rhyme off even before I knew who those people were.

She was a historian and a women's rights advocate, without ever outwardly labeling herself as such. She had a pensive disposition, always contemplative when she was seated. She didn't watch television or use her phone in her spare moments. Rather, she'd sit and think, and if something inspiring came to her, she'd frantically begin typing an essay or an opinion piece to be posted on some online publication.

And she was a good mom.

Why she thought I was special... it began from something horrific, and maybe that was why it was always doomed. I was only a year old when we started playing the monsters hiding game. I once decided to hide in this tiny space behind my crib, face down. And she just thought it was something cute, apparently. So she would encourage me to show her friends my hiding spot, and by repetition, I came to understand the value of knowing where to go when Mum said to.

We'd be reading a book or cuddling together, and Mum would announce, 'The monsters are coming, Nat! Run! Hide!' We would scream and laugh and I would run to my room and hide in my special place. We had fun with that, though I was too young to remember. It's just what she told me.

But one day, the monsters really did come. I don't know if I want to say all of what happened. I don't know if I can. Mum came tip-toeing into my room and pulled me out of the crib, waking me as she did it. And she looked at me, a toddler, and said something like, 'Hide in your special spot. The monsters are here. Don't move or make a sound until I come to get you!'

And to Mum, the thing that was 'special' was that I understood. I knew where to go, and I hesitate to say this, but I think the earliest real memory of my life is the realization I had on that day: it's not a game. The monsters are here. And that's all I did—I hid. I imagine they came into my room, but they never found me. They just found Mum, in her room.

People here are ruthless, capable of horrible acts, as I've already said. Maybe someone from another time would say, 'Yeah, there are disgusting people here too,' so I guess we were always like this. Some of the atrocities committed are for basic survival—a merciless pursuit of necessities, even at the expense of another's life. So when even 'good' people are willing to do that... it's why I'm always vigilant. Always expecting the worst from people.

So that night, I can't say what they did to Mum. But I'll just say that they left her to die, and they fully expected her to. But she didn't. She had a tremendous will, which I hope I've made clear, because I don't hold a grudge against her in the least. She did so much for me. And likely the most important thing she ever did for me was to refuse to die that night.

I have to assume that after that night, my mom wasn't the same anymore. But she continued to believe in me. Years later, she said no other toddler in history would have had the wherewithal to hide properly. I escaped certain death, she said. But she never talked about her own turmoil from that night, instead only focusing on how proud she was of me.

And for many years thereafter, we were happy. You know, as happy as you can be in this time and place, with a woman scraping by and her little girl doing just the same but on a different level.

She had such high hopes for me; I remember it all pretty clearly from about age seven onward, and so for the better part of a decade, I was her desert rose that was going to change the world. Outside of that dangerous optimism, one thing after another went wrong for Mum. So it came to a point where I was the only positive thing for her. When I was twelve, I was changing. I was so tall, and I hated it. And mum noticed things about me *that fed into her optimism.*

Now, I didn't say 'delusion', because it wasn't quite that. She saw that I was bright and learned quickly. She saw that I was strong and had a spine. She saw my growing collection of certificates and medals from school and sports and cadets. And I think my being so tall was a sort of false physical indicator for her too. At that time, I was nearly a head taller than she was. But by thirteen, I didn't feel good about much, despite the qualities and accomplishments I just described. And in high school, I didn't feel good about... anything really.

But she kept believing in me and more or less ignoring my depression, which I often took out on her. We were eating dinner one night, and I was in a foul mood for no reason I could verbalize—maybe that was one of the tougher aspects of it. Teenagers often don't know what's making them so angry. Makes them angrier to be unable to explain it, or at least that's how it affected me. And at dinner, when I was being a little brat, she finally broached the subject, demonstrating a careful, motherly tact:

She started with something simple and kind, like, 'What is it, Natalie? You can tell me. I hope I didn't do anything to hurt you.' Then there was a long pause, so she continued, saying she thought it would help me if I explained what had put me in a bad mood that night.

I responded quickly, as though I'd had it loaded and ready to go, but I know that in fact I did not have this planned. I'm not even sure if it was what I wanted to say, but I remember it clearly, and this is exactly what I said:

'I feel like I'm in a bad mood every night. It's so exhausting going all day pretending to be happy. So when I get home, it's impossible to keep it up, and then all you see is the worst of me.'

There was a change after that night. Like she noticeably started making more of an effort to ask me about my feelings and to make suggestions about how to improve them. The whole thing angered me more. I think if I thought about it hard enough, I would notice some other moments that contributed to the gradual erosion of her faith in my 'specialness'. Outside factors included her working multiple jobs, us going without proper heating and cooling occasionally—at times to the brink of death. What else... her failing romantic relationships, of which there were only two or three over the years. And then eventually her turning to drinking more and more.

Life's tough on everyone from time to time, but I know it was particularly cruel to Mum as the years went on. I wish I could say why. But there really is no 'why'. It's not like I'm trying to find an answer. I know that's just... how life unfolded for her.

Then at sixteen, when I failed my first crack at the driver's test, she laughed at me. That one I won't forget either. She was drunk, midday, and she laughed at me. She rolled her eyes. She told me only a stupid person would fail it. And she walked to her room and said, 'And I used to think you were special.'

She was never happy again for the rest of her life. Where she was once pensive, she became sullen. Once hopeful, now jaded. She died relatively young. Sickness got to her early, as she was depleted from a hard adulthood and too much drinking. I tried to stay close with her, right up to the end. And I think she appreciated that. Aside from that original time with the driver's test, she was never really cruel to me. She just didn't care about me the same way anymore. Didn't believe in me much at all anymore.

I don't suppose my whole experience with my mom has shaped a lot of my personality now. If anything, I think it has helped me to stay detached at work, which is important. Maybe I'm too detached outside work too. I'm aware. But I've taken to policing with a cerebral embrace, and I'm okay with that.

At that point, Natalie stopped talking. With the Incognito connected to her laptop, she decided to access the files for the first time. Up until then, she had only recorded. She began sifting through the files, listening to small excerpts so that she could label them with a proper title; otherwise, the recordings would have a timestamp, but no further information. She was surprised and a little embarrassed by the sound of her own voice, and kept thinking about how it was never quite strong enough. Clear enough. Normal enough. Despite being alone, she even occasionally cringed, slightly ashamed to find she had the vanity required to actively listen to a recording of herself. But for a time, she kept her mind on the task—label, reorganize.

After a while, she couldn't focus much on what she had said, because she kept finding moments where she wished she could backtrack, correct an error, switch a line, change her tone, add a pause. Frustrated at her inability to do something she thought would be easy, she resolved to never listen to the files ever again. And then she began a new recording:

I already explained that my dad was never around, but I do have some vague memories of my grandpa—dad's dad. Even when my mom grew tired and bitter, and as much as she had every reason to hate my dad, she didn't say much negatively about him. And she spoke really highly of my grandfather. She would remind me that he took care of us both after my dad left.

I remember Grandpa was a train man—a conductor. He died when I was just a girl, seven or eight years old. Under a specific set of circumstances, I can think of him: if it's quiet and I'm alone, and I close my eyes, breathe slowly and deeply, and focus intently. I'm alone a lot, but that sort of decompressed inward reflection is difficult for me. When I'm able to conjure the strength for it, I can see Grandpa's big smile, and remember him as a hulking giant of a man. There was a warmth and particular authenticity in his smile and in the wrinkles that smile accentuated around his eyes. Of course, these weren't things I was thinking of when I looked at him as a child. Just feelings that I've come to understand in retrospect after years of diligent effort to remember.

His size was reassuring too. He was a relatively tall man, but to me he was enormous. Those wrinkles, the smile, the kindness, and the size, they all came together to bring me a sense of comfort I've never felt with another man—or with anyone at all really—before or since. He had huge hands too, and it felt like they were so big that it was only his hands that hugged me, rather than his arms.

So it's a hug, a smile, and that feeling of completely relaxed assurance when I was with him. That's the collection of memories I have of him. Each of those, on its own, still feels like a collection; there wasn't one time he smiled at me that I remember, or one hug. I truly only have one clear and singular memory of him, but it is one that I cherish:

There was a time when I was very small and I had to take a passenger train ride by myself. I'd had a medical appointment in Toronto, seeing a heart specialist because of my murmur... Mum used to tell me my heart's rhythm held the lapping waves of the universe's largest ocean. She was so eloquent, when she still had that enthusiasm in her. Sometimes I didn't even know what she meant when she spoke, but the sincerity in her voice, combined with the deep eye-contact and all the gentle touches of my arms and shoulders, it all made me feel a specific joy that's never been replicated since I was very small. Maybe that type of joy isn't something anyone can experience again after they reach adolescence. I'm not sure.

I've gotten so far off track…

It was almost unbearable that day—the weather, I mean. A gusty winter day. And I was on the train home from Toronto, five or six years old, and the phone Mum got me specifically for that trip, it buzzed from an incoming text: it was from Grandpa, as he knew that I was on board that train. He was working on a freight train coming from the opposite direction, and he told me that they'd stopped, and that if I looked out the right side of my train, I could see him as our train sped by.

I was thrilled, and actually very nervous, because I didn't want to miss the opportunity. While on that epic journey by myself at such a young age, even a flickering glimpse of Grandpa was meaningful in making me feel secure. The train had a lot of vacant seats, so I darted across to the right side, and didn't dare look away from the window. After a few minutes, there he was. He was wearing a thick, tan coloured canvas jacket and an orange safety vest, and I saw he was staring into each window just as intently as I was staring out. He didn't have the advantage of seeing a lone figure in a bright vest, backlit by miles of snow, so he had to be sharp. But we did it. I was waving like a maniac before he could see me, and for the briefest of moments, we locked eyes and I saw his smile even with part of his face obscured by his coat and hat. He returned a broad wave of his hand and arm, like someone shipwrecked waving at a helicopter, only with all of the joy and none of the desperation. He appeared to be on the verge of laughter—likely so pleased that his plan had worked and we'd actually connected.

Saying it out loud, I'm now reminded of something else: his wingspan. As I said, he was sort of tall and he could cast an imposing shadow. Though he was lean, his thinness sort of accentuated how big he was across his shoulders, because the slim figure drew you to his length: the hands and the arms and a broad back combined to make a wingspan more fitting of someone two or three inches taller than he was. And I saw every centimetre of that length when he greeted me with that exuberant wave.

When I returned to my seat, I couldn't stop smiling. I had to excitedly tell a nearby traveller that I was waving at my grandpa. My heart raced, and I *put both hands to my chest to feel it. The lapping waves, but a rush of them in that moment. I've already said I had a murmur, but it's important to note that mine really wasn't like a normal heartbeat at all, as each beat was slightly distinguishable from the last, and the rhythm of my heart didn't have that kick-drum thump. I hesitate to even call it a beat. I did have a surgery to correct it a few years later, but from the day of that train ride until the day of the surgery, my own heartbeat, despite its wavering and weakened state, brought me a level of comfort in frightened or concerned moments, even after Grandpa was gone.*

"What if Dad didn't come home?" David asked his mother.

"Remember, Dad always comes home."

"But what if he didn't? You would have to do everything, like the dishes and the sweeping! I would help."

"I know you would, Davey Boy."

"That's what Dad calls me!"

"I want to call you that too, Davey Boy!" She rustled his hair.

"Stop!" he said, giggling and leaning into her.

"Let's get a cartoon on for you while I make dinner. Okay?"

"Okay! Batman!"

"Can we try something different this time?"

"Um... Superman!"

Sighing, Ava conceded. "Okay, Davey Boy."

She went into the kitchen and stood at the sink, looking into her partial reflection in the window. Just then, she saw a figure move quickly, as though trying to hide from her view. She paused, unflinching, and adjusted her viewpoint to peer into the shrubs and vines along the chain-link fence.

"Mom?" David called for her. "Can I have a little snack?"

"Sure," she said, turning her body, but continuing to look out back for an extra moment. "Sure, David. Just a sec."

Natalie left her apartment just long enough to walk down and up a flight of stairs three times. A spent force after three flights, she returned to her room, and treated herself to a hot water rinse of her hands and face. She breathed deeply over the sink, basking in the steam. She pushed out a short, hard breath, and sat at her laptop, then listened to the entirety of the last segment she had recorded.

Immediately after finishing, she selected all of the files on the Incognito and dragged them to the laptop's trash can. Quickly, she clicked to undo the deletion, then sighed in frustration, tapping her index finger on her desk. She moved the Incognito from her laptop to her phone, then returned to her bed, which by then was stripped down to the mattress. She brought her phone with her:

When I first got on with the service, my coach officer's name was Heather Kovacs. She's retired now. She was a good cop. She benefitted from her family line of cops—six generations, she told me. But that's how it is and always has been with any career, as far as I know. Nepotism everywhere. If you know someone, it's just a lot easier. Heather had a lot of stories about her dads, who were both cops. And about her grandmother on one side and grandfather on the other side—both cops. She would often repeat that 'Policing isn't what it used to be.' Or she would say, 'It wasn't always like this'.

I didn't like when she said that, because that kind of thinking implies that everyone before us had it easy. I know that's not really what she meant. But it's too general. At least, that's what I thought at the time. But when the snow melts and the crimes start piling up, I get in a dark place and think about what she said. I think there's some truth to it, though I didn't work a beat a hundred years ago, so I can't really know.

Like right now... just before he died, Briggs caught that guy who killed two people with a hatchet. Meanwhile, a fourteen-year-old kid overdosed last week, and there's been three arsons in the last two months, and they appear to be connected. It might have been like this fifty years ago, but I wonder how much further back you'd have to go before there wasn't stuff like that in smaller communities like ours. I know Terrace Bay has grown rapidly in the last couple decades, but it's still not a major metropolitan city, not yet. I wonder about what it would have been like to police here when it was a quiet town, and before everyone hated cops.

So Heather... she was strictly business, and I appreciated that. She had a long career because she had the ability to separate work from home. She taught me how vital that separation is. Though she had a family and played sports and such.

She worked with the OPP and patched over to GLRPS, always living in the same area up here. We've stayed in touch a little bit over the years. We went to see a movie together once after she retired. It was a ludicrous story about a time-travelling asshole named Blade.

Heather was the one who taught me a lot about interrogations and working undercover in cells. Most of my techniques are just variations of the ones she showed me. That was a time when I did a lot of my best work, I'd say... coaxing confessions out of people, knowing when to lean on them, when to stroke their egos, when to console them. Most of them want to tell you. Whether it's in the cell and they're desperate to brag, or in the interrogation room, where they're racked with guilt, or sometimes still want to brag. If you work at them too hard, they'll tighten up and you'll lose your chance. But if you play it smart, they find a way. That's how Heather put it. She said that if you work them right—mostly just opening the floor up to listen to them—most of them do the work for you. They're going to find a way to tell you.

Stay close to the bad ones, she told me, because they don't think they're the bad guys. And once they come to the conclusion that you don't think so either, that's when they'll tell you everything you need.

The last time I was assigned to interrogations was a year ago. I had about three minutes working on this suspect, and then one of the detectives came in and literally told me to screw off and let him do it. In front of the suspect. With the sergeant and arresting-officer watching through the two-way mirror. I stood off to the side, mostly in shock at the way he talked to me. I'm not sure why that kind of treatment has continued to shock me all these years, but it still does. I stood there and I watched him leaning into this suspect, grilling him and playing mind games in the most obvious and aggravating way. It was like watching someone else deliver a speech—reading off the cards, stuttering, mispronouncing words—while you sat in the wing, with the entire speech fully memorized. He was all grandiose gestures and misplaced pauses. Style without substance. A meatless performance.

Then when the perp started laughing at him, the detective looked at me like it was my fault. And he flipped his hands around as a way to tell me to get out. I walked out and right through the room where the others were watching. I wasn't embarrassed. I was furious. Why didn't the other guys stop him? And the worst part about it is that those guys will always think that I left out of embarrassment, not anger. That pisses me off. I'm sure they went around telling everyone else about how humiliated I was. Maybe they'd say they felt bad for me or knew the detective was wrong, but who cares? I don't care about that.

The arresting-officer followed me out after a few minutes, and he saw me sitting in the stairwell and he asked me if I was okay. I remember saying, 'You know how sometimes people leave rooms and sit alone because they want to be followed? This isn't one of those times.'

I wish I wouldn't have said that to him, because it's not like it helped. And I wish I wouldn't have told that story just now. It makes me feel worse. Some days... some days I feel like... I don't know. This life I live... it's a shadow.

This shadow of a life.

Days passed, and Natalie abstained from completing any more audio journals. For the first time in many years, she was reminded that the release that comes from self-expression also brings mental exhaustion. In restful silence, slowly, Natalie began feeling better.

She ventured down to the plaza of her apartment building twice; she picked up some take-out from the restaurant and bought a few supplies from the variety store the first time, and then went on the row machine in the fitness centre the second time.

She was lying in bed, thinking about returning to work within a day or two, her feet twitching with nervous energy. She sat up in disdain at her own inability to find sleep, and swung her feet over to the floor. Her feet planted, the nervous twitch was replaced by a constant shaking of one knee. She took a deep breath and stopped all movements.

She looked at her shelf of snacks, just out of reach: peanut butter, crackers, protein bars, trail mix. She looked at her desk, seeing her phone right beside the recording device she had taken from the Gavril residence. She reached for her own Incognito, and began to record:

Who gets to decide when a discontented person should be relabelled as a madman? And is it a false distinction?

She tossed the phone aside, onto the bed, dissatisfied at the sound of her own voice. Her knee began bouncing again, and she let out a frustrated grunt as she exhaled, twisting her lips and turning her head back to the desk. She picked up Lucian's recorder, and through her laptop, linked it to her apartment's speaker system. With no idea what to expect, she kept the volume low, stretched out on top of her blanket, and listened.

THE POWER OF THE HUMAN VOICE

Episode #21
April 6, 2019
Subject: Ron Hawkins, 38, recently laid off, former General Motors production line worker, Lordstown, OH

"Good morning, everyone. I'm your host, Leonard Nistor, and I'm here in studio with Mr. Ron Hawkins. And now, loyal listeners, sit back and behold, The Power of the Human Voice. Mr. Hawkins, let's talk about the past, and how we can bring back the essence of the best days you can remember."

What we need to do is get back to the times before everyone was a lib-tard and got offended by everything. People can't even take a joke no more. That was the good ol' days. Now you can't even give a girl a compliment because you gotta worry about her calling the cops on you for it.
If you want to talk about when my country was truly great, there's three times you gotta look at:
The day we signed the constitution, when what was ours was ours and we had a right to defend it. Then after the war, when we all could have two cars, a house, and a family, and the suburbs belonged to us and were safe. And the world knew they couldn't tread on us. Then the eighties, when we got tough on crime and crackheads.

And then also right now. That's four times. We're living in the right time because people are starting to realize we don't have to kneel to the Hollywood elite anymore—the socialist communist agenda. We're rising up and fighting back and things are getting better for every true American.

"So tell me, if—"

And now you're looking at me like I didn't already explain it to you. Don't think I didn't listen to your other episodes. I know where you stand. But now I'm here to tell our side, and you ain't been listening. And you better. Because the war's coming and you're gonna have to pick a side.

Episode #29
December 27, 2019
Subject: Samir Malik, 41, cardiologist and youth soccer coach, Detroit, MI

With these terrorist cells—alt-right, save-your-race types. They're not well trained, but they're messy. I've read a lot about them and seen several interviews. It's important to me, because I need to know about the people who hate me—what they're thinking, how their minds work, what I need to do to stay out of their way. People like your guest from several months ago, Mr. Hawkins. Those people are clear about their goals. Whereas others, like politicians on both sides of the aisle, exploit societal issues with twisted rhetoric, hiding their true intentions.

"Which are?"

On one side, they mask their fight for power as a fight for equality. On the other side, they're masking their race war as a fight for free speech or some other right that isn't actually being threatened. A race war or religious war— they equate to the same thing, I believe. I know that must feel like an odd way for someone to start, but my point is that it's a unique and strange time to be asking people about the past. People like myself are quite worried about their futures, and rightfully so. Please do not be confused: I'm in a better position than most people. But it's a scary time to be a—hmm—just to be.

I look at Facebook, something that started for the younger people and then became something totally different. And now posting on Facebook is like talking into a mirror. I lost several friends or acquaintances these past three years. People talking about themselves and their experiences or opinions in ways that aren't engaging for anyone but themselves. At first I laughed when people began posting overtly xenophobic conspiracy theories, or wildly unbelievable news reports from strange sources. But it eventually grew more tiresome. It frustrates me that adults are unable to separate propaganda from fact. And it brought out the worst in people, at least in my limited circle. I could always delete my Facebook page, but I do feel something of an obligation—to myself—to continue to see what the people I know have to say.

You know, because I'm different, I always noticed that people found it easy to be nice to me. They find it necessary to put in a little extra effort or patience to be nice. But also because I'm quite different, people find it extremely difficult to be anything more than just nice to me.

"How do you mean that you're different?"

Well, I'm introverted, and not in this way that people pretend to be as a means to get attention, which is actually quite an extroverted behaviour. I'm introverted and contemplative; my approach is always methodical; I admittedly don't have much of a sense of humour; I don't do well in social settings; I don't express emotions clearly. Ah ha, as you can see, I'm keenly aware of my own shortcomings. That itself is discomforting for some people. I think also that people hear my accent, they find out I'm a doctor, and then they feel as though they already have learned all there is to know about me.

But you know, for me, my childhood was not very pleasant. We were quite poor, with a strict household and an intense focus on my studies. That influence carried over well into my twenties. And I never married. So when thinking of the past... I think I didn't have many opportunities to nurture fond memories, probably unlike many of the other people with whom you've spoken.

I enjoy my work and I take some pleasure in my accomplishments at the hospital, but it is just work, ultimately. I think the best times for me often came on the football pitch. I don't look like it, undersized and growing a little soft these days, ah ha. But I was an adept defender in my youth. And coaching children has brought me some joy and some fun. And in thinking of a specific memory for me... there was a time when I assisted at the high school, and an excellent player—a very popular young man, handsome, athletically built, charming, and so on—he once surprised me by confiding in me. That was a meaningful moment for me, and completely unexpected. He was only fifteen at the time, but I know he'd been heavily recruited already to play soccer and basketball in university.

"Can you expand on how he confided in you, and why that was meaningful?"

Well, he was a player who was sort of just drifting through each drill, each practice, and even each game. And when I say drifting, I do mean effortlessly. Yet still, he was a dynamic player and a physical force. No leadership qualities, but always the leading goal-scorer. I only saw him play basketball once, but it was exactly what you'd expect, considering the athlete that I've just described to you.

But in the way he carried himself and the expression on his face, it was always quite clear that he didn't want to play. The boy was held ransom by other people's dreams and expectations. His parents and coaches and friends saw him as either someone from which to profit or someone to which it was valuable to cling for some other personal gain.

I didn't even ask him what was the matter or if he was feeling okay. I knew what the matter was, and I knew he was feeling the same way he felt every other day, when it came to athletics. Perhaps he was testing the news out on me, because I'm an unthreatening person. But I also like to think that he trusted me. He said, 'I don't think I'm going to play next year.' And I said, 'That's okay.' He paused but maintained eye contact. Looking far down at me. I think he was perplexed by my response.

And I didn't have to ask for an explanation. It's not my business anyway. But he turned away from me, facing back toward the pitch before saying, 'People get offended because I don't have the dreams they want me to have.'

Episode #38
March 17, 2021
Subject: Natalia Tojibaev, 31, librarian and tutor, Toronto, ON

First I would like to say that I feel honoured and privileged to be asked to share my thoughts for this project, if only over FaceTime. My primary concern is that people thought things would go back to normal by now, and in fact, many assumed the world would be better for people who are like me or similar to me in one way or another—immigrants, or first generation Canadians, or people of colour, or Muslims, or even women in general. But you can plainly see, no matter how you define normal, the world has not gone back to that. And however you gauge improvements for the underrepresented, you can't find much to cheer about for us.

I think a lot of people stopped the fight right after the election. They assumed this one specific change was all that was needed, or maybe they didn't have the energy left for anything else. I can say for certain that more is needed. I actually had a brick hurled at me by a masked man last month, and it hit my back—not my head, thankfully—so the damage wasn't much. But even with the shock of it, and me falling, and the squealing tires, I still heard the man—quite clearly—screaming about my hijab. 'Go home.' Some other things I'd rather not repeat. And it's been since then that I've started my meditation, as a tool for healing and a way to prevent panic attacks. It was my psychiatrist who recommended the meditation, initially.

Meditating, and more generally taking on this spirit of mindfulness, has helped me reflect a lot on the great memories I had, and the times in my life where I felt safer for the most part, and happier and healthier, with more of a positive outlook on just about everything I encountered.

This process led to me finding the work you've published, and that's why I reached out to you. I felt some urgency, given the shape of our society and my own bleak projections for the future. And I thought it would be useful for me and hopefully for others who might hear my story and be able to relate. I hope so, anyway.

Now… the specific time I wanted to tell you about:

We came to Canada when I was so young, I don't remember anything before. I do remember that I could tell, when I was six or eight, that my parents felt the stress of it—trying to re-establish themselves in a new place and set their roots. Trying to make things good for me and my brothers. I think my oldest brother carried a bit of the load too. My parents never said anything to me, but I remember their strained voices, hushed arguments, occasional frustrated sighs, and overall exhaustion. I remember sometimes wishing someone would play with me, but knowing I shouldn't ask… although I couldn't tell exactly why I shouldn't ask. I just knew.

But my parents were so proud of me. So, so proud. Whenever I did remotely well at anything, they were overjoyed. It wasn't that I needed to accomplish things for them to love me, because I always felt loved and I never felt the pressure to be great—to live out the lofty dreams most parents have for their kids. But it was whenever I was successful at something in the public sphere, like a spelling bee at school or an art contest at a summer festival, that

I could see and feel my parents' pride most clearly.

And I believe a part of the reason was that they were so happy to see me being an active part of Canadian things. Actually, just things in Canada— not necessarily Canadian at the core, like hockey or something like that. Anyway, I wasn't tied to many traditions, even within my faith. Of course, yes, I am a Muslim. You remember I mentioned wearing my hijab earlier. I used to wear it, I mean. I will definitely never wear one again.

Anyway, my family is Muslim, but my father is actually an atheist who just grew up in the Muslim tradition. And we don't have older family members here, who might have been raised with expectations more closely linked to Tajikistan or Islam or both. That's definitely not my parents. They told me even when I was a child, that their expectation was that I would live my own life. Make my own choices, and try to be the best person I could be while doing so.

So when I was twelve, I had been dancing at a local studio for a few years. We had recitals, and I won or at least placed in some meaningless competitions. I was pretty good by the standards of—I don't know—my own experience in that little studio and the area around it. And one time my instructor saw me warming up with some movements my mother had taught me. Old country stuff. And she asked me to show her more. Ultimately, I was asked to open our next recital with a little performance inspired by these traditional Tajikistani dances.

Big surprise: my parents were elated. And my mother wore this red and white dress to the recital. It had some floral pattern on it. And she had one of those elegant little sweaters over top. She was beautiful. And yeah, yeah, I did okay when I danced, but the key moment was when she hugged me afterwards, and she squeezed me so tight. And on the drive home, she couldn't stop talking about it. I was a pre-teen, so naturally everything my parents did was starting to annoy me or make me feel embarrassed, but not that night. It was different in a way that I can't explain, and I suppose that's why the memory stands out so clearly for me. It's the earliest experience I had where I might say... I've never felt better than I felt right then and there.

And I asked her about the dress. She told me she chose it because the colours matched Canada's flag. She was thrilled about the opportunity I had to express myself and be involved in activities in ways I might not have been able to, had we never come here. At that time, I was safe and I was supported and I was loved. And I don't think the future holds anything better, where I will feel all of those things together. I'm not miserable. But I'm realistic. It's not getting any better, and really, it's probably going to get much worse.

Episode #52
August 27, 2022
Subject: Desmond Baker, 79, retired carpenter, Muncie, IN

I've had a long life, and a pretty good one. But these days, I think most about my grandson, Aiden. He could do anything. He coulda been anything he wanted. But, you know... cancer's indiscriminate, they say.

I didn't like all the song and dance stuff when he was little. But when he grew up a bit and I saw how much he could impress people with that stuff. Man. He had these dextrous fingers. Slamming on the piano like Jerry Lee Lewis. And boy could he dance too. James Brown style. All the girls loved him.

But he wasn't just about that fancy dancy stuff. The ball diamond was where he would shine brightest. A three-tool player, y'see. He could hit, he could run, he could defend. Played centre field and would catch anything anywhere near him. The ball would get smoked, come hot off the bat, and I'd just say, 'Aiden's got it, don't worry.' The other grandparents couldn't believe it. And he could huck that thing from the warning track to the catcher's mitt. And straight too. And no one could draw out an at-bat like Aiden. Ten, fifteen pitches. Fouling them off and waiting for the right one. Or just drawing the walk. There's an undervalued skill, especially when you can run the bases like he could. He'd take second easy. He'd take third if the pitcher wasn't paying close enough attention. He had an eye for that. He could stretch a single to a double, hustle out an infield single, break up double plays, lay down perfect bunts, spray the ball all over the field. He was a nightmare for pitchers.

And you know, there's why I don't like all this anti-immigration stuff. I don't much go for politics, but if we don't do the immigration, where are we supposed to get all our goddamn ball players? Only them Dominicans had the kind of heat to keep Aiden honest. Otherwise, the boy'd have been a major leaguer out of high school.

"Did he play in college?"

Sure, yeah. Shoulda been an All-American, but there's backroom bias stuff going on for the awards too. He didn't care though. 'I just wanna play,' he'd tell them. He played at Auburn. I went down to watch a game his freshman year. That was his only season, before…

And when I was there, I'll never forget, he went 2 for 3 with a double, a stolen base, and an RBI off a sac fly. I'm telling you, the boy could play. And afterwards he took us to an old-fashioned type diner. I loved that joint. They had a genuine jukebox. Like a real one with all kinds of classic records in it. I picked three songs. That was one of my favourite days. One of my best memories—that whole day.

"Do you remember the songs you chose?"

Sure, of course. It was Sugar Sugar by The Archies, Respectable by The Yardbirds, and Once Around the Bargain Bin by Empty Echo California.

Episode #60
December 9, 2022
Subject: Marie Badalucci, 83, retired nurse, Flint, MI

I learned about your journals from a niece of mine, and she taught me how to listen to them from your website. I think it's a nice thing, what you're doing. Not a lot of nice things or nice people these days. Of course, fifty years ago I told myself I'd never say anything like that—like everything was better when I was young, or people have changed all for the worse—but all the same, the world hasn't ended up exactly how I thought it might. Do you ever feel like you're the only one who sees it? Sometimes I wonder that, but I think truthfully what's happened to me is the same as what happens to everyone. Except maybe not the people who have so much money that they live up in the clouds, above all our problems… I'm rambling.

"But I think you're onto something, Ms. Badalucci, and I think our listeners are enjoying what you have to say. Let's try to get a bit more specific though. I want to ask you about your memories, and some of the best—or even the worst times. Most elderly people like to tell me about something from the good ol' days."

Good days? I like to see the dad and his young boy from around the way. I see them when I'm watching out my window. They're always out walking.

The child with the tricycle or picking up sticks or jumping in the snow. Racing. Kicking a ball up the street. Or the dad picks him up. I could care less that he's Black. I see them so much, I don't know if he has a job even. But he sure takes care of that boy, and that's what matters. Likely works from home these days anyway.

He'll carry that boy for shoulder rides, and I can see the boy smiling ear to ear. If I've got the window open in the spring, I hear him explaining things to the boy. All his little questions and the why why why. It's lovely, really.

"But what about things from your past that are your best memories?"

Just what I told you. I like seeing the boy and his dad.

Episode #65
February 7, 2023
Subject: Ava Clayton, 27, personal trainer,
nutritionist, Walmart cashier, and graphic designer,
Ann Arbor, MI

The past is gone. I don't even like to think about it, and in fact I actively avoid it most days. My past is a bully that just pokes me and laughs at me while I'm trying to sleep, pretty much. No disrespect to what you do. I like listening to it—obviously—that's why I entered my name to be interviewed. I think other people either had better stories to tell, more positive stuff in their lives, or just find a way to put a spin on it that sounds nice for all us listening. I can't. I didn't try too hard to think of something nice for you, because like I said, I don't like to think about the past. And trying hard to think of something nice would end badly for me.

Once I was with all the kids from around my spot, and we were playing hide and seek at the park. This is when I was just eight or nine years old. And when it was my turn and I was it, and I was counting, they all went home. I don't know when they could have planned it. Or if only a couple of them had it planned and the rest just went along because they're cowards and they don't know what else to do, or whatever. I searched for thirty or thirty-five minutes maybe, before I went home. Even though I knew after just a couple minutes that I would never find anyone.

And that's my past for you. I don't cry about it, but that's just it. I'm sure you can tell we don't have much good to look forward to now too, as a people I mean.

"So the past is gone and the future is bleak, and you're living for today?"

I didn't say that either. I wish there was something to look forward to though. Like if something could be guaranteed. Even if it was an afterlife. I dream I could be someone to guide other people as they move on to that place, whatever it might be. So maybe that's where my head's at, when I'm not scrounging for clients or begging Walmart for extra hours to get through the next grocery trip and the next set of bills.

"And if the past is a bully, what is the future?"

I don't know, honestly… I'm so tired. And as much as I hate thinking about the past, I absolutely dread thinking about the future. I just can't imagine how it could get better.

#66: My Father's Legacy

Hello everyone. This is Gabriela Nistor, daughter of the late broadcast journalist Leonard Nistor, one of the great culture-protectors of the last generation; it has been over two decades since my father's last episode was released online. He and his interviewees shared their most cherished memories, often relating them to the broader ideas of making their country or our world into what it could be at its best. They spoke of returning to the days of yore, retaining culture, or striving for a greater future. All these concepts— considering what we remember and miss most, and what we value now—are quite different today than they were twenty or twenty-five years ago, given how much our world has changed and how most people's hopes have tapered. I plan to capture and help explain that shift in our collective ethos.

I've finally decided to continue my father's work, and I've been compiling interviews for the past six months. I plan to publish one per month now, for as long as it's viable and there are people willing to listen. My father died quite young—coronavirus complications—and listening to his interviews is the closest I've ever had to a connection with him, as I was just a little girl when he passed. I hope that continuing his legacy now can help his spirit live on.

And now, loyal listeners, sit back and behold, The Power of the Human Voice.

A Schoolboy's Mate
April 8, 2046
Subject: Bernie Pascal, 63, doorman, retired professional boxer, and former armed forces infantry soldier, Sudbury, ON

I lived in a boys' home for a few years when I was a teenager. It wasn't that hard of living. We ate good. They had a pool table. And when you lived there, you didn't automatically get a reputation. If you didn't want one, wasn't that hard to avoid it. But even if you wanted one, you had to earn it. You didn't just get to say you lived there so that made you something. Depended how people thought of the house anyway—to some people it just made you nothing. But anyway…

We had a wide mix of kids among us. All creeds. All colours. Lotta mix. Some total scrubs who couldn't fight for shit. Some kids who were hard. Like proper hard. Some kids you knew could be something good some day. I was kind of in-between for everything. But I could throw hands as good as anyone.

They had a system in place for when the boys had beefs we needed to squash. It helped us avoid fighting at school, at the dinner table, in the halls, in our bunks. They kept it in the gym. We ain't have a ring, but we had a set of wrestling mats that was donated by a high school. And once a month, we'd have Rings. Like I said, we ain't have a ring, but we called it Rings.

For the workers, it was a perfect strategy—us doing it once a month. That way, it was never too far off that you would say 'Fuck it' and just bash a guy. But it was mostly far enough off that you would squash it without fighting, or just forget about it, by the time Rings came.

It'd be a lot of us who'd say, 'Just wait until Rings, snitch'. Snitch or rat or motherfucker or whatever we said. 'You mine come Rings time'. But we was just boys, you know. Sometimes the heat would come down ten minutes later and we was just laughing and it was over.

But if Rings came and you had beef, it got squashed. At the start of each session, mans would say, 'If y'all got problems,' and we'd all go, 'Rings can solve 'em'.

If y'all got problems, rings can solve 'em. And mans would go, 'Today's the day.' And it'd be dead quiet. Like in them old MMA shows in Japan way back. You ever seen any of that? Crowd just quiet. No hoorahs or hollerin' shit. We waitin' for something good before we say what. They didn't let us anyway. No cheering. We clapped when the fight's done and we shake hands if we was the ones in there. That's it.

And it'd go like this: three names out of a hat, and up to two others who requested to be chosen. Each would call out an opponent. So three to five matches. You got chosen, and you stood up in the middle and had a chance to call someone out. But the thing was this: if that person said 'No, I don't want to fight,' then it was done. No fight. Si'down, son. And don't say shit about nothing. They did it that way to keep the strong from calling out the weak. They ain't want no mismatch. No bullies in Rings—nuh-uh. So when you had the chance, it had to be fair play. You got beef? You call that person out—not the smallest or youngest or the new guy who don't know how real it gets. Otherwise, you miss your chance.

So you call someone out. You just point and say their name. If you say anything else, no fight. They say yes or no, and that's it. We grappled for five minutes and we boxed for five minutes. They ain't want no kicks in the head or knees in the head. Easier to justify it as exercise if we kept gloves on. Even though we probably got hurt a lot more than if we woulda been able to fight MMA rounds instead. Strictly boxing makes it so it doesn't seem so barbaric. Sounds better to whoever makes the decisions. Cuz they ain't there to see how brutal the fights can be.

So they had us wrestle first so our arms would be tired out and we wouldn't be able to punch as hard after, I figure. But the person getting called out had one choice after saying yes. He could say, 'Just box,' and then the one doing the calling out had the turn at saying yes or no. Some guys just wanted to box, if they had real beef. Guys who did the grappling, they was doing it more as sportsmen, mostly. Friendlier competition. Not quite friendly. But friendlier.

And we had a couple guys come through who went on to be something in the fight game. Me, like I say, I was good, but didn't end up the best career. Just when I arrived at the house, Charles Lord was there, on his way out soon after—went on to box for Guyana at the Olympics and was a two-weight champion pro. I only got to see him in Rings once, and it was a bloodbath. Flatlined a guy who had the stones to call Lord out. Another while I was there, Vaughn Gibbins. He was already a junior national champ freestyle wrestler, and later got two national titles in university. Smart *motherfucker too. He a pediatrician now.* I followed him. I seen what became of the ones who got out of the system.

"Any particular reason why you chose to follow their lives?"

Ain't their lives, ha. I wasn't looking in their windows or nothing. I say I followed their careers. I think it makes me feel good, seein' that. Maybe I'm jealous too. But I don't think it's that as much. I got some good in my life, and in my career—my fight life. Plenty of the boys I knew in there just spent their lives running hustles and slinging dope. I always had a job. Still got one. Had two kids, both educated. I served. Saw combat. And you know, no slouch in the hurtin' business neither. Had eighty-four amateur bouts, three Golden Gloves—that's national, sanctioned. Not some phony novice or underground stuff.

Then I was a junkyard dog in the pros. I went 21-5-1 with 14 kayos. Most of them kayos was clean too. Got ripped off twice. Hometown judging. Home cookin', the saying goes. And the draw was... ah, draw made sense. Good fight. Point is, I earned a rep that if your man wanted a real dogfight, you had to book it with Bernie Pascal. And if your man's record was puffed up with soft-touches, and you think you wanna test it stepping up in class with Pascal... do so at your own peril. I was an equal opportunity ass-kicker. I don't discriminate. Whoever want it can get it. Maybe I lost some from rushing in with that attitude. I coulda had a title if I was more patient, maybe. But the way my younger years was, I never felt like I had time to wait for the sun to shine on me. I had to go get it, and I came up a bit short.

"And do you miss it?"

At my age, there's nothing left to do but miss things. So yeah, I miss it.

"I see. So that's the period which you remember most fondly... anything else?"

Yeah, one more thing. Same time, same place. The one I always remember most was Royce. If you followed the pro game at all, you'd know Royce 'Right Here' Reitnour. And when we was kids, it was always, 'Not Hoyce. Royce.' He'd never let it slip. Not Hoyce. Royce. It was to the point where some of us would actually call him 'Not Hoyce'. He turned pro a little too young. Lost a couple on his way up the ranks when he had no management, but ended up undisputed world champion. Was on all the pound for pound lists for a few years. Man he could move.

He only spent a year with us in the house, but he left an impression. He was sixteen and short, average build, pretty nondescript. But if you saw him *shirtless, he was diced. But shirt on, he looked like he couldn't punch his way through a wet paper bag. And when he was new at the house, he got called out in Rings. I told you that was a cardinal sin at the house, but this one knucklehead, he always tried to do it. He always called out the new guys, hoping to put hands on someone weak. They usually turned him down, which suited him just as well, cuz you know bullies ain't actually wanna fight. They just front. But Royce said yes.*

He'd been there about four days—and he was quiet. And the kid who called him out, his name was Max or Matt or something. He was almost a grown man, and looked it too. A bit doughy in the middle but hard up top and had some power. I went him once, a couple months later; we had real beef. And I whooped his ass too. But with Royce, it was different cuz we didn't know what Royce could do at that time. Neither did Maxy, or whatever his name was, but he learned quick.

Royce played him for a fool: slouched shoulders, no eye contact, lookin' like he was free lunch. Acting like he ain't even know how to hold his own fists. Like 'Where I'm s'posed to put these?'

Max come in cocky—just like Royce wanted—and that cut his chances in half. I mean, he ain't have a chance anyway, but even less when you think it's gonna be easy. I remember it clear as day: Royce come out chin tucked, but hands low like he ain't wanna be there. But the first punch Maxy threw, Royce countered it, WHAM. Whiplash right hand coming off a slip to the right. See, Maxy just pawed with a left jab, because he ain't had no reason to believe Royce could fight. That's what I mean when I say he got played for a fool.

Royce told me after, he like to do a chin check, like Roy Jones Junior. He would come out hard and test his opponent's chin, see if he could take a shot. If the guy could take a shot, Jones would back off, use his speed, just pot shot and break him down. But he had the stuff to find out right away if the dude could take it, where other guys don't have that kinda blinding speed to be able to just step right to his man and land a clean power punch in the first exchange. But Jones had that, so he could chin check you in round one. Royce had that too. Sometimes, that first punch was all it took to find out if your man was macaroni. And that's what it turned out Maxy was—an imposter.

His knees buckled on that first one, and then he was dumb, too proud. Instead of holding or running, he marched straight back into Royce, and I'm telling you man, Royce laid him flat with a two piece and a biscuit: that's that 1-2-3, that jab, straight right, left hook. All square on the jaw, and down Maxy went. Schoolboy's Mate. Now that's a chess term. Bet you thought I didn't know that. Four moves to checkmate just like four moves to the kayo. And didn't nobody call out Royce. Ever. Again.

Not Hoyce—Royce.

The Last Stop at Dawn Hotel
January 6, 2051
Subject: Brooklyn Vanetti, 25, civil engineer, Agawa Bay, ON

Our family lived in Kingston when I was a kid. We had a big, beautiful, old house. A two and a half story home that had been converted from a church rectory into a bed and breakfast and then into a single family home. It was over 150 years old and required a ton of expenses in upkeep and general maintenance. My parents adored it, regardless.

My friend once told me that what made the design of the house so unique was that it would surprise her: she'd be walking through the house on the main floor, looking for a bathroom or whatever, and then come to realize she'd walked in circles and ended up back where she started. It was easy to get lost down hallways or absorbed in some little enclave of the house, even as you got to know most of its features. Yes, she could find the stairs to my room, the kitchen, the back door. But even when you got to those stairs leading up to my room, they split at the halfway point. So while just walking to my room, there was always the opportunity to turn and go up the other way, if you wanted to change your mind and see what else there was to see.

A spacious reading area in a bay window over here, a library with an en suite over there. One room had a thick metal door with a spindle wheel handle; it had been a walk-in vault in its days as a rectory. That house had some secrets. And I found the best part about having that secret was sharing it.

Exploring the house was an adventure for newcomers—and I mean that when I say explore—you couldn't learn the whole layout in five minutes like a normal house, and not just because it happened to be big. So that's a part of my own life that I always remember fondly. Those early days. Especially when I was a teenager and started to have some semblance of a social life and some autonomy.

I wasn't a very interesting kid. That house was my intrigue. I liked having people over to visit. Even if they were people I hadn't met before or who I didn't really get along with at school, I knew that I could impress them or find my way into their… I'm not sure what. Their consciousness, their memories, their good sides. I wasn't really trying to get into any social circle. I was sort of disconnected in that regard. And the pressures of the social side made me too nervous until I was in my twenties.

Older boys went after me when I was new to the high school. But as I said, I was too reserved for that at the time. I didn't have those types of desires yet, and the boys honestly frightened me. But I did let a couple of them come to the house. It instantly gave me a power over them that I couldn't hold anywhere else. Arrogant boys and their one-track minds.

So when they came to my house—and this only happened two or three times, as the risk wasn't worth the fleeting joy it brought me—but when they came, they'd invariably want to get me alone, but there was often some way to sway their interest, albeit momentarily. The vault, which my dad used as a sort of arming room, with a hulking oak desk and vintage rifles in display cases; the tiny spiral staircase to the cellar, obscured by a throw rug; or the home theatre room, where the entrance was hidden by a framed floor-to-ceiling poster of my dad's favourite film. Just push and pull and there was the secret room. I'd let the boy sneak a drink from the bar in there, and that might excite him, but then I'd make him leave before he could convince me to lay on the leather recliner and turn the projector on. I had to stay sharp. So it was just on to the next room.

You see how I kept the control. I couldn't repeat it often, but it was really the only social gratification I ever got in high school. There was an intimacy of sorts, but it was the house, not our bodies or some emotional connection.

And many of the memories aren't my own, but my parents had several stories about interesting travellers who would visit our house. It happened because the house always remained listed as a bed and breakfast if you researched the address online. My mom contacted Google Maps two or three times, and the name of the B&B would be removed from Google for a few weeks, but it would always end up back on there: The Last Stop at Dawn Hotel. As a result, people would show up, often in dire situations, mostly in the middle of the night, searching for a place to stay.

A Big Bag of Rice and a Gun
November 15, 2062
Subject: Gary Petrovic, 44, maintenance worker, Government of Canada Food Production Plant, Ottawa, ON

I didn't have it long, but when I had it, I knew it, and I could feel it. So for me, the best times, the ones I wish I could live over and over, it wasn't about moments, it was about my confidence, I think. What I felt inside at the time, rather than the stories I could tell you.

I could tell you about meeting a personal hero of mine… or about a beautiful girl I was with or when I won my first marksmanship competition or a time the work I put in helped us yield a huge crop. Those are all great. But the energy pushing through my veins in those years, that is the truly great memory for me. I got some stupid trophy for my first competition, but that's just a trinket. My dog can play with it. The great part of that day was driving home by myself—radio loud, smiling, feeling the sun on me. That was a time when I knew I had it. I had it. The years haven't been easy on my face and my body, you can see, but there was a short window there, where I had it and other people could see it too. And knowing they could see it and feel it, that's my best memory.

But that's all gone. And that's fine with me. Because I feel I made the most out of what the good lord gave me. As I get older now, I'm staying as sharp as I can for as long as I can. I'm staying prepared because there's a lot of restless people, and I can feel their energy too. A lot of sicks and a lot of tireds out there.

People are constantly on edge now. We can feel there's a shift coming. I know the past couple decades have brought changes people my age or older might not have ever been able to imagine, but those changes are nothing compared to what's coming. That's in terms of how hard it will hit, how broad the repercussions will be, and how quick it will all come. I'm talking about changes that might mean the end of our civilization. Not necessarily the end of the species, but if people aren't prepared to fend for themselves, those people are going to be trampled on. And that's most people.

My dad told me about when people panicked over COVID-19. Absolute morons at each other's throats for toilet paper. Toilet paper! Like it'll mean anything when the world crumbles. And bottles of water, as if you can't just put a drop of bleach in a bucket from the lake. But people don't know about that, as like I said, people are unprepared for living in any way that is less than fully dependent. Been like that since the turn of the century. Can't change the oil in their cars. Can't fix their furnaces. Can't stop a leaky faucet. Why learn to do that when you can pay someone to do it for you? That's been the mentality.

Tell you what my daddy did, and it's the same as what I'm ready to do when it goes down. Everyone else stocking up on toilet paper, bottled water, frozen meat. Forgetting that if the world as we know it comes to an end, that frozen meat's just going to spoil when there's no power, and that bottled water is just a waste of money for something you could go draw from the river yourself.

Like I was saying, my dad bought canned meat—turkey, chicken, ham, tuna, whatever. Get your protein from something shelf stable. That, plus a big bag of rice and a gun. Carbs and proteins, no need for a fridge. Easy to store, easy to cook. Gets you the energy you need to get through the days.

So he's the one who taught me how to be ready for what's probably coming soon. I've got everything I need stored away. Maybe you think it's strange since I work for the government. But that doesn't mean I have to have blind faith in the government's ability to protect its people when panic sets in and we turn into animals. I'll be ready to protect my land. I don't want to get into the details of what I've got to protect and how I'll be able to keep living, because people listening don't need to know everything. But they should know that I've got what I need and I know the value it has, so I'm ready to fight to keep it. And I'm not the only one out there. There's plenty like me.

"And do you follow much of the political landscape? Is there something specific going on in government that has led you to think there's this great change coming?"

Lady, I worked my whole life in the fields before, and now I work all day in a factory—whatever they want to call it—doing all the grunt work no one else wants to do. Do you think I have time for politics?

"Maybe not."

It's not as much what's happening in government anyway. I believe politicians only care about us enough to get our votes, but that means they're obligated to do at least some bit of good. It was decades ago that we saw the shift where running for political office turned into a hobby for the rich, and that hasn't done the workingman any favours. So I know politicians are always trying to line their own pockets, and looking out for themselves first, but still, most times I think politicians are trying to help society, at least to some extent. So it's not that.

It's the unrest in the streets. That's what's getting me. It's people getting sick and tired of waiting for things to get better, of being told to keep being patient. And at the same time, it's this growing influence of big business. I don't even want to call it 'business' or 'businesses' anymore. It's the growing influence of those rich people in the shadows, in the towers. Come to think of it, I shouldn't call it 'influence' anymore either. More like manipulations. It's the divide they're creating, and the fire they're stoking. There's the rich guys turning to politics just for the hell of it, then there's the ultra wealthy ones, manipulating.

A man like me can't do anything about it. My great grandpa, who I was lucky enough to know until I was ten, would say, 'That don't mean but nothin' to me'. That's the sort of attitude I keep now. I'm through trying to change anything or inform anyone. And again, I'm not alone on that. There are others like me—some a little crazier or confused, maybe with a devil-may-care attitude, thinking their rights are more important than everyone else's lives. That's not what I mean. I mean it's not worth my time or effort to try to be that, that, that better person anymore. Like I said, I've just got my big bag of rice.

I can see you don't like to interrupt much when your people get talking to you. I think you want me to define things more specifically. But isn't that what dread is supposed to be like? Foreboding feelings are hard to pin.

I'll just say… there's a creeping menace. And it's the people's accumulated resentments.

Billionaires Rejoice!
August 18, 2068
Subject: Sofia Kutsenko, 21, public relations manager, The United People's Conglomerate, New York City, NY & Ottawa, ON

Thank you for having me on your program today. It's a pleasure to be here, and I'm really excited to share some good news from The Conglomerate for all your listeners.

"Yes, you're welcome, Sofia. I think first I should explain to everyone why this month's segment might feel a little different from others, and then I'd like you to give some background information about The Conglomerate and the details of the recent merger. So, I'm here today with Sofia Kutsenko, who is the regional PR representative for the United People's Conglomerate, or UPC. The UPC began as a right-wing lobbyist group and political financier."

Sorry, I'm just going to stop you right there, as there is a lot of disinformation about the UPC and what we do. As your listeners will glean from our name, we are for the people, and—

"Excuse you, but I'd like to finish my introduction, and then I assure you that you will be the one taking over and in full control of the remainder of the segment. I'm not sure if you've listened to my program before, but the way it works is—"

I'm sorry, but I wasn't aware that there was a strict format to be followed. And we at the UPC, for the people, are against such fascist ideas that restrict free speech and other constitutional rights. And that is the type of information the mainstream media is avoiding telling the public.

"Right, well you don't sound sorry. And allowing me to complete my introduction would not be in any way relatable to fascism."

Are you sure about that?

"Yes, and I think you should ensure you understand the definition of the word before you start throwing it around in an effort to frame me as a villain to my listeners. I think you underestimate your 'people's' ability to see through your inflammatory rhetoric."

Do I?

"I'm sorry, do you want me to answer that?"

You see, it's this type of control and subjugation of voices that we are trying to fight against. We at the United People's—

"Saying 'People's' in your title doesn't mean you're actually for the people. That's just further pandering on your part. Further assumption that the people are too stupid to understand whose interests you actually care for."

It sounds like you've already made up your mind about what sort of interview this is going to be. And about what our group stands for. If you won't listen, then it's not my job to change your mind.

"Isn't that your job though? Aren't you the public relations chairperson for *the UPC?"*

Indeed I am, but again you're missing my point.

"Okay, then let's take a step back."

Yes, with pleasure.

"I'm here with Sofia Kutsenko, and rather than discuss her memories—traumatic or beautiful—or the specific times in her life she'd like to revisit, she's here to talk to you about the UPC, and the ways the UPC wants to make our world great again. The UPC has offices around the world, including one in Ottawa, and its main headquarters in New York City. I'll have Sofia take over now, to tell us more about how the UPC is going to impact all of our futures."

Thank you, Gabrielle. Though you went a little off-kilter right at the end there.

"It's Gabriela."

Right. Well citizens, here we are. We've arrived at a very exciting new frontier in our civilization, and I am here to tell you that the United People's Conglomerate is a North America first organization, committed to enriching the lives of Canadians and Americans above all else. We will deliver to all those wonderful families out there who've struggled in recent years. We will be guiding you as we return to the glory days—a resurrection of the greatest times we've had as a society.

The UPC is a collaboration of like-minded freethinkers; a strong front of self-made businesspeople who don't mind ruffling some feathers in order to bring jobs, food, money, garbage, safety, energy, and prosperity to Americans… and Canadians.

I personally come from a modest upbringing, and I know struggle. I knew that with hard work and dedication, I could succeed in this world. And look at me now. I'm just like you listeners out there, and I'm telling you, success is possible. Prosperity is possible. One of the first initiatives we've taken on is to take the lottery system out of the hands of the government. We've loosened the fat cats' grips on control of the winnings, so as to help you—the people—get your fair share. By combining the resources of two countries, we've found a way to immediately help the hard-working folks at home, giving you more opportunities to win, and more opportunities to win big.

We've got many brilliant billionaires on our team, and they're using their combined brainpower, global experience, negotiation tactics, and business acumen to make great deals here in North America, ensuring your safety by *contributing to the success of our heroes in the armed forces, and taking power away from our foreign enemies who continue to seek to undermine our Christian values and break up the solidarity of our great nations.*

There are precious few politicians like those from our greater times, and we are using our influence to bring back strong leadership, and to enhance the teamwork and joint projects between Canada and the United States. We want political leaders who will be allies to the hard-working public, who will not give free handouts to people who are trying to steal your tax dollars, and who will create new, safe, affordable, hurricane-proof infrastructure and housing for those who've truly shown they deserve the best.

That's what the United People's Conglomerate is all about, and we are taking power from the hands of big government and giving it back to the citizens of Canada and the United States.

New World Order
October 9, 2068

Good day to all you listeners out there in the universe. Unfortunately, this will be my final broadcast. The government grant that allows me to continue my program has been denied for 2069. It is a grant that I've received consecutively every year for twenty years, and that means I will no longer be able to keep up funding to produce and release content. Further, all of the advertising that gives me extra funding has been stripped or cancelled—I must say under pretty mysterious circumstances—meaning that I no longer have any advertisements or sponsorships to even close out this calendar year.

I should admit that a member of the UPC has reached out to me to offer sponsorship, but only if I hand over full creative control to the UPC, and allow them to choose all my interviewees, write all the questions I get to ask, and control all topics discussed. I've respectfully declined the offer. Since then, every episode of The Power of the Human Voice has been wiped from all streaming platforms affiliated with the UPC, including Amazon Reads, Google E-Books, and Apple iBooks. There's been some effort to snuff out the controversy in the news, as my program was one of hundreds of podcasts, songs, and both fiction and nonfiction books that were deleted from millions of devices owned by private citizens around the world. Orwell or Bradbury would have had nightmares about this type of purge. In fact, several of

Bradbury's works were amongst those purged. Orwell's 1984 is one that the UPC and their affiliates have been able to rebrand and make their own through some clever marketing and redacted excerpts, so it's still available for purchase. Life imitates art, as Oscar Wilde might tell us.

As has been happening on-and-off for decades, one political side cheers the erasure of some content it deems offensive, setting a precedent before the other side gains power and uses that precedent to eliminate wider circles of content, silencing critics while repressing opportunities for education and understanding. Heaven forbid we come to empathize with the perspectives and experiences of others.

This particular purge was a business decision, supposedly. Copy and distribution rights, duelling companies, judicial proceedings too complex to explain to us average citizens. In short, no clear reasoning has been presented. Democracy cannot prevail without a robust free press, dear listeners.

I'll be moving forward with other ventures in the near future, hoping to be able to keep a roof over my head in these trying times. I can still be reached on my social media accounts, which will be listed following this closing segment, wherein I've selected a set of three songs that were mentioned in previous episodes of the program. Please enjoy John Henry was a Steel Drivin' Man by Steve Earle & The Dukes, Once Around the Bargain Bin by Empty Echo California, and Nevermind by Leonard Cohen. Be safe out there, dear listeners. The pullers of the strings have tightened their grip.

This is Gabriela Nistor from The Power of the Human Voice, signing off.

December 27, 2081

Okay, hello. This is Lucian Gavril. I've... I'm continuing the work of my late mother, and my grandfather before her. I've meticulously catalogued and scrutinized all of their work, and I want to stay true to their grassroots efforts—giving the floor to underrepresented voices, and letting people tell their own stories with limited disruption or analysis on my part. I don't want to betray the authenticity that evolved from the work my mom and granddad did.

From the outset, I should say that I'm not a talented media man, and any form of public speaking—pre-recorded as it may be—is not something I'm strongly suited for. I have big shoes to fill: Leonard Nistor, with his velvety smooth voice, disarming nature, and prolific body of work. Then Gabriela Nistor, who operated with such clear purpose: fearless pursuit of the truth in an effort to produce something meaningful.

I don't know exactly why I've decided to do this, and why now? I can't answer that, but maybe actually doing my own recording will help me figure out why I began reviewing all their work in the first place... if that makes any sense.

I dreamed of this—of conducting such interviews. Of the doors it could open, the healing it could cause, the resolution it could bring... of all the potential storytelling has. And so, here I am.

Natalie had listened to interviews all night, until she found herself drifting in and out of sleep. Then she listened to more and more throughout the next day. It was nearing dusk when she turned the playlist off after hearing Lucian's own introduction. She resolved to have a hot meal and get ten hours of sleep before returning to work to start her shift the next morning.

She started with a glass of water, pulling it back all at once, in heaving gulps. Next, she began roasting three faux chicken breasts on a pan with mixed vegetables. She stood in her tiny kitchenette, leaning on the countertop, staring at the oven while crunching ice chips from of a cup. Minutes passed. She received a text from Pete:

Coming over. Tell asshole at gate to let me in.

Natalie called down to the guards at the entrance to her building to inform them of Pete's arrival. She then began scrambling to prepare for a visitor, but quickly came to realize there was nothing to do. She kept her apartment clean, and she didn't have enough possessions to necessitate tidying. She lit a scented candle and cracked her door open for Pete to enter. Shortly thereafter, he knocked gently and pushed the door open with a measure of hesitation.

"Hey. Brought you a soup."

"Thanks. Come in. You can sit there at the desk."

Pete sat down. He didn't look around. He just waited for Natalie to put the soup aside and join him.

"I'd offer you a tour, but... this is it."

"None of my business anyway—it's nice." He waited a beat before moving on. "I got the notification you were coming back on tomorrow. I just wanted to check in to make sure you were feeling good. Because if not, you've got more sick days you can use, or I can figure out a way to get your vacation started early. It's not that hard."

"No I'm fine. I need to get back, honestly. I haven't been sick for about two days now, but just trying to catch up on sleep before starting my rotation."

"That's what I figured you'd say. I wanted to be sure though. Because... I know you don't have much else. No disrespect. But... you're like me, I know. You do other things, like your defensive tactics training, but that's mostly just an extension of the job. So..."

The silence hung in the air. Pete looked around for the first time. The room was warm and the candle's scent was subtly sweet.

"I know you care about me, Pete." Natalie almost couldn't believe she said it, but it couldn't be taken back.

"Hmph," Pete grunted as the two briefly locked eyes. He then pointed to a framed photo on the wall. "I see you've got a good picture there from when you finished training at the college. Does it mean something to you still?"

"I guess it does. I was happy. We went through hell. And I was already looking ahead to how it guaranteed me an early end to my working life. I don't know if that's a good thing or a bad thing. Maybe bad—to be looking ahead past the entire career. But that's how I felt. And I knew I was well prepared for the job—for the stresses it would put on me. For the dangers. For what it would do to me."

"I don't think it did to you what it does to most. Most of them when they get the badge, they gain something, but they lose something too. Confidence comes, opportunities come. But I think a lot of them lose a bit of their humanity. If they're brazen and cocky and got into it for the wrong reasons, then they lose that bit of humanity right away. Or over time, if they're not prepared for what they're about to be exposed to. Not prepared the way you were."

"You're right. You get something, but you lose something else. It's true… Do you have many pictures? Keepsakes around your apartment?"

"Yeah, a few. I kept a sketch from a training partner. I framed it. He finished a test early and it took me forever to finish. And while I was typing, he drew a picture of me. Just ballpoint pen on lined paper. But he drew it upside down, so it's skewed and some of my features are obscured. I like that. So that's the only art I have. Then it's photos from training and missions and handshakes with the mayor and medals and challenge coins.

"You know," Pete continued, "I went to Oakshot's house once. He invited me for dinner with his family last year. And I was shocked—because he's such a diehard. Fully committed to the fuel injected mentality. But walking through his house, you would never know he was a cop. Pictures of his wife and kids and their vacations. That was it. Big smiles and pushes on swings and laughing together. You wouldn't believe it. There was so much laughter in that house. It made me nervous, but… in a good way. I never had anything like that when I was a kid. There was no laughing in my apartment. I admire Oak for that. His kids will be… if nothing else, they'll be well adjusted. It really shouldn't have been a surprise though. The job is only what he does for pay—which is how we should all think of it, as long as we stay vigilant. But after being there and listening to how he and his wife talked to each other, I know the badge just isn't as important to him as it is to me. It doesn't have to be important to him because he has other things."

"I'm here for you, Pete."

"I know. Thank you. I've always got your six too. On duty or off."

"That's why you're here right now."

"Yeah."

The two friends lingered again in comfortable silence, Pete

studying his own folded hands, and Natalie watching him.

"What was the best time of your life, Pete?"

"In what sense?"

"Like what was the best moment or the best stretch of time, something you just wish you could relive if you could get away from the here-and-now for a while."

Pete gave the question a long consideration.

"I can remember what I think were some of the best moments of my life. But even then, thinking about reliving them... the whole day? The memories turn sour with time. The moment itself is nice. When I wrestled as a kid, or went to a concert, or when I was in the army, or when I made sergeant. But then I think of how lonely I was at the time. There was no one to share the success with. Or I think back to that time that seemed so great, and realize I wasn't as happy as I thought I was—or as I was pretending to be. I think the photo is enough. A picture is easy, simple. It looks nice on the wall. I don't think about it all too much. Really, I have a hard time thinking of myself as ever being truly happy. Not for much longer than it takes to snap the picture, anyway... Listen to me, I open my mouth off-shift for the first time in forever, and I don't know when to shut up. Point is, I'm here for you now, and I came to make it clear I'll be here for you tomorrow and all the rest of the days too. I'll let you get some sleep."

He got up and moved to the door quickly. "Rest up, Ross." He turned to smile at her only after he'd opened the door. "See you back at work soon."

Still seated, she returned the smile as Pete left. She continued to look at the door for a moment when he was gone, then turned her head toward her window, her desk, her single plant. She pushed out a long, slow breath and started to feel the weight of her eyelids. As she began to doze off, she was shaken by the sound of her oven's timer.

She ate her dinner, returned to her bed, set an alarm, and fell into a deep, dreamless sleep.

Cormac was back to work—telework for the time being. Having burned through his allotted leave, and with the service setting strict time limitations for when an officer needs to recover from being injured on the job, he was forced to start working again or hand in his badge. An HR representative for the GLRPS did tell him he was entitled to a small severance, should he choose to retire early, but he knew he wouldn't be able to find sufficient work, given his limited formal education and inability to complete arduous manual labour; the explosion had taken his left leg and two fingers from his left hand.

There was no way he could afford one of the new, supremely effective prosthetics that had been developed since private enterprise took over much of Canada's medical field. Ten years earlier, human genetic modification became a fully legal, limitless service offered in the private sector. After that, the floodgates opened for private industry to work its way into public health, medicine, and science much more. Thus, the price of high quality prosthetics soared.

So Cormac worked—first from a hospital bed and then from home, taking calls for the telephone reporting unit, where dispatchers sent low priority calls: stolen bikes, internet scams, Facebook rumours.

He hung up the phone after another dubious call: a citizen searching for confirmation about "suspicious poors with dark complexions" roaming the Landfill Lofts, pretending to be collecting charity donations. It was something Cormac had come across a week earlier, and a month before that while he was still a detective too; an old home security camera still frame, circulating Facebook, occasionally re-emerging in a new town, along with unverified claims made by the person doing the reposting: 'These poors have been seen in the Loft area'. 'These immigrants are tricking people and ransacking their homes'. None of it was true. Not when the rumour first started in Toronto three months prior, not when the same photo began circulating amongst Terrace Bay citizens, not this time either.

Cormac took care in standing up, grabbing a crutch, and hobbling toward his balcony. He left the outdoor light off, feeling the fresh air as he stepped into a starry darkness. He could see a light on in a room in the next building, and he thought it might be Pete's—he knew Pete lived in that building, on about that floor, but it had been a while since he'd been over there.

He watched the yellow glow for a moment, until the light inside went out. At that, Cormac turned to look forward, leaned his hands onto the balcony's railing, and then hung his head.

Back on shift, Natalie arrived to a service call in the heart of Terrace Bay. Aleem arrived in his cruiser shortly afterwards. The call was related to two neighbours arguing over a shared driveway. Aleem joined Natalie as she spoke with the complainant, a heavyset elderly woman wearing a nightgown. When the woman saw Aleem at her door, she moved as though she was going to let him in, but then stopped; she grabbed a puffy winter coat from a hook behind the door, put it on with arduous effort, zipped it up to the top, and then opened the door for Aleem, scampering away as she pulled the knob.

It was a story the officers heard often. A driveway shared between two residences: a new neighbour moves in and starts parking across the imaginary line, or two long-time neighbours suddenly have some unrelated grudge, and begin using the imaginary line as a conduit for their disgruntled energy.

They listened to her version of the story, asked questions, took notes. The woman's bone-weary, middle-aged son sat at the kitchen table with his chair turned to face the officers; he stared at his feet the entire time, occasionally letting out a cartoonish sigh.

Afterwards, the officers went to the other neighbour to get his side of the story. The complainant is usually more flustered, nervous. The one accused of misusing the space is first surprised, and then prone to either fits of laughter or rage, or sometimes laughter that turns into rage. The officers listen calmly to both sides, saying very little, eventually finding a simple compromise that settles the issue, or at least deters either party from calling the police for a few weeks.

Aleem could feel the complainant peering through her window at him and Natalie as they interviewed the other party, and then as they walked back to their cruisers too. He was trying to contain a laugh. "That parka," he said, and Natalie smiled at him. "Is this your first day back?"

"Yes. It felt like I was off for a year."

"Time is strange with this job. The days usually crawl by, but the seasons seem to slip past."

"And the days-on last a lifetime, but the days-off are gone so quickly. It's like they didn't even happen."

"Planning vacation gives me too much stress," Aleem confided. "I found my blood-pressure would rise when I'd look at my calendar to plot out a block of days, or when I'd sift through websites to search for flights and destinations. I don't like thinking about it because it reminds me of how quickly it's going to be over and done with."

"And then you're right back here, one step away from drawing a chalk line down a driveway." She smiled again.

"It's the anniversary of my start-date on the job today," Aleem said, as he passively kicked at some pebbles on the pavement. "Nine years ago today was my first shift."

"Congratulations. I'm sorry the date came on the heels of the raid. I wish the circumstance was better."

"That's fine, thank you. It's another anniversary for me today too, actually. It's been three years since I returned from assignment in Bay City, Michigan. That was a good experience. Three months deployed there. I mostly worked on the marine unit. It was good to feel like I was starting fresh, but with a better base and a clear head going in. I liked not knowing anyone too."

"Does it make you feel sad that it was so long ago?"

"No, not really. I like these reference points even though they put distance between now and the good memories. The mental math anchors me to today, and it's a reminder that those moments were real. They have an established time and place when and where they happened. So I like to think about what I was doing around today's date when I was, for example, twenty years old. I like working through the index of my memory, thinking about something that happened to me around that time—someone that I met, or a place that I went. I think that type of reflective thinking keeps me sharp."

"Good perspective," Natalie said, nodding as she looked back at the window of the complainant's house. She watched the woman move the curtain to hide, and heard her son yell something indiscernible.

"Let's get back out there before someone from oversight sees us," said Aleem. He started to move to his vehicle before Natalie stopped him.

"I want to try to get surveillance set up to help me with the missing person case I'm working." She paused while he turned, closing his door, giving her his full attention.

"They closed the file on the case while I was off. Brooks took over and closed it after two days. I don't even know if he did any work. He wouldn't talk to me about it. It was like he'd already forgotten. I'm nervous to ask to return to the case. You know how they'll treat me if it looks like I'm questioning a man's work, especially after management has signed off on it. I just think that he's out there and could be brought home and given the help he needs—he's got a family. And I know he was mixed in with the Freedom Fighters, so there could be a connection there too. I just don't know how to explain it to management without sounding like I'm obsessing or just making guesses. They're always quick to ridicule. It gets so tiring to try."

"Try why?"

"Just try. Any inspiration, any effort. It just gets crushed. I'm left feeling like I should apologize for having ideas."

At that, something was sparked in Aleem. He was resolute, moving a half-step closer to Natalie, looking her in the eyes when he responded:

"Never apologize for advocating for yourself and your ideas. Because even if you don't get the desired outcome, you've now created a space wherein your voice must be heard. It's the same as exercising your agency through a complaint, or standing up for yourself in any way. You've created a situation in which your concerns must be taken seriously, where people know they'll be held accountable. Advocating for yourself shows a strength that exists beyond the physical. People will remember: 'That person will speak up. Be careful of that one, she'll push back'. They'll always have to be mindful. But only if you say so.

"Will it mean that some officers won't like you? Sure. But those aren't the ones worthy of your energy. Maybe it will also mean you'll have a hard time getting promotions or special assignments, like I've had lately. But, the fact will remain—people will know they need to be mindful of you. It's an important kind of respect that you must force them to give you. The worst case is you get denied. But you will have tried. And you will have planted the seed. And those are admirable feats."

"I guess I'm just sick of having to be the dissenting voice."

"I feel the same way. But the dissenting voice is a dangerous one. It's needed in a field where people are so worried about upholding the status quo. Justice must supersede tradition."

Dressed in their ceremonial uniforms, several officers from the GLRPS arrived at the funeral service for Cst. Oshun Briggs. A partition wall had been removed, making space for extra chairs and opening the room into a large, high-ceilinged, brightly lit space. Enormous windows allowed for the morning's natural light to enter, bringing out the colours in the many floral arrangements that had been placed along the perimeter of the room.

Pete offered Cormac a chair, but he refused. "Fuck that," he whispered. "I'll stand with you." They stood beside each other along the back wall, and Cormac kept his eyes forward, watching the dais, waiting for the ceremony to begin.

The service was led by one of Briggs' lifelong friends. She was tall, wore a black pantsuit, had long, wavy, red hair, and spoke softly but clearly. Her husband—flanked by their two daughters—sat in the front row, chin high, looking at her proudly. Terrace Bay's regional chief, Calvin Till, was in the aisle seat of the second row; his boots had a mirror shine and the crisply ironed creases of his pants were visible from across the room.

Briggs' brother, Terence, approached the podium to deliver the eulogy:

"What can I say? What can I say about the little brother who managed to one-up me at everything we did?" At that, good-natured laughter rippled through the crowd. The sound was louder than Natalie expected for a funeral—these people came to celebrate a life. It was then that Natalie fully took in just how densely packed the room was. So many people. And many people were crying, but also smiling, holding hands, looking at each other to bask in the moment, nodding along as Terence spoke. They measured their reactions carefully, but were excited to oblige Terence in the mood he set. This was an adoring audience.

"As much as I tried to be the role model, to be the better athlete, the better student, the better musician, the better neighbour, I always found Oshun was surpassing every feat. Damn you, brother. When we were teenagers, I remember him knocking on my door, entering bashfully—hat in hand—and telling me the only reason he joined all the same clubs as me, took up the same interests as me, was because he admired me so much. And I have to admit, I cried. I cried and we embraced. He consoled me. Like usual, the little brother became the big brother. And over time, I came to like it that way.

"I didn't know anyone else quite like him. And that makes it even harder to see him go so early. These cops—and I'm so glad to see many of you here in this room—they don't get a lot of respect, but they put their lives on the line for us every day. Oshun knew the hazards of the job, and many of us closest to him were surprised to see him take it on. Though he was always a big, athletic kid, and he excelled in law, in civics, in anything he put his mind to, I actually always thought he'd be a veterinarian. The guy was such an animal lover. If we'd go to a house-party where the host had a dog... forget about talking to Oshun because he was just going to hang out with the dog all night.

"An avid bird-watcher, a painter, and a saxophonist—who would expect this guy to be a police officer? But he did it, and he excelled at that too. He said he wanted to help people, and I'm proud to say that he did just what he set out to do.

"But." He took a deep breath. "My brother had his demons too. And they came from the job. When you officers go every shift, through all the years, bottling things up, that pain or trauma is going to manifest itself somehow. Oshun attempted to end his own life two years back, and I know from another personal experience, that when a life ends by one's own hand, their pain doesn't end with it—it just gets passed on to someone else.

"I'd imagine many of you didn't know that Oshun nearly took his own life, because it got hushed. And because as soon as he recovered, he went right back to suppressing all his emotions and holding in the effects of everything he saw on the job daily. I say this with great consideration and not with anger, but with the way Oshun's last few years went, and the way he died... the police service failed him. I hope my words stick with you officers that are here today: don't expect to be taken care of. And if you're in one of those positions where you're supposed to be supporting the health and wellness of the officers, or you are able to make changes to programs and processes, please take my words to heart.

"Now let's not leave it there. Let's not dwell on the ending and on those awful people who took my brother from me. Those people that I know will be brought to justice." He paused, holding a severe stare in the direction of the officers standing tall along the back wall of the room.

"Let's think about something else for a moment: Oshun was a good cop who made big arrests, kept our city safe, and took on daunting challenges with a smile. That was another thing I hated. I hated how he would smile in moments when other people were shaking in their boots! Myself included. We'd be lined up for a race, or squaring off to fight some clowns at a bar, and I'd say, 'Man, can you stop smiling for a second!'

"Now, one of the reasons Oshun enjoyed policing was he said

it made him thoroughly appreciate every last second of his vacation time. But what did he do with all that precious time? For the last five years, he took our grandmother on vacation with him. I'm over here trying to find a day to take my brother to lunch; meanwhile, he's jet-setting with Grandma in Copenhagen or Helsinki. Damn you, Oshun." He pointed up to the heavens, smiling and holding back a tear as his voice cracked at the sound of his brother's name.

"Oshun never married. I suppose I'm thankful that he didn't have a partner or kids to leave behind with his untimely passing. But the selfish part of me is wishing he'd have had a son or daughter. Because I would have loved to see all my brother's skills and talents passed on to someone new, and just to be able to see how those abilities bloomed and what unique and interesting hobbies and challenges another little Briggs would have taken on. Likely with a smile.

"He was a talented artist with an iron will, a loyal and considerate friend, a dedicated police officer, and simply, a wonderful man. Oshun Briggs was the most fascinating and exceptional person I ever knew, and I am proud to say that he was my brother. I will think of him often, remember him fondly, and miss him dearly. Damn you, brother, until we meet again."

At the conclusion of the service, with Briggs' family staying for a luncheon, other attendees splintered into small groups in the parking lot.

"I'll wait," Cormac told Pete, opting to stay behind and wait for the crowd to disperse. "You go ahead."

Without a word, Pete nodded and made for the door. Natalie hurried her pace a little to catch up to him, and they exited the building together.

"Terence's eulogy was beautiful," Natalie said. "I feel awful now to admit how little I knew about Briggs." She stopped at Pete's vehicle, expecting a conversation.

"Yeah, he had a lot that I didn't know about." Pete was distracted, rushing. "I have paperwork to do. I need to get back to the station." He entered his car and left, with the same severe look that he carried like it was an obligation.

Natalie remained, standing alone. Two other officers walked by, looking at her with mocking smiles.

"When are they gonna build a fire for that witch?" one said to the other, his voice more than a little too loud. And they howled harder than the combined laughter of everyone at the funeral service.

"Make it quick, I'm busy." Deputy Chief Nathan Crawford said, after looking at Natalie only long enough to establish that she was in fact standing at his doorway.

"Sorry to bother you, sir. I would have gone to Gilchrist, but he was called for a meeting with oversight early this morning. I tried to run my idea by him, but he said he couldn't deal with it today because this meeting was unexpected, and apparently he's going to be gone all day."

"Why are you telling me Gilchrist's business? And why do you seem so interested in what he's doing with oversight?"

"I... I'm not. I thought it was important to establish why I've come to you instead of my inspector."

"Well, it's not, and this is already feeling like a huge waste of my time. And the service's. And what are you doing leap-frogging the chain of command? Are you new? Do you not know that you're to go to your staff sergeant?"

"Pete had some paperwork to do, and then his meeting with Briggs' family shortly after the funeral, sir. I know he's busy with that and I didn't want to waste any more time. I'll be quick. I want a case reopened."

"I don't do that."

"What do you mean?" Natalie was taken aback. Crawford was shockingly dismissive, even measured against the standards to which she'd become accustomed.

"I mean if the case has been closed, then it's disrespectful of you to try to reopen it."

"Well, if I may, it's a missing person, and I—"

"Oh brother. Another missing person? Is it a child?"

"No."

"A young woman?"

"No."

"Give me a quick description of the person and the scenario."

"Adult male, with a wife and kid, precarious work situation, recent mental health struggles, potentially tied in with a domestic terrorist organization."

"Not interested. There's no case there. A competent officer already did all the work that needed to be done, and found nothing. He's gone. He's dead, or he'll reappear. And what do you mean, '*if I may*'? What kind of insubordinate talk is that? Check the base in your tone when you speak to a superior. No *you may not* reopen a case. There's plenty of fresh work for you to do. Get back on the beat."

Dejected, Natalie left the office and was on her way back to her patrol car when Pete stopped her: "Ross."

She turned. "Yes?"

"I'm sorry about before, after the funeral. I took that eulogy pretty hard. The part about the failure. Us failing Briggs. I already took responsibility, but it hit differently to hear his brother talking about it there."

"I know, I understand. It's okay."

"You look like you're pissed."

"More than usual?"

"I see it. Flustered."

"I wanted the Gavril missing person case reopened. I still think he's in with the Freedom Fighters somehow. Either they've got him locked away somewhere, or he's pushing product with them, trying to pay for his kid's schooling. Crawford said no. He wouldn't listen to me."

"Well if it's related to that crew, I wouldn't bank on getting any support anymore. It's my call, so yes you can do some more leg-work on it if you want, but I don't like putting my name to that if Crawford kicked you out of his office just for asking."

"It could be something with Daryl Vickshaw and whatever he's got at his scrapyard. Maybe he's got a bunker there too. I think we've got lots we can move on here, beneficial to both cases. I think—I think there's something very dangerous happening. Something menacing. Something dire."

"I respect your stance here, Ross. And I have faith in your intuition. But this is a losing battle, and your man Lucian might be a lost cause at this point. You want there to be a villain here that we can take down easily, but you're looking for a poor guy who has lost control amidst all the struggles of this world that we're all limping through. It's one helpless person in a sea full of helpless people, all barely treading water. And the villain is on a yacht, not even bothering to look down at us."

"Untouchable?"

"I think so."

"Then maybe our whole vocation is a losing battle."

Feeling heat rush over her, she walked away. "I'm going on break," she said, without turning to look at Pete.

"You've made the right choice, Elroy, listening to me," said Zach, as they walked toward the door of the scrapyard's front office. "You just needed someone to get you to remember that light that's inside you. Remember when I told you about that light?"

"I'll never forget it. Some call it darkness, but we see it for the light that it truly is. I remember."

"Good. Good, patriot. Now let's get this gear and complete our destiny." Zach knocked at the door. "I'd just walk in, him being my family and all, but he's a private type. I respect that."

"What is it?" Daryl Vickshaw hollered from inside.

The two Freedom Fighters shared a puzzled, amused look. "Came to collect, brother. We already got the reserves from Donnie's gas station. Now we need the supplies you said you had organized."

"It's all in the warehouse."

"So come on and help—"

"Busy! I'm busy!" Daryl paused, collecting himself. "Look, I already organized it. Got the stuff in bags. Printed the frames yesterday, assembled all parts myself, and test-fired too. Plenty of ammunition, the vests, everything you need."

"Okay well, if you're not—if you're busy—we'll go get the gear and next time you see us will be on the news. Mickey is standing back and standing by."

"K."

They shared another puzzled look, no smiles this time, and wandered back to the truck, pulling around to the warehouse to find the door open and two heavy canvas bags waiting for them. With nimble fingers that moved swiftly from muscle-memory, Zach and Elroy each loaded an AR-15 assault rifle. After loading, they checked that their spare magazines were packed, estimated the total ammunition, put on their vests, and unzipped the other canvas bag to reveal dozens of smoke bombs, tear gas balls, and flash-bang grenades. Elroy was giddy with excitement, and he turned to Zach to reveal a toothy grin.

"Be still, my heart," he said with a lively laugh.

Zach clapped him on the shoulder and they embraced, sighing in relief and laughing some more.

Unaccustomed to taking her break so early in the day, Natalie wasn't hungry. Though she worked with her belly in a near-constant state of emptiness, she was used to only satiating herself at a certain time of day; further, her frustrations left her without the patience to prepare a meal.

With her headphones on, she slipped her hand into her vest pocket to retrieve her phone. When she went to attach her Incognito, she realized that Lucian's was already attached. She had a sudden panic and looked up as though she'd been caught doing something bad. Collecting herself, she decided to continue listening to Lucian's recordings:

"This is Lucian Gavril, new host of The Power of the Human Voice. We're talking with regular people about their memories, and about their hopes for what they want our world's future to hold; in the spirit of the program, we are trying to connect those two things together—past and future. You may

yearn for some golden era from long ago. So we are asking people: what is that for you? On a personal level, what is the time to which you wish that you—or we as a collective—could return? Perhaps something from when you were a child, or maybe something from before your own time. What does it mean to you to be asked about going back to a better time? What do you think about? Or is the past not enough? Should we be forging an entirely new path? Is there hope for a better life for you and for all of us? These questions may seem to disrupt each other, to pile on top and erase each other. Yet somehow, as my mother and my grandfather both found, a story always emerges. Something authentic, something relatable, something powerful. So please, loyal listeners, sit back and behold, The Power of the Human Voice.

"*Today I'm joined by Karla Valdez, my childhood friend who recently returned to Terrace Bay after two consecutive terms in the Prime Minister's cabinet. Good afternoon, Karla.*"

Good afternoon. Thank you, Lucian. Since this is a new beginning for the program, I thought I could start with a review of how my last several years working in the federal government have shaped my thoughts regarding what the people of Canada want, what we need, and—specifically for your show—what about the past makes people reminisce through a glossy, nostalgic lens, and why.

I entered government at the federal level during a crossroads period, as powerful lobbyists and corporations actually fully became a part of the government itself. Right alongside that change, I noticed several other things happened: there was a significant shift in how and where government resources were allocated; the spectre of foreign terrorism re-emerged in a meaningful way on the podium, in the media, and in public discourse for the first time in many years; and the conversation turned from making the future better to bringing back past greatness, which is also something we've seen before as a society, but not for many decades, at least amongst the vast majority.

I hesitate to say this, but I was disappointed in our government's inability to make positive change for our citizens. No matter what, there always came another bureaucratic misdirection, another source of disruption, another disparate idea crashing down from someone whose influence spreads a much wider net than mine. There were often promises of progress to be had, but the promises continued to ring hollow until the day I left my post.

My passion has always been with increasing opportunities for the youth. I managed to improve some school breakfast programs, and I did whatever I could to increase funding for arts projects, particularly for disadvantaged youth. But everything I managed to accomplish really resulted in me taking from one to give to another. They were all lateral moves. It usually seemed that every positive thing we did was predicated on stripping the worth off something else we needed.

The worst part of all this is that you would think that I was in the best possible position to enact the changes I thought were necessary. But I simply couldn't do it. Maybe no one who takes up public office is ever able to live up to their own expectations. But I came to find there was a large—and ever-growing—dissonance between the most powerful people in office and the average citizen who existed outside of that alabaster authority and upper class access. Every story of a real, average citizen holds no emotional weight amongst the powerful people who make the decisions. You could show the UPC every episode of The Power of the Human Voice and it wouldn't resonate with any of them. They are separated from the masses—they've no skin in the game.

Therefore, us people on the outside—and I felt like an outsider when I was there—are left romancing past encounters, whether on programs like yours, or in day-to-day conversations. 'Remember when? Oh that was the best. If only it could be like that again'. We've painted our pasts in Nabokov's false azure.

And the worse our present-day gets, the more apocryphal our visions of the past become. Would we remember our childhoods so fondly if our todays were pleasant, peaceful, and prosperous? Would the lives of our hardworking great grandparents be enviable if we weren't worried about flash floods, forest fires, and a dwindling supply of drinkable water? If we could go back and relive cherished moments, would we be able to simply forget the struggles and injustices of the world we left behind?

The zeitgeist of the Canadian people is clearly reflected in the praise we heap on our supposed 'great' history, and in the platitudes politicians use to dissuade the public from complaining about their current positions. It's shocking to me that people can't see the paradox in those two things. Be thankful for what you've got, says the UPC—often disguised as the government so as to avoid blame. But also, dream about escaping your nightmare, by focusing on how great things could be if only we returned to the past.

All this in spite of how the national discourse of glorifying the past changed completely when the bodies of thousands of Indigenous children were found in mass graves of residential schools across both the US and Canada. Another common power move is for lobbyists to remind us that our history should be remembered, honoured, appreciated, respected—but only the history we like; only that which is chosen. Not those unmarked graves. Not those human lives. Months went by, and their history was not chosen. We can't blame today's officers, priests, and politicians for decisions made so long ago. Oh no no. Forget it. And if you try to make people remember, it's such an exhausting battle.

I speak from my own experience when I say this: the same type of rhetoric that was used to tell people to shut up and sit down on the back of the bus still persists today. Every time a young person has an idea for change, you can hear the sentiment echoed in one way or another: shut up and sit down.

The past is a prop—a symbol—and we should never underestimate its power over the people. The power of the chosen history.

"A moving insight, and certainly a well-informed perspective, Karla. Thank you. And for you... What holds power over you?"

Well, I'm alone, you know. And I'm alone by choice. I had a plan for how I would accomplish the most I could in my life, and it never involved children or time spent—and I won't say 'wasted', because I'm certainly not interested in judging anyone else's choice—but time spent with a partner. I basically navigated through life just exactly as I imagined I would, until right now. I reached something of a summit, and as you see, I'm disappointed in the result. So now I suppose I'll be left to reflect on some of my life's choices, but not as a way to mope or wallow. That's not how my mind works. But it's definitely enough to give me pause, and to make me plot my next move very carefully.

With that in mind, I suppose it's my ambition that holds power over me. And sometimes it seems it does so in vain. I aspire, and fate chuckles. I still feel that I have an obligation to try to make this world better for people, so that is what I will do, one way or another.

I do already have something in mind, but I don't want to say too much now, since it's just a preliminary thought. But I can tell you this: ancient Aboriginal teachings will tell you that the interfaces between land and water are considered places of power. I may start from there.

"From where?"

Those places of power belong to the people, and not just the wealthiest ones. And that is all I will say for now. Thank you so much for hosting me, Lucian.

Hello listeners. It feels strange to say that opening greeting, since I've not yet been granted permission to release these interviews online. But that's just for the time being. I don't have anyone to interview today, but I felt compelled to share something with all you future listeners out there in the universe.

I've been having a recurring dream lately. As I think is typical of recurring dreams, I didn't actually realize it was recurring until it had happened three or four times—maybe more. I've also never had such lucid dreams, where I feel like I'm actually in control of what is happening around me, which makes the dream stand out all that much more for me. It all feels so real, particularly because I do think I have full agency in this dream universe. However, I know, even as it is happening, that it is separate from my waking life. I know it's the dream world, because of certain points, such as... in this world, I live in the house where I grew up. And in this world, my old friend Remy is often with me, but he has bright yellow hair, which is something the Remy in my waking life has never had.

Anyway, in this dream, I have a strange job, shrouded in mystery. Even to myself, there are details of the job that I don't understand and I don't want to understand. I am part of this group, called The Syndicate. And we bag and tag dead bodies. Every time a truck pulls up, we off-load it in my garage, and it's just bodies. Faceless bodies. I don't mean that I don't know them—I mean they don't have faces. Just flat surfaces instead. And all our faction of The Syndicate does is put them in these big black bags, and we use these bizarre, cartoonish, oversized sort of nail guns to PTHUNK—put a tag on each bag. The tags are meaningless to me. They've got writing on them, but it's a language that I can't read. Bag them, tag them. Put them back in the truck. Don't talk.

Remy drives the truck. He brings them. He eats an apple while we bag and tag. He drives the truck away. That's it.

This is only the second time in my life where I can remember having a recurring dream. As far as I can tell, this one is meaningless and relates to nothing I've ever experienced in my life, except that Remy is there and it's in my childhood home.

The other recurring dream I've had is much more connected to my own trauma: my dad had a horrible accident at work once when I was a teenager. He went into a coma. In reality, he woke up a few weeks later and more or less returned to normal. But in this recurring dream I have, he never wakes up, and my family and I are left struggling to adjust. It's this slow, miserable nightmare. And I wake up with tears in my eyes, often pounding my fist into the mattress, and it always takes me a few seconds to realize that it's not true. Dad woke up. And now I'm awake too.

"Welcome to The Power of the Human Voice. I'm your host, Lucian Gavril, and joining me via video chat today is Elroy, who prefers to use only his given name. Elroy is part of a movement known as the National Force of Freedom Fighters, and we actually met recently through a matter unrelated to my podcast work. Shortly thereafter, I reached out to him again via the group's website, which I must say I was surprised to see had government approval. Elroy, the floor is yours."

All right, thanks. So I wanted to set the record straight about who we are and what we fight for. We are free men who are proud of our history, proud of our heritage, proud of our culture. We think of it like this: pride, for us, is the opposite of shame. We resist the popular leftist agenda of shaming us for who we are and what our forefathers accomplished.

We fight for free speech, for chartered rights, and for Western values. We are not terrorists, despite what the mainstream media used to try to say about us. That's why when you told me you actually wanted to hear our side of it, I was glad to do this interview. You're not one of the brainwashers in the mainstream, and you actually want to listen to what we have to say. In fact, you're one of us. I know there's a light inside you too. I saw it when I first met you. And that light, it has a purpose. Just like my light. So that's why I'm here.

As for the Freedom Fighters, you may see us doing patrols, protecting the streets, protecting public property likes parks and sidewalks. We refuse to let these things get ruined by junkies or protesters, and we as Freedom Fighters have not just a right, but an obligation, to protect them. And no, we are not cops. We do what the cops are unwilling to do. Like a softy toy is going to teach someone to never loot or riot again. It's a farce. Talk to real people out there—not media types—and you'll see that we are revered in the community.

They call us heroes. But we don't like that either. We are anti-heroes. The true anti-heroes that the world needs. The hatchet men you're afraid to ask for but you know you want.

Now we've recently linked up with some financiers. They've added the money, which means we've got the tech support, the hardware, and the bankroll to back up the muscle, the brains, and the skills we already had. So ask yourself, how would we get that kind of financial support if the people didn't agree with our cause?

And we've got boots on the ground. We make our presence known so that people who think the same as us know they don't have to be afraid anymore. Just like in the glory days in 2016, when the patriots before us relearned that we are kings and we don't need to act ashamed and hide our pride anymore. We know there's power in numbers, and our numbers are growing daily. You've seen our compound, yourself. You've seen our people—our soldiers. Not some rubber bullet snowflakes. People ready to do whatever it takes.

Truly, there's no stopping us now. The people have spoken. We've got something big cooking. They don't want me talking about it, but it doesn't matter. I can do what I want now and I know it won't change the end result. Better for you to hear it from me so no one else takes credit. Amanita wants it one way, but Paul and Evan want it another way, and we do it our way.

"So are you going to tell me the specifics?"

There's change coming. And when it happens, you'll know it was the National Force of Freedom Fighters who liberated Canada.

I'm sorry again, as I've not been able to keep up with bills these days, so I don't have an internet connection right now, and I've had to cancel my latest interview. I made some money recently, but it went straight to our son's education. Family comes first. However, the good news is that since meeting my last guest, Elroy, I've continued to have steady employment, which should bode well for this program. But without a guest today, instead, I thought I could check in and tell you something strange that happened to me earlier.

I took my boy, David, to the park. We were lucky with lots of sunshine today. We went and we had a really good time. Usually it's hard for me to connect with him. He used to talk so much—constant questions, always wanting to learn. But lately he's so introverted, and I guess I am too. Maybe I don't see him enough, between this project and with my contract work with the Freedom Fighters. Anyway, David and I just hadn't talked much lately. Ava balances us out, but I don't always like being around her anymore. I can't be near her because of the way her aura radiates. Light just beams off her. It's exhausting.

This day started out great. We were laughing and chatting on the walk there. Then we were climbing on all the playground equipment, and racing around and going down the slides. But then I noticed there was this cartoon picture up beside the top of one of the slides. And the picture shows a huge playground with all these little cartoon kids having fun, and the sun shining above them, and it's sort of this very nice but completely forgettable scene—except there's one solitary image in there. It's a boy on the ground, with his knees pulled close and his head buried in them with his shoulders hunched. It's a cartoon designed specifically for this park, so why is there a kid alone and crying in there? It doesn't make any sense. And he has ashes smeared on his clothes and skin. And as I looked really closely, I could see there were words written around him, in a circle all the way around his little body. And the words are written in a light grey, so you can barely see them on the white background. It said 'Misery Simulator'.

I couldn't play with David after that. I couldn't focus. I couldn't explain it to him either. We just went home.

Another fresh batch of bodies last night. Seemed like more than usual. Most of them were charred. Some fell into ashes when I tried to tag them. The work is so tiring. Monotonous plus hard on my back, lifting all the dead weight. And I was deducted pay for the bodies that turned to ash. I needed that money. We needed it. I woke up today and I could feel the pain all up my spine. I'm used to hard labour, but not like this. Not with the demoralizing aspect too. I tried to explain it to Ava, but she doesn't get it. You have to experience it. It's tough to keep my dream life separate from my waking life, but I suppose I have to, if no one in my waking life can ever understand.

There's an infinite number of devastating situations for which most people are completely unprepared, because they honestly believe it could never happen to them.

When I saw the fire, I didn't think, I just reacted. I dropped the leash and ran straight for the house. Frank chased right in after me. It wasn't like you'd think, because the movies can't show you how hot it really is. And people understand that it would be hard to breathe, but they don't know about the stabbing pain in your eyes, how hard it is to see between the blinding light of flames and suffocating fog of smoke and the black night that surrounds it.

After two breaths, it was like I had crushed glass in my lungs. And I'm still not thinking. It's not even registered to me yet that I'm truly here. I'm about to die and I have no idea where the kids are. I've never been in this house. I've never met this family. I don't even know how many people I'm looking for... or if there are kids at all.

And yes I got one out. But only one of them. And not Frank. And people called me a hero. But I didn't see it that way. I think about that other kid every day. And I dream about that burning house. Every single night. I hate sleeping. There's no peace for me anymore.

You spend all your days thinking your life is this one thing, this one way. And then one day it's something completely different and you're no longer at all the person you were before, or maybe you never were that person. And that's not something that happens to everyone. But that's what happened to me.

'He knew who he was, but he couldn't come to terms with why he wasn't like everyone else'. That's what a tattoo said—along the top of a bicep, all the way down the wrist—on one of the bodies last night.

This time was different though. Some of the bodies were still warm, and some of them were breathing. Slowly. Way slower than what's normal for a human being. I don't know what to say about it, because Remy says we aren't allowed to ask questions. The cash comes, so I can't complain. As soon as I open my mouth, one of the other guys gives me a look. No talking anymore. We don't talk about anything. I don't know when the rules changed, but now we're just mute the whole time. It's like every shift is different now; I can feel how The Syndicate is prepping us for July seventeenth. All systems off.

Remy's hair was the normal dark brown, almost black. Not bright yellow anymore... he's trying to tell me something. I think it was Waking Remy sending me a message, since we can't talk. The Syndicate is after me. When

I'm in my dream world, they can tell what I'm thinking. They know that I know that we're not getting what we deserve. Not enough compensation, not enough information. Not for a job like this, where all we do is slug and break our backs, and dozens of people have lost their lives every time. Who are these people? Are they other members of The Syndicate? Other people who think like I do, and talk too much about things that are supposed to be left unsaid? What is this work that we're doing?

Remy knew to warn me. And he was able to cross over. Which means the people that are coming for me must be able to cross over too. I think I know who they are. That pawn I interviewed a few weeks ago—he's one of them. They've got me driving the truck here in the waking world. I'm the Remy here. I think they'll try to get rid of me next shipment. But I'll be ready. I can still be a hero. I've just gotta get through a few more nights of bagging and tagging. I need to stay alive until then though. One more night at home. One more recording tomorrow morning. Then I'll be on the move. I'm the problem.

David's body was in the truck. He was older, maybe sixteen. But it was him. Burns covered much of his body. And the others were watching me closely when I bagged him. They wanted to see what I would do. I was scrunching up my face and pawing at my nose, pretending I had to sneeze. But I think they knew I was holding back tears. These monsters. They're coming for my family now too. It's too late for me. But I can punch a hole in their operation—just a few more days.

If someone finds this, just know I did what I did to save other people from the Misery Simulator. I don't know how they got it inside my head and plugged me into their world. But they did it. And I will stop them from doing it to someone else. They'll be the ones whose lives are burned to the ground this time.

This poem was in David's pocket last night. I snatched it before I bagged him:

I thought you two were heroes
With love just for me
But you are not a hero
And neither is she

Once when I was young, someone asked me about my grandpa's program, and how it made me feel, given that I didn't really know him. I didn't know what to say about that. But the person asked me what I would ask my grandfather if I could see him that day. And I said... I'd ask him if he's proud of me.

This is Lucian Gavril, signing off from the final segment of The Power of the Human Voice.

"Carter is in your zone right now while you finish desk duty, so she'll keep an eye out—though it's not much to go on—but I wanted to tell you anyway," Pete said to Aleem, standing up straight but resting a hand gently on top of the front desk. "There was a report of suspicious activity. A truck—"

Just then, Natalie entered the room, out of breath, her lungs searing: "Pete, I need to tell you something."

"Just a second," Pete replied, without looking at her, then continued talking to Aleem. "A report of a truck with snow on the windshield, and someone loading a barrel onto the back. The barrel was taken out of a mechanic's garage over on Virgil Avenue. The person who filed the report said they thought the truck was white or light grey, but it was still dark out, five o'clock this morning. He said there's never anyone around the garage—or at that business at all—until closer to six. So when you're out of here, follow up with the business owner. See if they've noted anything missing from their stock."

Aleem had been looking at Natalie. He nodded at Pete's instructions, then extended a hand, palm up, offering the floor to Natalie.

Still, she hesitated, looking back and forth between the two men. "I... I took something from the Gavril house. I didn't mean to tamper or overstep, I just took it because I left in such a hurry when I was sick." She waited. The men waited too. "Or I don't know why I took it."

"Ross." Pete turned his head to Aleem and then directly back to Natalie. His expression didn't change. "You sound distressed, and I want you to know that you need to be careful, but right here right now, it is safe to say whatever you need to say."

"If there's a problem," Aleem said, giving Pete a quick nod of agreement before returning his eyes to Natalie and continuing, "we're the ones who can help."

Composing herself, Natalie continued, "I think the Freedom Fighters are the arsonists, and I don't care what upper management and oversight want. We should pursue this. The recordings on this device make it clear to me that Lucian Gavril—my missing person—is in a dangerous mental state, and the Freedom Fighters are likely the serial arsonists. And if they're not, Lucian certainly thinks they are anyway, and I'm not sure where this could all lead."

"There's a recording." Aleem was forthright, with an almost-imperceptible tinge of guilt in his tone.

"What's that?" Pete said.

"We should go see Chan in evidence. I'll explain on the way."

They left quickly, and as they entered the hallway, they ran directly into Deputy Chief Crawford.

"Where are you three going in such a hurry? And why all together? I see why Gilchrist complains about all the waste on your platoon," he said, stepping in front of them. Just then, Natalie received a phone call, showed her phone to the others, and excused herself. Crawford continued, "Canizales, I need to speak with you privately. And you," he looked at Aleem, "get on the road."

Pete followed Crawford's orders, and Aleem moved on, quickly breaking into a run the rest of the way to the evidence room.

"Ross, it's Inspector Gilchrist."

"Yes, I can see your name on my phone."

"Yeah, I guess I'm just surprised because I didn't think you'd answer if you knew it was me."

Natalie didn't speak. A pause with a purpose.

"Well, I wanted to ask a favour of you. Oakshot is back on today. Oversight wants time to review the case, but they saw no reason to keep him off. They're hard-asses, but they know we're understaffed. Anyway, I want Oak to ride with you for patrol today. Don't tell anyone. I just know it will be good for him. I read your file since we last spoke. You've got a great track record. Canizales also spoke very highly of you. I'm still going through the gamut and have been getting grilled, in and out of meetings with all these oversight guys I've never even met before. Look, I may be in a bit of trouble here; I think I let Pete and you guys off the leash too much. So please just see if you can teach Oakshot a thing or two. He's been in cells all morning."

"Understood. I'll go get him before I start my next patrol."

"Thank you."

"And... good luck with the Oversight Committee."

"Yeah... Yeah, we'll see."

"Don't sit down," Crawford instructed Pete. "This won't take long. A complaint has been submitted against you—claims of excessive force and harassment. This Elroy Maitland is saying he's had cruisers tailing him ever since he was released on bail. Further, he claims this isn't the first time he's noticed he's been tailed; he says your men have been staking out his residence consistently for quite some time."

Pete knew it was futile to try to interject and defend himself. He waited, and Crawford continued to explain.

"He's threatened the service with a lawsuit for the harassment, and his statement throws around a lot of accusations—planted evidence. Tampering. He thinks you've got a grudge, and he named others. He had badge numbers. Specific dates and details of incidents. All with officers under your command... Are you going to say anything?"

"I'm waiting until you're finished, sir."

"I'm finished."

"I can assure you that Elroy's claims are baseless and he's balking. He's trying to get out from under the mess he's made, and the thought that you're buying what he's selling makes me certain that he's a flight risk. This is a guy who is going to be serving serious time unless he has pertinent information that he's willing to share regarding the various arms dealing, criminal affiliations, and terrorist projects that he's a part of."

"You guys," Crawford chuckled. "You guys and that word, 'terrorist'. Not everyone who gets booked is a terrorist or a Nazi or whatever other buzzword."

"May I finish?"

"No. No, I didn't want to get into it like this with you. You've been given an order and that order is this: leave Elroy and his people alone. He'll have his day in court. We don't need the negative press and the protesters and the lawsuits. Leave him alone. That's it."

"What zone are we in?" Oakshot asked Natalie as she pulled him from the holding cells at the station. "And thanks for getting me out of there. I hate working cells."

"We're assigned to zone one, but we're going out of town for a bit first."

"So as soon as I'm back on, you're taking me off scheduled duty so that we can both do something against orders together? Shit." He chuckled. Natalie began to respond, but Oakshot started softly making trumpet sounds, apparently not actually concerned with getting a reply, and then he stopped as an idea dawned on him: "Let me get a snack first."

With a coffee and a cookie, Oakshot entered the passenger side of Natalie's cruiser. He watched as Natalie spoke, outside the vehicle, with Aleem.

"I've confirmed it. New evidence. Undeniable. Elroy and his morbidly obese friend are on a neighbour's surveillance video, clearly starting the fire on Memorial Street. The one where the child died. After I told Pete, he was right back into Crawford's office, getting torched for insubordination. But Crawford couldn't deny the evidence. They were going down to see Chan to watch the video when I left. I just wanted to catch you before you left too. Are you going to look for your missing person?"

"Yes, I just need to look at the scrapyard in The Wilderness. I think he might be there. In the area, anyway. Or worse, maybe just his body."

"I'll keep an eye out too. I know it's not much help. But I'm patrolling in zone three anyway, so that I'll be near the Freedom Fighters' compound when the call comes that they're wanted for arson."

"Don't rush in though."
"I won't."
"Good luck."
"You too."

Natalie and Oakshot exited the parking lot and began driving west, with The Blade on one side and mansions on the other. They drove slowly, mindful of the dense pedestrian traffic in the area. Oakshot leaned forward, looking past Natalie to admire the large and well-maintained mansion properties: healthy green grasses, trimmed hedges, white picket fences, wrap around porches, rooftop terraces. "That one's even got a garden," Oakshot commented, as though Natalie was admiring right along with him.

Soon, they entered The Junk neighbourhoods west of The Blade. Oakshot split his cookie in half. Steam emerged from the coffee cup and the mingled scents of fresh coffee and cinnamon spice filled the air as he dipped one half into the cup. He held the cookie in a moment too long, and it fell apart and plopped back into the cup when he tried to bring it to his mouth.

"Dammit," he said with a smile. Natalie's hands gripped a little tighter on the steering wheel. He ate the other half of the cookie all at once, without dipping, then hastily took a drink of the coffee as he chewed.

Looking out the window and squinting a bit as the sun poured in, he remarked, "I don't mind doing this. I hope we find your guy. I'll just be so much happier when this—when my own thing—blows over and I can get back on some bigger action. I can't wait to crush a door again, honestly. You'd think I'd want to avoid it after the last one, but that's not it at all. I want redemption—for all of us—from the last raid. I shouldn't say I want to forget it, because that would mean forgetting Briggs and Cormac. But... I don't know."

"You'd forget your own mistakes too then."

"True. Hard to do better next time without that memory. Why are you driving this way, anyway?"

"I just want to check my missing person's neighbourhood before we leave town. It'll only be a minute to drive by his house."

"This route reminds me of driving through Pennsylvania toward Michigan, when I was a kid. Pennsylvania was nice. Scenic. But it got dumpier the closer we got to Michigan. By the time we were in Michigan, the roads were awful and all the billboard advertisements were either for fireworks stores or anti-abortion crusade groups." Oakshot pointed at a house that had been abandoned before it was fully built. "And this place! Every time I drive past, there's someone new wandering in or out of that skeleton of a house. It's like it's on a loop, like in a video game."

After passing by the Gavril residence, Natalie and Oakshot began their drive north, into The Wilderness. They drove past a former public school—recently converted into a joint venture between a gene editing lab and a cosmetic surgery clinic—and a pair of old farmhouses. Both farmhouses had been purchased by government contractors, and the demolition crews were hard at work, tearing the houses down to make space for another monstrous building, in the same style as The Blade. Another blade-style building could potentially double the city's population, allowing for a gentrification of the old town and its lower-income residents, partially built properties, and crumbling houses.

"They're not hiding it," Oakshot quipped.

"What's that?" said Natalie, her eyes fixed on the road but her mind drifting elsewhere.

"They're not trying to hide anything anymore. Get rid of *the poors* as soon as possible. Push them out to The Wilderness. Like every city that bids to host an Olympics. Terrace Bay's going the way of Toronto now. I couldn't afford to live here if they didn't set us up with housing." Oakshot paused, though he again didn't seem concerned with getting a response from Natalie. Eventually, he turned to her with a wry smile and said, "It's the illusion of progress."

Natalie's phone buzzed in her vest pocket. She answered the call, from Ava: "Hi Ava. Is everything all right?"

"Lucian's truck is gone. I didn't know whether to report it stolen, or just assume he came and got it. That's why I called you instead."

"Okay, yes, I'm glad you called me personally. I'm back on the case now, and I've got some leads. I'll talk to a few colleagues and get them to watch for the truck. Given your neighbourhood and the weather we've been having, I wouldn't be surprised if it's just been stolen. Was there any broken glass on the driveway? Or sign of forced entry into your home?"

"Nothing that I've seen."

"And what's the make, model, and colour?"

"It's a big four-door Ford, light blue. It has a plow on the front, and he's got his company logos all over—on the sides, on the bumper, on the windshield. You can't miss this truck."

"Yeah, I remember it now."

"I think he's gone. I think he's gone for good."

"I wouldn't say this if I didn't mean it, Ava, but I don't think so."

Ava sighed before replying, "One of our pictures is gone too. He took it right off the wall… it's the only thing missing. I'm ready Natalie, if this is it. Text me if you think I should report the truck stolen. Be safe today."

When Natalie hung up, she felt Oakshot looking at her, but she kept her eyes on the road.

"We could turn around," said Oakshot. "Makes no difference to me. We can try to find that truck. I know you put a lot of work into this case."

"Well, what we're doing now is part of the same case. I think he might be out here in the woods somewhere. I have to figure the truck was stolen."

"They'd have had to go in the house and get his keys, likely. I heard most of what she said to you—no sign of forced entry and the truck obviously wasn't already idling. Seems like it'd take a pretty slick thief to do that, so not an addict, or it's just your man come home then took off."

Natalie thought about it. She turned the details over in her mind, considered the likeliest possibilities. She remained unconvinced, having a hard time settling on an outcome that she didn't want to believe.

"Maybe I'm too wrapped up in this," she admitted.

"It happens. Can't be helped with the volume of calls we get. Something's bound to stick to you. A victim that reminds you of yourself, or something like that. I don't mean to make assumptions, I'm just saying."

"Wait." Natalie put her hand to Oakshot's forearm, not quite holding it, letting her fingers rest gently. "Pete and Aleem were talking about a suspicious truck with snow on the windshield."

"Pft. Good luck finding a truck based on that description, after the thaw we've had."

"Lucian's truck has his business name in big white letters at the base of the windshield. The description fits. What else would it be? Not real snow, not this morning."

"I'll call it in."

"No. Well, yes. Do it. But send Aleem and Pete both texts too. Tell them I think this is severe—potentially very dangerous. Lucian might have stolen something extremely corrosive or explosive. Tell dispatch that too."

Aleem stayed close to the Freedom Fighters' compound, hoping he wouldn't get any service calls, and expecting to be able to complete an arrest of Elroy soon. But twenty minutes went by, then thirty, and still there was no word from base. No word from Pete. He circled the blocks, gradually expanding his perimeter, but returning to complete the loop at his starting point, the compound. He reached the outer block of his zone, then continued his route, this time making his perimeter gradually smaller. Still no word from base.

Worried he may have already aroused some suspicion, he decided to drive past just once more, then avoid the compound for a while. He turned the corner onto Elroy's street, and noted an unmarked black sedan parked across from the compound. "An overseer," he whispered to himself, recognizing the clean lines, matte black paint, and dark window tints of the Oversight Committee cruisers.

As he looked directly at the overseer, movement in his periphery drew his attention back to the compound's entrance: Gavril Plow: Snow, Tow, Contract Work. Despite its filthy exterior, Lucian's truck was unmistakeable.

Laser-focused, forgetting the Oversight Committee, Aleem fell back several car-lengths, creating space, slowing down below the speed limit, allowing another vehicle to turn in front of him. His eyes remained fixed on Lucian's truck in the distance as he radioed for backup.

Pete rushed to his cruiser and sped toward the compound, maintaining constant contact with Aleem, who remained in pursuit. Meanwhile, Cst. Carter joined from a nearby zone, filing in behind Aleem's car.

"There are two people in that truck, Staff. Hard to make out the one on the passenger side; he's quite small or he's hunching down to hide, but there's definitely someone sitting there," said Aleem.

"I'm a few blocks out. Get close now. Assess their reaction when they see you. If they don't flee, go ahead and flash your lights, pull them over somewhere with open space."

Aleem passed the car ahead of him and pulled in close behind the truck. The truck slowed down a bit, typical of anyone who notices a police car, but there were no other warning signs. Aleem briefly sounded his siren and flashed his lights, then followed as the truck began a gradual and seemingly hesitant process of pulling over.

"I've got a bright blue, full-sized, Ford pickup truck, licence plate Victor Bravo Delta Yankee 126, pulled over on the shoulder on the 400 block of Egerton Street. Data reads that this truck is registered to one Lucian Gavril. This is possibly a stolen vehicle and definitely in possession of stolen goods in the bed—perhaps toxic or flammable. Preparing for a high-risk vehicle extraction."

With swift expertise, Carter pulled up near Aleem, angling the nose of the vehicle in and blocking much of the road. Coming from the opposite direction, Pete turned in, perpendicular across the road.

Flanked by Pete and Aleem, Carter stepped out of her cruiser with her firearm drawn and aimed. Her fellow officers did the same, and Aleem began with instructions. This was a routine they had practised in training and tested in the field many times, but the pressures remained high regardless of experience.

From within the vehicle, Zach and Elroy had exchanged a defeated look when they were first stunned by Aleem's siren. Before they'd even stopped the vehicle, they began their backup plan.

"Are you ready to die, patriot?" Elroy said, with complete conviction.

"Not today, Elroy." Zach's voice was steady. "Quickly now, you call Mickey, tell him to meet at Daryl's. I'll call Daryl. They have more supplies. They'll finish the job. And you and I will see another day to continue the fight for freedom."

They quickly linked hands, then scrambled to make the calls. Soon, Aleem began his firm, loud, clear instructions. Zach followed along with a steady hand, removing the keys and placing them out the window and on top of the vehicle, doing exactly as Aleem commanded, while he had his brother-in-law on speakerphone:

"We're cooked, patriot. Pigs are about to bust us as we speak. Mickey is on his way to you. Finish the job. Scorched earth. Spare nothing and no one. The message must be clear. Poison the water. Bomb The Blade. Burn the landfill. Make sure the world knows the National Force of Freedom Fighters. Let them see your light."

On the other end of the call, Daryl Vickshaw agreed to the terms and wished his brother-in-law good luck. Standing beside with a long and boney hand on Daryl's shoulder, Lucian hung up the phone for him. Severely beaten and duct taped to a desk chair, Daryl was helpless.

Outside the scrapyard, Natalie and Oakshot walked through the sparse woods, looking for tire tracks, freshly shovelled dirt, tools, clothes, cigarette butts, embers, ashes, food scraps—any sign of recent human activity.

"Why don't we just go in there? The building is right there. If he's got nothing to hide, he won't mind us looking around."

"Not this guy. I've read his file, and we've seen what his friends and family are capable of. If he's got Lucian mixed in with their business, either we're too late, or we'll have to find out through questioning the others, once Aleem hauls them in."

"Then Ross... really, what are we doing out here?"

"I don't know," she admitted, frustrated at her own uncertainty.

Still, they looked. They meandered closer and closer to Daryl Vickshaw's property, until they were mere metres from the front gate. The wind had risen steadily during their search, and the chains dangling from the wrought iron gate clinked and clanged.

"Gate's wide open for us, boss. Cross the street and we're in," Oakshot teased.

"No. Not today." Natalie took one look through the gate, toward the concrete building ahead, wearing an expression as though she was staring directly through it—not really looking at anything at all—just thinking with her eyes open. She was entranced by her own feeling of helplessness, frustrated that she simply didn't know what to do.

Then a tall, slim figure walked slowly past the window. And back again. And again. Pacing back and forth methodically, but with arms flailing violently.

"He's in there," she said, as she moved in on the building,

drawing her softy to the ground. Oakshot followed suit, drawing his firearm.

With three pistols pointed at them, Zach and Elroy were laying flat, face-first on the pavement. Elroy studied the back of Zach's head while sucking in breaths, trying to stop himself from hyperventilating—this felt very different from the time at his compound. Zach maintained a blank look, moving slowly, following instructions. Even as he dragged himself across the ground, army-crawling forward at Aleem's command, his expression remained listless. It was as though no one was watching him and even Aleem wasn't there—just a voice he followed.

It wasn't until a small crowd of onlookers gathered—each holding up a phone, ignoring Pete's calls to step back and disperse—that Zach's demeanor changed. As Carter cuffed him, he cried out like he had awakened from a nightmare; shocked gasps rang out from the crowd. "Police brutality! Get off me! I'm not resisting!" he screamed. Even Carter was surprised, despite her ample previous experience making arrests.

"Just keep working," Pete coached Carter, his firearm still pointed at Elroy on the pavement. "Do it right. Nothing fancy. Nothing aggressive. Just get him in the car."

All the way up and into the car, Zach hollered about his rights, his lawyer, his liberties, his freedom, his family, his needs, his demands.

When both Freedom Fighters were cuffed and in the cruiser, they were smiling. Elroy's anxiety had been squashed by Zach's performance, and he was beaming as the rear passenger door shut. They shared a look and a laugh, noticing the dirt and red imprints the pavement had left on their faces.

A search of the truck revealed all the contents of Daryl's canvas bags, as well as other tactical gear, blueprints of The Blade, a barrel of pure cyanide, and both incendiary and fragmentation bombs. Further, tucked under the seat on the passenger side was a framed photo of the Gavril family. Minutes later, Aleem entered the cruiser to take Zach and Elroy away.

"Hey can I get my cuffs put to the front? This is inhumane. It's a human rights issue. I'm not an animal. It hurts," Zach requested, his voice calm in a complete reversal from the moment of his arrest.

"Absolutely not," Aleem said.

"Wowwww," an elated Zach said, turning his head and lifting his eyebrows while he looked at Elroy. His whole face was a smile.

"So funny," Elroy chuckled.

"Is it?" questioned Aleem as he shifted into reverse. "Or are you just laughing because you think you're supposed to?"

"Police! We have the building surrounded. Step outside slowly and with your hands high," Natalie ordered.

There was no response. No voice. No frantic movement. Nothing. Oakshot looked to Natalie, ice in his eyes. She gave him a subtle 'no', shake of the head.

"We will enter the premises if you don't exit slowly in the next thirty seconds," Natalie proclaimed. She jerked her arm like she was starting a tiny lawnmower, retracting her softy. Then she drew her service pistol—a Glock 17X, law enforcement model.

Natalie held her left hand to her heart and filled her lungs like she was atop a mountain—the act itself slowed her heart rate and cleared her mind. With a renewed vision, she radioed for backup and advanced toward the door. Oakshot lowered his pistol, aiming to the ground as he followed. Natalie announced herself again and entered, scanning the room in milliseconds, finding her pistol aimed at the chest of Lucian Gavril, who stood motionless beside Daryl. With a hand on Daryl's shoulder, Lucian looked like he was posing for a photo.

Daryl had been beaten to a nearly unrecognizable state—his face a swollen and bloody mask. The residual effects of exposure to pepper spray were visible around Lucian's eyes, with his repeated blinking as his only movement. Daryl could barely lift his head to look at Natalie—who had lowered her pistol—and his vision was so diminished that he wouldn't have had any idea who she was if not for the effect of the uniform.

"Shoot him," Daryl mumbled. It was all he could muster.

"Get on the fucking ground!" screamed Oakshot, pushing his gun in a pulsing motion as he emphasized the last two words. "I will put one through your skull right here in this dump if you don't!"

"Stop!" Natalie said to Oakshot. "No weapon, no weapon. He doesn't have a weapon. Lower your pistol, Oak." Hesitantly, Oakshot listened.

"Lucian," she began, "My name is Natalie Ross, and I'm here to make sure this situation ends without you or anyone else being hurt any further than they've been already." Finally, Lucian reacted, simply shifting his weight to one foot. Natalie waited, but he didn't speak or move any further.

"I know your wife. I met your son, David. Ava's been looking for you, hoping you'll come home. I just spoke to her on the phone, and whatever has happened already or whatever you're thinking you want to do here, it's not worth dying over. It's not worth never seeing them again." Lucian's knuckles went white as he tightened his grip on Daryl's shoulder.

"I'll cuff him," Oakshot said, and he took one step forward, but stopped himself, looking at Natalie for confirmation as Lucian—with blood on his hands and a vacant stare in his eyes—squared his shoulders and readied himself to fight.

"No. Just wait," Natalie implored him.

"Officer Oakshot here is going to take care of the man in the chair, Lucian. And his colleagues—Elroy and the others—they've been captured. We know what happened. We know they started the fires. We're preventing further suffering, Lucian. We've stopped them, and your recordings helped us—Ava showed me your work. You did it, Lucian. You're a hero. Now... don't give them the chance to say you're the villain. David may not understand your pain, but he will never be able to forget the choice that you make right now. Never."

"How?"

"How what?"

"How did you find out about the Misery Simulator? How did you catch them after weeks of nothing? No leads, no follow-up. Like you didn't even care."

"We found footage. It's all recorded, Lucian. I'm telling you: it's over."

At that, with little hesitation and both his facial expression and body language completely unchanged, Lucian relented. He began walking toward the officers, and Oakshot lifted his gun again: "Hands high. Walk slowly."

"I'll take him outside," Natalie intervened. "Backup is en route. Untie this guy. See if you can patch him up at all. Radio for an ambulance too."

"Got it."

Lucian listened and turned, presenting his hands and accepting instructions willingly. Natalie cuffed him, noting how vascular his forearms were—veins like blood-pumping branches.

As Natalie escorted Lucian outside, Oakshot began cutting the tape to release Daryl. He kept his pace measured, giving himself time to think, offering Daryl sips of water and brief words of reassurance while he worked at the tape.

"What's your name, sir?"

"Daryl... Vickshaw."

"Okay. Here, have a drink. We keep these bottles handy." He watched as Daryl lifted his head, took a pull, looked to the ceiling, and spit most of the water out onto his own face. He then wiped at the blood with the shirtsleeve of his one free arm.

"Here, take my hanky. I always carry one." From his pocket, Oakshot retrieved a black handkerchief with white polka dots. "This one's a relic, but I keep it fresh." Daryl looked at him out of the side of his eye, taking the handkerchief begrudgingly, then wiping his eyes and snorting bloody snot into it. He tossed it on the ground.

"Can you hurry up?" Daryl had regained his senses.

"Sure, sure. Is this your business?"

"Yeah."

"So you own this building and property?"

"Of course."

"So what's here is yours?"

"Yes, obviously, you fucking asshole. Now just get that psycho out of here and leave me alone." He coughed and sputtered at that, burning through his energy reserves.

"No problem," Oakshot said, finishing all his knife-work to release Daryl, who first touched his toes, then sat up again, arching his back and stretching. Oakshot looked around some more and then pointed, saying, "But over here—that pepper spray—was that his weapon?"

"Oh yeah. He brought that."

"Did he bring anything else?"

"Holy shit, no! Fuck off."

"So everything else here is yours?"

"Yes! Now listen: this is my land and my property and I have a right to defend it, and you are no longer welcome here. So I want you the hell out. Now!" He tried to keep screaming, but coughed up blood and keeled over, sitting back down. Oakshot let him feel the weight of the silence.

"Okay, you're under arrest for all these stolen family photos on the wall."

"What?"

"I recognize at least two people in different photos, both of whom I've written up reports for after property thefts," Oakshot explained. He shook his head with a scoffing laugh, a little too self-assured as he reached for his cuffs.

With her patrol car miles away, Natalie sat Lucian down on a parking block surrounded by tufts of choked yellow grass. She stayed two metres away, dropped to a knee, and spoke softly to him. "What do you need from me right now?"

He continued to look at the ground: "Help."

"That's what I want to do. Yes, you are handcuffed, and at some point we're going to have to get the full picture of everything you've done and all the places you've been since your disappearance. But I'm here to listen first. Ask questions later. If you have a need that must be fulfilled, we are going to handle that first." Again she waited, her posture relaxed, continuing to look at Lucian.

"I'll ask you three questions, and I want you to think about them. Prioritize if one is more important than another right away. And maybe these questions will help you think if there's something else you need: Have you eaten? Do you need medication? Would you like to speak with your wife?"

Lucian sighed. "Would you believe me if I told you that I'm a man who wants for nothing? Or I was."

"Until recently?"

"Until the fire."

"When other officers come, I want you to know that you're my priority. I'll be the one with you. Contact with your family, and a trip to the hospital for medical evaluation will be prioritized well ahead of anything else... and I do believe you, Lucian. You may not believe me on this, but I've come to know you over the past few days. I respect you. I care about you. And I am here for you."

Lucian looked at her, then past her, to see another car pulling in through the gates. Noting Natalie's uniform, the driver—Mickey—sped up as he swerved around piles of junk and moved to ram her. She turned, stood, and jumped out of the way. Midair, her foot was thumped by the car with a loud but nearly painless impact.

Lifting his feet and pivoting on his butt so that he could grip both hands to the outside of the vehicle, Mickey heaved himself out of the car and rounded it from the rear, advancing on Natalie. Lucian stood, his hands still cuffed and his feet pressed against the parking block, only to have Mickey shove him over. He fell with enough force to do a backward somersault, ending up on his side, unable to break the fall.

Natalie seized the moment, playing up what appeared to be a lower-body injury, limping backward, a pleading look on her face, eyeing the building's front door and expecting Oakshot to emerge.

Inside, Daryl found Mickey's arrival a blessing: Oakshot

looked out the window while he had his cuffs in his hand, and Daryl, still oozing blood and badly concussed, turned to attack Oakshot: he grabbed Oak around the waist. He first tried to tip Oak over, and then after failing, bit Oak's neck and began an attempt to pry his pistol from its holster. He held the butt of the pistol, but couldn't release it. Oak abandoned his cuffs and grabbed his attacker's hand with both of his own, pushing down with all his force then peeling the fingers back. Daryl squinted and screamed, blood now lining all his teeth; one loose tooth rattled as he screamed, then fell out, click-clacking across the floor.

The man was a bull, but in an incredibly weakened state. When plans A and B failed him, he just as much gave up as was simultaneously overpowered and defeated by Oakshot, who tripped and tackled him, turning him over with relative ease, reaching to find the cuffs on the floor close by, and finishing the job as chaos ensued outside the building.

Glancing behind him at the fallen Lucian, then turning to look at Natalie, Mickey touched his chest pocket, then reached back to his rear waist, as though checking that his pants were pulled up enough. But he noted Lucian's obvious limitations and Natalie's apparent helplessness, then laughed a big belly laugh, and slowed down to match Natalie's backward-stepping pace.

"Look atcha," he said, "like a little girl." He looked her up and down, licking his lips, still drinking in exhausted breaths, but savouring the moment. "All them little toys around your waist, but too scared to even use one. And your poor leg. Your poor leg."

He grabbed a spring-release knife from his chest pocket, taking obvious pleasure in springing it open. Natalie rounded the corner of the building, getting Lucian out of her background for when she prepared to draw. She made an obvious shift of her head, showing her change in focus to let Mickey see the fear the knife brought her; she even managed a little gasp.

"No no, honey. Don't worry about the knife. It's not this thing in my hand. It's me. I'm what you need to fear."

"You can't do that," she pleaded.

"But do you think that I won't?"

With Lucian out of sight and Oakshot still in the building, Natalie drew her softy and slammed one rubber bullet into each of Mickey's quadriceps.

"Oh you fucking slut," he cried, falling to his knees. He propped himself onto one knee, planted both his hands onto that support knee, and forced himself up with all his effort. Without trying to take another step, he reached back at his waistband again. But he struggled, like he couldn't find an itch. Like he couldn't quite reach a bug biting his back.

Finally, with sweat dripping from his beard and pooling all over his shirt, he got the pads of his thumb and middle finger onto what he was searching for: he snatched a fully loaded, .40 calibre Glock-22 pistol from his beltline. The gun's comically large, extended magazine housed thirty-two rounds of ammunition. He exhaled a stimulated sigh as he felt the grip of the gun, but his triumphant movement was rushed. His knees buckled as he moved to whip the gun around and point it at Natalie, and he sent the pistol flying into the wall of the building.

In a shocking moment of clarity, he realized the magnitude of his misstep. He looked at Natalie like a wounded dog; she had already drawn her service pistol and had it aimed at his face. "Step to your left," she said, fully in control.

"It hurts," he said, limping a little line dance.

"Get on the ground."

Hunched over, he held a hand up to signal her to be patient, then he reached a thumb and one finger into the tiny fifth pocket of his jeans, despite Natalie's urges to stop. He pinched an Incognito device and pulled it out, showing it to her and then letting a thick rope of spit drip from his mouth onto the device; he rubbed it in to erase the device's contents. Natalie let him have it. Despite the show he made of it, the act brought him little satisfaction. From there, he tried to move carefully to his knees upon Natalie's command, but he involuntarily collapsed instead, provoking a feeble groan.

By the time she got him sprawled out, cuffed him, and

brought him back to his knees, he had regained his breath enough to continue berating her. She remained silent in spite of all his slights, until he finally gave up trying to antagonize her.

"You got lucky," he muttered.

An oversight agent came to speak individually with all officers involved in the apprehension of the Freedom Fighters and their affiliates. Closed-door meetings.

Each interview lasted twenty to thirty minutes. Each officer was made to sign multiple documents during their interview—*I will not disclose information, I will not protest the decision, I was given the opportunity, the GLRPS is not responsible.* Each interview ended with a forced handshake: "The Oversight Committee thanks you for your service."

The service's public relations work was a marvel, as it ran in opposition to the fates that befell the staff. There were irreconcilable contradictions between what was said, who was punished, who was congratulated, and how those same people were treated. Aleem and Natalie were suspended without pay, but were told to pose for a photo-op with Deputy Chief Crawford before being escorted off the premises. At a follow-up press conference, Chief Till mentioned Aleem and Natalie by name, commending them for their hard work and rigorous pursuit of justice. Next, Till pinned a medal onto Canizales' chest, congratulating him for his tremendous efforts and many years of service. Pete was forced into early retirement a week later—restructuring chain of command, budget cutbacks, operational needs.

When the press started publishing articles on the arrests, the only photo used was one of Deputy Chief Crawford, flanked by Canadian and American flags.

Your life is not a movie. It is a still frame. A single photo. If you're remembered at all, it will be for one thing. Probably the worst thing you ever did. That was what Aleem said to me when we left the station after getting suspended. We went to a park bench and just sat there for an hour or so. I'd never heard him talk so much. He's a person that I always knew was really smart, but he only spoke in echoes, validating what other people said. People used him for confirmation—'If Aleem nods, I know that what I said makes sense'. I'd done that before. But he only ever said anything else if he knew what you were doing was dumb. That's why most of the false-alphas don't like him.

They fired Chan on the spot. He was walked out right before Aleem and I. Oakshot didn't get suspended. They just put the blame on me, so they could keep him in uniform and working a beat. I'm not mad at him about it. It's just what happened.

Since our suspensions ended, they've transferred Aleem to cells, permanently. He'll be counting prisoners until he retires. They've kept me in uniform too, but they only cycle me through cells, front desk, and the telephone reporting unit. I'm never on the road. Once recently I got called to interview a perp that no one else could crack, but I doubt that will ever happen again. Most of these guys would sooner let a guilty person go than be forced to admit that I got the job done for them.

I never talked to Gilchrist again after we talked on the phone on my last day in the field. He seemed nervous. I've never been in the oversight offices, but I can't even envision how suffocating the atmosphere must be if it makes such high-ranking guys get that anxious. He ended up getting promoted to chief and transferred out to Duluth. I'm sure he had to sign a few documents first, like me.

For a few weeks, they didn't replace Pete or Gilchrist. Deputy Chief Crawford became interim inspector and staff sergeant, though they never changed his title to show that. He was there as a fix-it-man, making sure there wasn't anyone else who would go against orders, keeping everyone in line. Pete was old school, but in a way that worked—a way that people understood and respected. Crawford is old school in a way that doesn't make any sense. Like the way people think that everyone else should suffer because they had to suffer back in their time.

After Aleem and I talked at the park, I went to the hospital's psych ward to visit Lucian, but he had already been removed from the unit—under suspicious circumstances. Brought elsewhere before he could be evaluated, the doctor said. He's serving time now. He got absolutely fried in court. No consideration for his psychological state, or trauma suffered, or previous *heroism, or the fact that he had a family to care for. Almost no mention of the arson. Lots of discussion of his violent acts at the scrapyard, lack of a steady job, living in a low-income neighbourhood, limited formal education, dubious ties to foreign countries through relatives, and the one time an officer found him drunk in his basement. It was all so one-sided, almost laughable the way the prosecutor pandered to the jurors, grandstanding like a complete clown. But it worked. I guess I had too much faith in the jurors' ability to be reasonable and see through the lies. I don't think that will ever happen to me again; I'll never find myself surprised because I expected someone to think critically or be kind or do the right thing or be considerate or think before they speak.*

I did some amateur psychological research about Lucian and his symptoms. Coupling that research with the podcast recordings and my own experiences with Lucian and those close to him, I've come to think he suffered from apophenia: as he was overwhelmed by the traumatic memory of the fire and constant despair of his economic situation, he came to find connections in things that were actually unrelated. The difference here is that ultimately there was a connection—the arson and the Freedom Fighters he'd become affiliated with. And that is where my theory gets jumbled. But I still think that connection was a coincidence. What else could it be? The man led an imagined life within his dreams—a fully developed mock life. Wherein he had a different job and different priorities. He's finding symbolism and connections in things that happened in his dreams, and cartoon drawings, and graffiti—or did he even actually see those things? I don't know. It doesn't matter now anyway. I can't do anything for him except try checking in on his wife and son while he's in jail.

I talked with Ava on the phone once and we went for lunch about a week after Lucian was taken into custody. She's extremely resilient, but I worry about how she'll maintain now. I tried to offer some reassurance, but that's a dangerous thing to do. You have to be careful about guessing or imagining how things might turn out okay. She already pulled David out of school, but she didn't really have a choice. She can teach him a lot at home—the practical stuff that he can help with. My biggest worry is that they'll have to move out if she can't afford the bills or a new roof or something else. I'm not sure if they have anywhere to go except out to The Wilderness. She'd have a chance of getting on as a servant or property manager when the second Blade is finished. There'll be some high-end real estate there. That could be okay for them. It would give them a guaranteed place to stay, though she would likely have to quit her psychology work.

When Aleem and I were at the park, we talked about how we'll be remembered. I was thinking about legacy… which is a totally useless waste of time. But maybe the strange situation we found ourselves in is what made me think of something I usually wouldn't value at all. A legacy. Suddenly, when I found myself reprimanded for doing something good, a legacy became important for me. How will I be remembered? Aleem probably wasn't in his own best mindset to give me a clear answer. Certainly not a glass-half-full one. But he wouldn't do that anyway. I guess the reason others don't like him is the same reason that I do like him.

I'm over it now—the legacy thing. What other people think about me is not my problem. In terms of the accomplishments and the notoriety you could get out of policing, even if you get it, that stuff never really amounts to much. I saw they pinned a medal on Pete in front of the press, right before they kicked him out the door for insubordination. Masking it all under the guise of operational needs, of course. And I've talked to Pete a few times since then. He calls the medal 'a toy' and said he threw it in a box. I asked why he didn't just get rid of it, but he said he's worried someone will ask him to see it one day. Loyalty to the service can never cease, even in retirement.

And Oakshot and I made a big arrest there in the scrapyard, and the follow-up search led to a great haul: the 3D printer that produced the guns for the Freedom Fighters, blueprints for more advanced firearm models, child pornography, emails about human trafficking, ethnic cleansing, eugenics, forced sterilization. Vickshaw was into some deranged stuff. We know he was part of the Freedom Fighters' desire for a crescendo of cascading violence. Elroy's words, not mine. That was repeated in one of his manifesto videos. 'A crescendo of cascading violence.' To what end? I don't even think the Freedom Fighters could answer that.

I'm sure Vickshaw cracked like an egg and fed them great information on the groups that are operating these rings, but they've not let me in on anything. There's been a concerted effort to separate me from the case. They don't want me digging any deeper. I haven't heard anything at the station or seen anything on the news though, so I don't know if anyone will be brought to justice.

So with policing, you can try to coast through, stay safe, follow orders, wait for the end. But if you catch some early sign of glory, or you come in *wanting to make significant change, the job wears you out quickly. I wish I had a way out of it now, to be honest. But I'm too tired to start over. I'll just grind it out at the front desk until they let me go or I die.*

I was a huge part of what could be a breakthrough case, but I don't even feel any better about myself now. Why should I? If the leads aren't pursued, what did I get out of it? What does anyone get out of it?

Daryl had Sofia Kutsenko's phone number in his contacts. She had a pseudonym: Amanita Virosa. I'd like to meet her. Her voice was so grating, such a put-on—in the interview on the podcast, I mean. It's clear her conglomerate is a pack of billionaire vampires. But I'm not so sure that it's about just hoarding wealth anymore. What would the UPC have any interest in the Freedom Fighters for?

Ava listened to all of the podcast entries. She said it was hard. Harder than she thought it would be. But she was glad she did it. She says we should find a way to release everything—somehow get government approval, or find a way to distribute it without approval, and continue the work of getting people's voices heard. She's right—this world could use a dissenting voice.

I don't know if there's a way. I don't want her to do it though. She's got David to take care of. I wouldn't want her in jail or worse. We're meeting tomorrow, on my first day of rest. I'm sure we'll talk about it then. Maybe there's a way. Maybe.

This novel could not have been completed without the help of the following people: **Heather Fleming, Grant Fleming, and Erik Mortensen**. A thank-you is not enough, but that's what I've got for you: thank you so much.

Furthermore, to the following people, thanks for the edits, suggestions, notes, inspiration, and/or expertise: **Brian Velocci, Tamas Dobozy, Jason Wiersema, Ezgi Kapcak, Will Sheane, Jen Skolsky, Nick Lord, Seema Shahjahan and Dave Nebbs.**

Specific linguistic, cultural, and regional expertise came from Brian, Seema and Will. Regarding construction, architectural design, and survivalist techniques, Brian and Jason contributed immensely. Dave, Erik, Jen, Tamas, Brian, and Grant provided professional, historical, and academic perspectives (as well as further readings and research advice). Heather, Seema, and Ezgi added particular insight to develop the female voice, paramount to the story. Nick and Tamas each offered inspiration and editing notes that they may have thought to be insignificant, but in both cases, their readings of my work and the subsequent encouragement they provided were huge boosts in my push to complete this story. Erik, Grant, and Heather provided that type of boost constantly, as my most cherished sounding boards and committed editors.

This novel's author photo was taken by **Cynthia Gagnon-Job,** and the cover art was designed by **Nicole Drury**. Associated art was created by **George Dimacakos**. Thanks to each of you for your skill, effort, and time.

Finally, to anyone who read this novel (whether you liked it or not), thank you.

Wade Fleming earned an MA in English Literature from Wilfrid Laurier University and worked as an adjunct professor at Lambton College before transitioning to a career in law enforcement. He currently lives in Ontario with his wife and sons. Wade considers himself an achiever, neither over nor under. He can be reached on Instagram @catmanduu22

Manufactured by Amazon.ca
Bolton, ON